Praise for the
T. C. LoTempio

"Nick and Nora are a winning team!"
—Rebecca Hale, *New York Times* Bestselling author

"A fast-paced cozy mystery spiced with a dash of romance and topped with a big slice of 'cat-titude.'"
—Ali Brandon, *New York Times* Bestselling author

"Nick and Nora are the purr-fect sleuth duo!"
—Victoria Laurie, *New York Times* Bestselling author

"A page-turner with an endearing heroine."
—*Richmond Times Dispatch*

"Excellently plotted and executed—five paws and a tail up for this tale."
—*Open Book Society*

"Nick brims with street smarts and feline charisma, you'd think he was human . . . an exciting new series."
—Carole Nelson Douglas, *New York Times* notable author of the Midnight Louie mysteries

"I love this series and each new story quickly becomes my favorite. Cannot wait for the next!"
—*Escape With Dollycas Into a Good Book*

"I totally loved this lighthearted and engagingly entertaining whodunit featuring new amateur sleuth Nora Charles and Nick, her feline companion."
—*Dru's Cozy Report*

Books by T. C. LoTempio

Nick and Nora Mysteries

Meow If It's Murder
Claws for Alarm
Crime and Catnip
Hiss H for Homicide
Murder Faux Paws
A Purr Before Dying
Bell, Book and Corpses

Urban Tails Pet Shop Mysteries

The Time for Murder Is Meow
Killers of a Feather
Death Steals the Spotlight
Cats, Carats and Killers
A Side Dish of Death

Cat Rescue Mysteries

Purr M for Murder
Death by a Whisker

A Side Dish
of
Death

Urban Tails Pet Shop Mysteries

T. C. LoTempio

BEYOND THE PAGE
PUBLISHING

A Side Dish of Death
T. C. LoTempio
Copyright © 2025 by T. C. LoTempio.
Cover design and illustration by Dar Albert, Wicked Smart Designs

Beyond the Page Books
are published by
Beyond the Page Publishing
www.beyondthepagepub.com

ISBN: 978-1-960511-98-0

Acknowledgments

As always, kudos to my wonderful editor, Bill Harris, who fixes more than he should have to and makes me look good. Thanks to my agent, Josh Getzler, and his team at Hannigan Getzler. And my heartfelt thanks and appreciation to all my loyal readers—without you, there would be no Shell and company!

To the late, great Princess Fuzzypants.
You will always be a much-loved member of the Pet Shop family!

Prologue

Saturday evening
June 11

The wind howled loudly outside the Fox Hollow Inn, lending a macabre touch to the murder mystery skit that was being enacted. Suddenly there was a loud crash of thunder and all the lights went out, leaving the room in total blackness. I hadn't given the signal, so the power outage had to be a result of the storm. I started to inch my way slowly forward, blinking as my eyes gradually became accustomed to the darkness. There was a loud wail, more of a yowl actually, and then the lights came back on. I heard another loud wail, this time from the hallway. "That sounds like a cat," someone yelled out.

I sucked in a breath. "Dahlia!" I cried out. No sooner had I uttered the cat's name than there came another loud crash of thunder. The side door to the room suddenly banged open and a dark, furry form streaked inside and whizzed past us. "Dahlia," I cried again. I moved forward and reached for her, but Dahlia was too fast for me. She eluded my grasp and sped back out the side entrance. I didn't hesitate but went right into the hallway after her. No sign of her. I turned left and went around the corner, and then I saw her. She was on her hind legs, pawing almost frantically at a door at the very end of the hall. I moved cautiously forward and said in a soothing tone, "Here, Dahlia. Everything's going to be all right."

The cat turned its head to look at me, and then let out another loud wail. She pawed again at the door, her nails scraping against the metal. I inched closer. "What's wrong, Dahlia? Is something in there?"

Dahlia threw back her head and let out another bloodcurdling wail. "Ow-*orrrr!*"

A knot started to form in my stomach, and I felt the hairs at the back of my neck start to rise. I stepped forward and gripped the door handle. It swung inward at my touch, and Dahlia darted inside ahead of me. I stepped inside and paused, letting my eyes adjust to the darkness. I felt along the wall and my fingers found a light switch. I flicked it on and the room was instantly flooded with bright light. I gave a quick look around. The room appeared to be some sort of storage area. There was steel shelving on the walls, filled to the brim with boxes. There was a pile of

1

them in the middle of the tiled floor, and Dahlia jumped on top of them. She stood there for a moment, back arched, and then she jumped off. Her motion caused the boxes to tumble sideways, revealing the body that lay underneath . . . one that definitely wasn't part of the show . . .

Chapter One

Two days earlier . . .

"That fundraiser looks like it's going to be very interesting." The woman reached up and patted her short gray hair. "I can see why the event is nearly sold out."

"Absolutely," replied her companion, another gray-haired woman in a black dress. She patted her cross-shoulder bag. "I'm glad we got our tickets early."

I was standing in the middle of the lobby of the Fox Hollow Inn, my cat Purrday at my side. The women moved away, still chatting, and I paused to study the giant sign that stood on a tripod in the middle of the lobby. The skyline of Manhattan was depicted against a purple background. Dark clouds hung overhead, and a large lightning bolt cut one of the clouds in two. Beneath it in large letters was the caption:

> *Help Us Help the Fox Hollow Shelter and*
> *Celebrate National Adopt a Cat Month!*
> Murder in Manhattan
> The guest list is long—the suspect list longer!
> Everyone is expecting a spectacular dinner and drinks—
> not a blackout and . . . *Murder!*
> Come join the fun! Saturday night—Appalachian
> Room, Fox Hollow Inn.
> The festivities start promptly at eight—don't be late
> *or else . . .*

The lettering was all in black except for the word *Murder*, which was a bright red with little droplets of blood dripping from the *m* and the *r*. At the bottom of the poster, two feet peeped out from beneath a white sheet. Over in the far corner was a drawing of two cats, paws entwined. Beneath that, another caption, in bold blue: *Visit our adoptable cats and kitties during the dinner. Fill out an application and become a proud parent!*

I chuckled. My mother, Clarissa McMillan, was spearheading this event for the Fox Hollow Animal Shelter. She'd done another fundraiser for them a few months ago, an antiques roadshow that had been very successful.

She'd gotten the idea for another fundraiser, this time a murder mystery dinner, and once Marianne, the shelter director, mentioned the cat room was desperately in need of expansion, it was a done deal. She was convinced this fundraiser would be even more successful, and why not?

After all, who didn't love a good murder mystery? Me in particular. And my friend Gary even more.

My name is Shell McMillan. In another life I'd starred in a popular TV show, *Spy Anyone*. The show had been canceled at around the same time I'd broken up with my fiancé, who was also the show's director. I'd been at loose ends for a while after that until a telegram from my mother brought the news of my Aunt Tillie's death. She and I had always been close, so it was not surprising to learn that she'd left me not only her Victorian mansion in Fox Hollow, Connecticut, but her business, Urban Tails Pet Shop, as well. Needless to say, I was at the point in my life when a change was very welcome—even if I had to move three thousand miles away to do it.

Gary Presser had played my husband on the show. He'd originally come to Fox Hollow to try and talk me into returning to Hollywood to star in a spin-off series and had ended up helping to clear me of a murder charge. He'd decided he also preferred small-town life to the hustle and bustle of Hollywood and had taken up residence in the huge mansion Aunt Tillie had left me until he found a suitable place of his own. I was still unsure whether he'd decided to stick around Fox Hollow because he truly did like small-town life or if he was just hooked on solving murders—something that seemed to cross our paths with more regularity than I'd prefer.

I heard a loud meow and my gaze traveled to the cat who squatted at my feet. "I'm not forgetting about you, Purrday. I know you like mysteries too," I said. I'd also inherited the one-eyed Persian along with everything else, and right from the beginning it was apparent the cat had a flair for detection. He also had an uncanny sense of knowing when I was in trouble and had rescued me from a tight spot more than once. I reached down and gave him a quick pat on the head. "Let's go or we'll be late meeting with Louise." When the cat didn't move I added, "Today's Thursday—the inn lunch special is always the fish of the day, and I bet Louise could scrounge up a small piece for you."

Purrday's ears flicked forward at the word *fish*, and he sat up immediately and totted happily along beside me as I moved into the lobby proper. Louise Gates, the inn's owner, had several rescue animals, and when she'd learned about this fundraiser had promptly offered to provide the venue and the dinner, gratis. She and her late husband Bill had both worked at the inn for years, and when the former owner put it up for sale, they jumped on it. Though the inn was originally more of a bed-and-breakfast, the Gateses were determined to revitalize it to keep pace with Fox Hollow's other hotel, the more upscale Mountainside. They'd spent a small fortune redecorating, and it showed. The front entrance hall had a tile floor done in a marbled gray, black, and white pattern. The walls were wainscoted in oak, and a massive crystal chandelier sparkled over the large oak desk that sat right in the center of the lobby. I made a beeline for the desk and the attractive girl sitting behind it. She glanced up as I approached and her features arranged themselves into a pleasant smile. I noticed the name tag pinned to her jacket read *Summer.* "Good afternoon. Can I help you?" she asked.

"Yes," I said pleasantly. "I'm Shell McMillan. I have an appointment with Mrs. Gates."

"Ah, yes. This is about the Saturday fundraiser, right?" She raised her hand and pointed toward a set of beveled glass doors at the other end of the lobby. "I think Ms. Gates is still in the restaurant. Do you want to wait here while I'll page her, or . . ."

"Not necessary. I'll find her, thanks." I headed straight for those glass doors, Purrday at my side. Sure enough, Louise was there. I spotted her chatting with a couple at a table in the center of the room. She was dressed impeccably, in a powder-blue suit that set off the red highlights in her dark hair and matching pale blue heels. I felt a bit frumpy in my Urban Tails sweatshirt and jeans, but I squared my shoulders and pushed through the doors. Louise glanced up and saw me headed her way. She murmured something to the couple, then wended her way through the tables toward me.

"Ah, Shell. And Purrday, too. Welcome." She made a "follow me" gesture with her hand and I fell into step beside her. We walked across the restaurant and through the glass door at the other end, then down a narrow hallway into a neatly appointed office area. A large cherrywood desk took up most of the space, with two comfortable leather chairs flanking it. A tall file cabinet made of the same dark wood occupied the far corner. Once we were seated, Louise removed a large ledger from the middle drawer of the desk and started leafing through it. "Everything seems to be in order for

Saturday," she said. "I've called in extra staff, and I believe Summer has the proceeds from the ticket sales from our allotment. I'm pretty sure the last ticket was sold just today."

"That's wonderful." I brushed an errant curl out of my eyes. "My mother wanted me to ask about the menu. You have finalized it, correct?"

"Yes, about that." Louise nibbled at her lower lip and clasped and unclasped her hands in front of her. Finally she rose and went over to the file cabinet, jerked open a drawer and pulled out a thin file folder. She walked back to the desk and placed the folder in front of me. "This is the menu Venery gave me yesterday," she said, tapping her forefinger on the folder. She raised her gaze to meet mine, and her eyes glittered with barely suppressed anger.

"To be honest . . . that man is impossible. I could just kill him!"

Chapter Two

For a second I was totally flummoxed. "That man? Are you talking about Venery? The chef from the cable show?"

"None other," Louise said bitterly. "The man's been nothing but a thorn in my side ever since he arrived on his high horse."

I mentally reviewed everything I knew about Reynaldo Venery. He was one of three chefs on a popular Connecticut cable show, *Culinary Surprise*. I had never seen the show, but I knew that Venery was the most popular of the chefs, and also the most temperamental. The man had a huge fan base and following and his videos on recipes regularly garnered over a million hits on YouTube. I knew my mother had pulled out all the stops and been at her most persuasive in order to get Venery to commit to doing the fundraiser. She hadn't given me any details on how she'd finally gotten him to agree and I knew better than to ask. I also knew that Louise had worked as a sous chef, so she was no lightweight when it came to the kitchen. In as calm a tone as I could muster, I said "What exactly has he done, Louise?"

"For one thing, he's completely redone the menu I planned," she said. "I know part of the deal was that he was going to have input, but he's taken over the entire thing." She pulled a sheet of paper out of the folder and handed it to me. "This is the menu he gave me yesterday. When I was a chef I worked with much simpler fare. I've never seen cuisine like this."

I took the paper, read what was printed on it once, and then read it a second time. When I'd finished, I looked up at Louise. "When I was on my old TV series I used to dine out at upscale restaurants that served pretty much every item Venery's got on here. Some of them actually sound worse than they actually are. Gnocco frito, for example, are actually spiced crisp dumplings, and nodini is warm bread knots."

Her lips twisted into a wry smile. "Then I imagine you're acquainted with funghi? At first I thought he was saying fungus."

. "Funghi are seasonal mushrooms. They can also be referred to as truffles. They're considered a delicacy and can run into quite a bit of money." I remembered the fancy restaurants I used to go to in Los Angeles where funghi and truffles were regular items on the menu. "Just one can cost anywhere from thirty to seventy-five dollars. I know chefs in LA. who have paid twelve hundred dollars a pound for them."

"Good Lord," Louise moaned. "The inn's doing well, but I hadn't counted on footing a two-thousand-dollar bill for mushrooms."

I slid the paper across the desk. "This isn't the menu you originally planned, is it, Louise?" I asked.

"Heck, no." Louise opened the middle drawer of her desk, whipped out a sheet of paper and handed it to me. "This is the original menu I made up BCRV."

"BCRV?"

Her jaw clenched and she shot me a forced smile. "Before Chef Reynaldo Venery."

I scanned the sheet. There were a lot of familiar, popular items on it that I knew were big hits. Pepper Steak stir-fry. Chicken cordon bleu. Mini Reubens. Vegetable lasagna. Roast beef and gravy. Linguini with pink vodka sauce. Flounder stuffed with crabmeat. Garden salad. Assorted cheeses and croutons platter. My mouth watered just looking the list over. "This looks fabulous, Louise. Did Venery say why he changed the menu?"

Both her arms flew up in the air. "Why? Does he need a reason? He's renowned Chef Reynaldo Venery, that's why! He didn't offer up any explanation, he just stuck that on my desk with a Post-it informing me that he thought this menu was better suited to his talents. His talents, hah!" Louise's lips twisted into a bitter smile. "Obviously cooking roast beef and linguini isn't fancy enough for him. He's always been headstrong, a know-it-all."

I raised a brow as I looked at Louise. "You sound as if you're well acquainted with him."

Louise hesitated, then shrugged. "Anyone who watches that cable cooking show of his knows what a food snob he is," she said. "He's not catering this out of the goodness of his heart. He knows his name is in the program. He's using it as an excuse to show off. He treats me as if I know nothing about the food industry when actually I started out as a sous chef in New Orleans years ago. Bill managed the inn before we bought it, and I worked in the kitchen here for years." She gave me a pleading glance. "I know what sort of cuisine my customers prefer. I'm afraid if he goes through with this menu the event will be a terrible failure."

I had to agree with Louise. While Venery's menu was perfect for an upscale crowd in New York or LA, it would undoubtedly end up a disaster here. I cleared my throat. "Why don't you speak with my mother, Louise? After all, she's the one who convinced Venery to do the benefit. I'm sure she could persuade him to change the menu back to its original form."

Louise stopped massaging her forehead and turned to look at me. "I don't want to bother your mother," she said. "Clarissa is one of my best customers. She went to the trouble of getting Venery specifically because she thought his name would sell tickets, and it did. But this highbrow cuisine . . . I'm just not confident people will love it."

"And I think my mother will understand that. You're right, Venery is probably just showing off. He doesn't understand that folks here are twice as impressed by a good roast than they would be with all these dishes with the fancy names."

Louise nodded. "Plus, the man's been nothing but rude since he arrived. He's been rude to the entire hotel staff. The first thing he did when he met my staff was give them a lecture on the care of his precious knife."

I blinked, not certain I'd heard correctly. "His knife?"

"Yes. It has a custom handle, silver with a leaf design. Apparently it's been in his family for generations. He considers it his 'lucky' piece. He uses it on his show and takes it everywhere."

I brushed my hand across my forehead. "He does sound a bit . . . eccentric."

"That's putting it mildly. The man's a master at making enemies, always has been. All the sous chefs hate his guts. Even though they all know the dinner is for charity, I wouldn't put it past any of them to try and sabotage his fancy-schmancy menu."

"Well, we definitely can't have that." I reached out and touched her hand. "Tell you what, Louise. Why don't I speak to my mother about this? I'm sure once I explain the situation to her she'll be happy to help."

Louise's face lit up. "Would you, Shell? Like I said, I hate to bother her but . . . I admit it. I'm desperate."

I patted her hand. "I agree. Why don't you have a word in private with the sous chefs and let them know there's a good possibility you might be going back to this original menu. I'll go see Mother right now and call you when I'm done."

We left the office and made our way back toward the front of the inn. As we started to cut through the dining room, Purrday suddenly stopped and let out a soft meow.

"Oh, my," Louise said as she looked down at my cat. "Is something wrong?"

"Not at all. He just knows today's the fish special," I said.

"He does, does he?" Louise's eyes twinkled and she bent over and said to Purrday, "It's Boston cod. Do you like cod?"

Purrday sat back on his haunches. He pawed the air, and his pink tongue darted out to lick at his lips.

"I'll take that as a yes," Louise said with a laugh. "Let's see if we can scrounge up a nice piece for his lunch."

We made a sharp turn and went down the short hallway that led to the kitchen, but as we approached, angry voices could be heard coming from behind the large doors. "Uh-oh," Louise murmured. "It appears His Highness is having one of his snits."

Louise pushed the door open a crack and motioned for me to stand beside her. I peered into a large bright room with miles of stainless steel counters, most with cabinets underneath, punctuated by the occasional sink and state-of-the-art range. Dozens of copper-bottomed pots and pans hung from racks built into the low ceiling. There was a large island in the center of the room, and I could see several men and women in white aprons and caps huddled in front of it. Behind the island stood a good-looking olive-skinned man in a white chef's tunic. A tall chef's cap was perched atop black hair that curled out from under it and around the sides of his head. I recognized him at once from pictures I'd seen on the Internet. That was Chef Reynaldo Venery. His face was very red and he was gesticulating wildly with his hands. I looked at the faces of the rest of the staff. Some looked bored, others actually appeared to be frightened.

"This is not the way you make gnocchi," he snarled. "The pasta should be light—this is as heavy as cement." He dipped his finger into the stainless steel bowl in front of him and popped it into his mouth. "Yech," he cried. "Too salty. Who's got such a heavy hand with the salt?" His head shook to and fro like a metronome and his hand reached up to stroke his goatee. "If it is this bad now, what will Saturday be like? *Mère di Dieu!*"

Louise stepped back and let the door close before Venery could be made aware of our presence and shot me an apologetic look. "I'm sorry, but this isn't the best time to interrupt, trust me."

"I can see that," I said. I looked down at Purrday, who was regarding both of us with wide eyes. "Sorry, fella. No cod today."

Purrday's eyes widened. If ever a cat looked about to cry it was Purrday. "Ow-orrrr?"

I knelt down and rubbed his ruff. "Tell you what. Let's make a stop at the Fin and Claw on the way back to the shelter. I think Buck has a flounder special today."

That elicited a warm purr from my kitty. I rubbed his head and stood up just as more loud shouting reached our ears. Suddenly the kitchen door banged open and Venery himself strode out. "I want to see improved Gnocchi when I return," he yelled. "Or we will all stay until you can get it right." He turned, saw us, and his face darkened. He inclined his head toward Louise, then he swept his chef's cap off his head, tucked it into his pocket, and strode past us and down the hall without another word.

I looked first at Venery's retreating back, then at Louise. "Well, he's certainly . . . forceful. And not a word of apology to us, either, for his behavior."

"Oh, that's typical," said Louise. "The first day he was here I had a line outside my office. They all wanted to quit. I had to promise them all double time this week to make them agree to stay." Her hand dove inside her jacket pocket and she whipped out her cell phone, looked at the screen, then at me. "I'm sorry, I've got to go put out another fire. Please, please, let me know what happens with Clarissa."

Louise hurried off and Purrday and I retraced our steps back to the lobby. As we rounded the corner, I spied a tall man standing in front of the reception desk. Something about his build and the way he carried himself seemed very familiar; too familiar, in fact.

"Oh, no, that's impossible," I said softy. "It can't be!"

But the next second the man turned around, and I froze as my worst fears were confirmed. Staring right at me was none other than my ex-fiancé, Patrick Hanratty.

What in blazes was he doing here?

Chapter Three

For a minute I was so stunned all I could do was stare. The first thought that passed through my numbed brain was how good he looked. His ash-blonde hair was a bit shorter than the last time I'd seen him, but he still had the same broad shoulders, narrow waist and muscular legs that filled out the Brooks Brothers suit he had on to perfection. His eyes met mine and they narrowed for just a fraction of a second; then his lips split in a smile, the same smile that in the past had never failed to dazzle me, cajole me into doing whatever he wanted.

Of course, all that was *before* I'd caught him in a very compromising position with one of the script girls on our show. He'd tried to charm his way out of that one but it hadn't worked.

I could think of only one reason for Patrick's appearance here . . . my mother.

"Shell," he said. His gaze raked me up and down appraisingly, and then he held out his hand. "It's good to see you. You look fantastic."

I took an involuntary step backward and ignored his proffered hand. Instead I cocked my head to one side and said in as stern a tone as I could muster, "Patrick. What are you doing here? Making good on a promise to my mother, perhaps?"

The smile faded a bit when I stepped out of reach, but now it was back in place again. "I have been speaking with Clarissa," he admitted. "I was hoping I'd run into you, Shell. I wanted to find out how you liked the present I sent you." He paused and scanned my face. "You did get my present, didn't you?"

I stared at him. He couldn't be serious! The last time I'd seen him I was storming out of the penthouse we'd shared in Los Angeles, dragging my suitcase and carry-on and telling him to bite me. He'd made no effort to communicate with me since until a few months ago, when I'd gotten a note and a very belated birthday present from him, a comedy and tragedy charm bracelet. He'd ended the note with the words *I've missed you.*

Too bad I didn't share the sentiment.

I squared my shoulders and stood a little straighter. "Yes, Patrick, I did receive it."

"So?" he prodded when I fell silent. "You liked it, right? I remembered you admiring a similar piece of jewelry, so when I saw that one I figured it was just the thing."

Before I could reply I heard a loud meow, followed by a sharp hiss. Patrick looked down, then back at me. The corners of his lips quirked slightly upward. "Friend of yours?" he asked.

I reached down to give Purrday a pat on the head. "It's okay, fella," I said. I looked back at Patrick. "This is my cat, Purrday."

Patrick's eyebrows drew together as he looked from me to Purrday and then back to me. "This is your cat? What happened to the Siamese your mother gave you? Kahlua, right?"

"I'm impressed you remember her name. As I recall, you were more concerned with the hairs she might leave on one of your expensive cashmere sweaters than anything else." Patrick winced but didn't respond, so I continued, "FYI, I still have her. Purrday belonged to my Aunt Tillie. I inherited him along with a house and a pet shop. And I have another cat too, a stray Purrday found in the backyard. Princess Fuzzypants."

"Wow, three cats, a business and a house . . . you certainly have settled into a new life, haven't you?" Patrick swiped his hand across his forehead. "And speaking of new life, how's Gary doing? Your mother said he's been freeloading off of you for a while now."

I frowned. It certainly seemed as if my mother had been keeping Patrick up to date on what was happening in my life—from her point of view. "That's her opinion. I wouldn't call it freeloading. He's staying with me until he finds a suitable apartment. In exchange for room and board, he does the cooking as well as help out at the pet shop."

Patrick let out a loud laugh. "Gary Presser behind a cash register? Selling kitty litter and kibble? Now that's a sight I'd pay dearly to see."

"He's quite good at it. Better than you'd think."

Patrick cocked his head at me. "You have to admit it's a convenient arrangement. I'm betting Gary's not in a hurry to find that suitable apartment." He leaned in a bit closer to me and lowered his voice. "You know, I always thought he had a bit of a thing for you when we were working on the series. Those love scenes sometimes seemed a bit too realistic—on his end, of course."

"You've been listening to my mother," I said between clenched teeth. "There has never been anything romantic between Gary and me. If anything, he's the brother I never had." I swiped at my forehead. "Gary's not the guy you remember, Patrick. He's changed since he came here to Fox

13

Hollow. He's less full of himself."

Patrick's expression was one of mock surprise. "Are you saying Gary Presser has mellowed?"

"Yes, I suppose I am." I looked him square in the eyes and added, "Enough about Gary and me. We're getting off topic. Why are you here in Fox Hollow? I thought you were in France working on a movie."

"I was," he said. "The picture wrapped a few weeks ago. Your mother called last week and invited me to her murder mystery dinner fundraiser since I missed her last one. I have to admit, I was a bit surprised she got involved in doing another one so quickly."

I shrugged. "You know Mother. She enjoyed planning that last one, so once the shelter director mentioned the cat room needed expanding, she jumped right on it."

"Yes, she did sound very enthusiastic. Clarissa really warmed to this murder mystery idea. She was very insistent that I not miss this one. She thought I might have a few tips—pointers I could share with the cast. But don't worry," he said quickly as he saw me frown, "I'm not here to offer advice, trust me. I didn't come here just for your mother's fundraiser. As it happens, I have other business here in Fox Hollow."

I raised an eyebrow. "Other business? What sort of business could you possibly have here? Are you scouting small towns for a location for a new movie?"

"God, no. Nothing like that." He took a step closer to me and said in a low tone, "What I'm about to tell you isn't public knowledge, but I know I can trust your discretion. As you might recall, my plans for the spin-off of *Spy Anyone* went out the window when both you and Gary pulled out."

I held up my hand. "I didn't pull out, because I was never in to begin with. Gary bailed on you."

"Because he found a more satisfying life, right? Fine, if that's how you see it," Patrick responded. "Anyway, I'm in the midst of preproduction planning for a new TV series. I would be both director and producer."

I took a moment to digest that tidbit before I replied, "Well, that's very ambitious. Another spy show?"

"Hardly. This is totally different from anything I've ever done before. It's a reality show—a cooking reality show where amateur chefs compete under the tutelage of pro chefs for a large cash prize."

I let out a low whistle. "Wow, that is different. Whatever made you get into that?"

He shrugged. "Good directing jobs are hard to come by these days and cooking shows are quite popular, as you know. Plus, I've always been a fan of excellent cuisine."

"I remember," I said dryly. "We always ate out at the very finest restaurants in LA. Although that was mainly because neither of us could cook, or wanted to learn."

"Right," he said with a laugh. "Anyway, I've got two chefs signed up already who are coming off of big wins on major cooking shows and now I'm hoping to sign the one who'll be our headliner—an established chef, the main draw." He let out a giant sigh. "I've been after this guy for a while now to have a sit-down so I can outline just what it is I have in mind. He mentioned he'd be in Fox Hollow this weekend, so it would be a good time for a meet."

A little warning alarm went off in my head. "A chef, you say, and here for the weekend? You can't mean . . . are you here to meet with Reynaldo Venery?"

He gave a quick look around, then put a finger to his lips and whispered, "As I said, this isn't for publication."

"Oh, really, Patrick. Who would I tell?" I sputtered. "If I were you I'd rethink your choice. I've seen Venery in action. The guy's a real jerk."

"Maybe so, but he's a jerk with a big following, which could be crucial to the success of my new show."

I wagged one finger in the air. "You should be careful what you wish for. A guy like him could end up being more trouble than he's worth. Surely there are other popular chefs you could convince to be on your new show. I can think of a dozen right off the top of my head. Marc Murray, Tiffany Faison, Jet Tila—"

Patrick held up his hand. "Do you think I haven't tried to sign top names? They either have prior commitments or are out of my price range. I'm still courting sponsors. I'm open to suggestions, though." Patrick glanced at his watch. "I have some time before our scheduled meeting. How about I buy you a late lunch and you can tell me all the reasons why you think my hiring Venery is a bad idea?"

I gave my head an emphatic shake. "I don't think having lunch with you is a good idea, Patrick."

He jammed his hands into his pockets. "Okay, I guess I can understand why you'd feel that way. I know I was a real cad to you, Shell, and I have no right to even be speaking to you, but . . . once upon a time, whether you

15

want to admit it or not, we made a pretty good team. I always respected your opinions."

"Could have fooled me," I muttered.

Patrick reached out and grabbed my hand. "I mean it, Shell. I'm asking for your help. You've always had good instincts. If you don't think Venery is a viable option, I'd love to know the reasons why."

I pulled my hand away. "Regardless of what I think, it's really your decision, Patrick," I said stiffly.

"Ow-owrr!"

We both looked down. Both of us had temporarily forgotten about Purrday who'd been squatting off to one side, apparently observing. Now he made his presence known. His ears flicked forward and his lips drew back, exposing his sharp teeth. "Ow-orrr," he yowled again.

Patrick gave me a laconic grin. "Seems your cat agrees with you," he said. He knelt and extended his hand toward Purrday. My cat looked at me, then inched forward and sniffed at Patrick's fingers. After a few seconds he took a step back and settled next to me, his tail wrapped around his front paws. Patrick chuckled. "At least he didn't bite me—unlike Kahlua."

"She did that in retaliation for you pushing her off your cashmere sweater. And as I recall, she didn't even break the skin." I glanced at my watch. "I really should be getting back to the pet shop," I said. "So, if you'll excuse me?"

I started to step around him, but he moved to the side, blocking me. "I'll be here through the weekend, Shell. Maybe you can find some time and we can have lunch . . . or just go somewhere and talk." I opened my mouth to protest, but he held up his hand. "I meant what I said, Shell. Whether or not you feel the same, I still regard you as a friend. Just think about it."

I gave him a tight smile, then turned on my heel and walked away, Purrday right beside me. I reached the double doors, and before I pushed through them, I turned my head to glance over my shoulder. What I saw gave me pause. Patrick stood beside the front desk, chatting amiably with Summer, the young receptionist.

Standing across the hall by the elevators, watching them, stood Chef Reynaldo Venery. He was looking straight at Patrick, and if looks could kill, my ex would surely be six feet under by now.

Chapter Four

Gary was behind the pet shop counter looking intently at his tablet when Purrday and I arrived some twenty minutes later. He glanced up, saw me, and gave me a cheeky smile. "Hey, Sunshine! Robbie said you went over to the inn to get the final menu." He paused and gave me a probing look. "Is everything all right? You look . . . upset."

I tossed my bag on the shelf underneath the counter and fisted a hand on one hip. "I am upset, but it doesn't have anything to do with the event . . . not really."

Gary frowned. "What's that supposed to mean? Didn't you get the menu?"

"Sort of. It turned out that Louise was having a bit of a problem with Chef Venery. It seems they have very different viewpoints on what the menu should consist of."

"Ah, so Venery is living up to his reputation, eh? I kinda thought that might happen," said Gary. "The guy's a pompous ass on that show, and I got the impression he wasn't acting."

I leaned an elbow on the counter. "I didn't realize you were a fan of *Culinary Surprise*."

He waved his hand. "I watch all those cooking shows whenever I get the chance. Where do you think I get most of my recipes from?"

I chuckled. "Well, I got a chance to see Venery in action. Louise took us to the kitchen to get Purrday some cod, but instead we were treated to Venery giving his sous chefs a lecture on the correct way to make gnocchi. And he wasn't too nice about it, either."

"Sounds about right. If you'd ever seen the show, you'd have known Venery makes Gordon Ramsey look like a choir boy."

"He sounds like a real character. Louise said he gave her staff a lecture on his special knife."

Gary rolled his eyes. "Ah, yes. Silver handle, leaf design. It's a family heirloom. He always finds a way to use it on the show."

"Well, I promised Louise I'd ask Mother to speak to Venery and see if she could get him to be a tad more agreeable about the menu. I tried calling and texting but so far no reply. I bet she's got her phone shut off."

Gary leaned closer to peer intently at me. "Venery isn't the only reason you seem flustered though, is it?"

I sighed. "No. As Purrday and I were leaving, you'll never guess who we ran into."

"Wait, let me guess." Gary put his hand across his eyes and started to hum. A moment later he lowered his hand and said, "Could it be . . . Patrick Hanratty."

"Gary!" I reached out and punched his shoulder. "You rat! You knew he was here!"

"Ow!" Gary rubbed at his shoulder. "Before you hit me again, I only found out a little while ago. Clarissa came by looking for you and she mentioned that she'd invited Patrick to the fundraiser and he was supposed to arrive today. She didn't say anything about him staying at the Fox Hollow Inn, though. I'd have guessed he'd be bunking at the Hilton. It's more his speed."

"Yeah, well, I think Patrick has his reasons for wanting to stay at the Fox Hollow Inn."

"His reasons? And what might those be?"

I was spared answering by a very loud meow. We both looked down. Purrday had knocked my tote bag out from under the counter and was sticking his head inside. I bent down to retrieve the bag and extracted a medium-sized container from its depths. "Sorry, fella," I said. "I forgot about your treat from the Fin and Claw."

Gary looked at me. "Treat?"

"He got cheated out of some cod thanks to Venery acting like a jerk, so I got him some flounder as a substitute."

A customer came up to the counter carrying an armload of cat toys. While Gary rang up the sale, I took Purrday back into my office, got out his bowl and spooned the flounder into it. He squatted in front of the bowl and started slurping it up almost immediately. I left him to his treat and returned to the shop floor, where Gary was just handing the bag of toys to the customer. Once she'd left, Gary looked at me again. "We didn't finish our conversation. You were going to tell me why Patrick decided to stay at the Fox Hollow Inn."

"He said he didn't come just for the fundraiser, that he has other business here."

Gary had been arranging a stack of flyers on the counter and now he paused. "Other business? What kind of business could he possibly have in Fox Hollow?"

I lowered my voice to a half whisper. "He told me this in confidence, so don't repeat it to anyone."

"Shell." Gary shot me an injured look. "Who would I tell?"

"Olivia, for one." Olivia Niven, who ran the local dance studio, was my BFF. She and Gary had been dating since he'd arrived in Fox Hollow. "She told me how you like to gossip."

"Yeah, about the old Hollywood crowd." As I continued to stare at him, he dropped his gaze and added, "Okay, I may indulge in a bit of gossip about some of the inhabitants here from time to time. But this is different." He made a motion of locking his lips and throwing away the key. "Trust me, mum's the word."

"He's decided to produce and direct a reality cooking show."

Gary's jaw dropped. "A reality show? You're kidding? And cooking, no less?" He reached up to rub at his forehead. "I guess when you stop to think about it, it makes a crazy sort of sense. Pat always loved eating, but he hated cooking. So, what? He's here scouting a location for the show?"

"Not exactly. He said he's here because he scheduled a meeting with a chef who he's trying to convince to be on his new show."

"A chef from Fox Hollow? Who on earth—oh, no!" Gary sucked in a breath. "It's not . . . he's not meeting with Venery?"

"None other. He thinks that Venery will be a big draw for his new show."

"He probably would be, but I doubt the ratings would be worth the trouble the guy would cause," said Gary. "Patrick must be desperate."

"He said that he approached other chefs but they all either had prior commitments or were out of his price range." I tapped my forefinger against my chin. "As I was leaving, I happened to see Venery standing over by the elevators. The look he was giving Patrick wasn't what I'd call friendly. It was positively . . . venomous."

Gary shrugged. "I wouldn't worry about it, Shell. Venery gives everyone dagger looks. You've never seen his show."

"What's that about dagger looks? Wait, don't tell me. You have to be talking about Venery?"

Gary and I both looked up to see Leila Simmons approaching the counter. Leila was a reporter for the *Youngstown Sentinel*. She and I had become good friends when she'd recently helped me unravel a puzzling mystery. She eased a slender hip against the counter. "So what has Venery done now? Anything that will make a good story for my paper?"

"Well, if you call antagonizing the inn's entire troop of sous chefs a good story, then you're in luck," I said. I gave Leila the CliffsNotes version of what I'd witnessed earlier. "The man's a jerk," I finished.

Leila's nose wrinkled. "You can say that again. It's hard to believe the guy's supposed to be such a ladies' man."

Both Gary and I stared at her. "Venery a ladies' man? You're joking," I said.

Leila shook her head. "Alas, I wish I were but I'm not. The man's conquests are legendary. If it's female . . ." She spread her hands. "Google him sometime and you'll see. He's dated a lot of beautiful women, from nineteen all the way up to ninety. And while we're on the subject of ladies' men . . ." She leaned closer to me and wiggled her eyebrows. "I heard that Patrick Hanratty checked into the inn late yesterday. He's your ex, right?"

I made a face at her. "Unfortunately, yes. I ran into him when I went to pick up the final menu for the event from Louise. It wasn't exactly a moment out of one of those Hallmark movies."

Leila clucked her tongue. "Too bad. I thought maybe a reconciliation was in the air."

I gave her a stern look. "Not as far as I'm concerned."

Leila grinned. "I'm sure Josh will be happy to hear that. Have you mentioned your ex is in town?"

"I haven't seen Josh all week," I responded. "Between his schedule and mine, we keep missing each other. I'm just hoping he can get Saturday night off for the fundraiser." My boyfriend, Josh Bloodgood, was a homicide detective on the Fox Hollow police force. We'd met when I'd been his number-one suspect in a murder investigation. Fortunately, I'd been cleared and our relationship had grown from there.

"Speaking of the fundraiser . . ." Her hand dipped down into her tote, came up clutching her wallet. "My editor is having a hard time finding a ticket. Of course, it didn't help that he decided yesterday he wanted to go." She rolled her eyes. "I told him I'd see what I could do. I thought I might be able to talk Vi and John Kizis into selling me their tickets. Vi wasn't that keen on going, but John finally talked her into it. I thought maybe you guys might have one left?"

"I'm not sure," I said. "Robbie's in charge of ticket sales, and he's out making deliveries right now." I pulled out my phone. "I can text him and ask."

I sent off a quick text to Robbie and got an almost immediate answer. Nope. "Sorry," I said, as I showed Leila the text. "Have you tried Gruber's

Deli? Or Hanson's Home Goods?'"

"They're next on my list," said Leila. "I'd sure love to find one and score some brownie points, especially since my review is coming up." She snapped her fingers. "Say, what about the inn? Think they might have any left?"

"Louise said she was pretty sure they sold the last one," I said. "But you could check. The receptionist, Summer, was in charge of the ticket sales."

"I'll definitely do that," said Leila. She paused as her phone let out a loud beep. She looked at the screen and frowned. "Oh, wow. Have you seen this, Shell? It's a weather alert. They're predicting a monster hurricane to hit here sometime Saturday night."

"Great," I said. "Well, the event is still a couple of days away. Let's hope the weather bureau is wrong as usual."

Leila left and Gary looked at me. "I hope that storm does pass over, although it probably would lend a lot of atmosphere to the murder mystery play."

"Atmosphere like that we don't need," I said. "Let's just hope it's not bad enough to keep people away." I glanced at my watch. "I really should try and find Mother. I need to talk to her about the Venery situation ASAP."

"I think she said something about going over to the shelter. She said she had to introduce Marianne to someone," Gary ventured.

"Introduce . . . oh, it must be the social media person," I said. "The original blogger Mother got had to back out because of a family illness. Mother was going crazy trying to find another influencer since there are only two days till the event."

"Well, apparently she got someone," said Gary. "As per usual, she didn't share any details with me."

I grabbed my purse from underneath the counter. "I'm going to go over to the shelter now. With any luck, she'll still be there."

I gave Gary a thumbs-up and hurried out the door. The shelter was only a five-minute walk from the pet shop, and I covered the distance in record time. I stepped into the main area and saw a young teen volunteer behind the desk. "Good afternoon," I said. "I'm Shell McMillan. I believe my mother, Clarissa McMillan, is here meeting with Marianne."

The teen smiled. "Yes, she's here. They're meeting in the conference room off the cattery. Do you need me to show you?"

"Thanks. I know where it is."

But before I could move down the hall, we were both startled by the sound of voices, raised in a loud argument—and they were coming from the direction of the cattery!

Chapter Five

I turned and hurried down the hall toward the cattery. When I pushed through the door, the first thing I saw was my mother standing in the entryway to the small conference room. A slender brunette woman in a bright blue tie-dye dress stood beside her. The woman seemed familiar, but I couldn't think why. Their gazes were riveted on two other women standing in the cattery proper. One was the shelter director, Marianne, the other a slim fiftyish woman with short spiked hair framing a round face. That face was, at the moment, a bright red and the woman was shouting at Marianne.

"I tell you, I filled out the adoption application online Saturday. Apollo is mine," she fairly screeched. She jabbed a chubby finger at the cage. I glanced over and saw a small snowshoe Siamese in there. The cat lifted his head and stared straight at me with his bright blue eyes, almost as if he were trying to apologize for his role in this situation.

Marianne's voice was low but her tone had an edge of steel to it. "And I told you, Ms. Dalton, we were unable to verify the information on your application. The Costas came in Monday and took a shine to Apollo and filled out the application. *Their* references checked out."

"That's poppycock," Ms. Dalton sneered. "My references are all reliable people."

"Maybe so," Marianne returned, "But my staff were unable to contact any of them. The phone numbers you gave for your personal references were out of service. And as far as your veterinary reference, well . . . did you know Dr. Wolpner retired last month?"

"How would I know that?" she snapped. "I haven't had to contact him since Jiminy Cricket passed."

Marianne raised an eyebrow. "Jiminy Cricket?"

"My late husband's beagle." She paused, tapping her finger against her bottom lip. "There might be a *slight* chance I could have gotten those other numbers mixed up," she said at last. "I didn't have my address book with me, and my mind's been mush the past few months. But still!" Her finger left her bottom lip and shot straight up in the air. "Someone should have contacted me!"

"We tried," Marianne said smoothly. "Several times. You didn't respond."

Ms. Dalton looked surprised for a few seconds but quickly recovered. "My phone's been acting up," she admitted. "I need to get a new one." She raised a hand and brushed it through her hair, making the spikes stand out even more. "I'm sorry to act so difficult," she said in a more mollified tone. "It's just that I feel a greater effort should have been made to verify my information before you just up and gave my cat to someone else!"

"What is important in pet adoptions is to get the right home for our animals," Marianne said smoothly. "I'll call one of the volunteers in here and you can look over our other cats. We've gotten some more in since you were last here. Perhaps one of them will appeal to you."

Ms. Dalton frowned and crossed her arms over her chest. "Are you implying that I'm not capable of giving Apollo a good loving home? That's a load of you know what!" She thrust her lower lip out like a petulant child. "I saw him first!"

"True," said Marianne in a tactful tone, "but Siamese can be a very difficult breed. The Costas own another snowshoe Siamese and want Apollo as a companion for him, so they're familiar with the breed." When Ms. Dalton remained silent, she continued, "I think we can find you an even better fit than Apollo. There's a sweet little cocker spaniel that just came in the other day. The owner is going into a nursing home. I know you said you wanted a cat, but, since you have had a dog in the past . . . I thought you might consider her."

Ms. Dalton frowned. "Well . . . maybe. Can I see her?"

"Of course." Marianne turned to my mother and said, "If you'll excuse me, I'm just going to take Ms. Dalton over to the kennel area. I'll be back shortly."

My mother waved her hand. "No worries, dear. Take your time."

Marianne took Ms. Dalton's arm and escorted her in the direction of the dog room. Once they'd gone, I called out, "Mother! I need to speak with you."

My mother's head jerked up. She looked at me and smiled. "Shell, darling! I went to see you earlier at the pet shop but you had already left." She made a beckoning motion with her hand. "Come here, there's someone I want you to meet." I walked over and my mother laid her hand on the other woman's arm. "I'd like you to meet Charisma Walters. Charisma, this is my daughter, Shell. Her pet shop, Urban Tails, is one of the event sponsors."

"Charisma Walters," I said. "Of course. I thought you looked familiar.

I've seen your photo on your blog—you and Serendipity."

Charisma Walters was one of the top internet influencers in Connecticut, possibly the Eastern seaboard. She'd been the owner of a successful PR firm in Hartford. Two years ago at the ripe old age of thirty-two she sold it for a pile of money and decided to concentrate on internet marketing instead. She started a blog, *Charisma's Corner*, and within three months had over fifty thousand followers. In the short time she'd been blogging, it seemed that when Charisma spoke, people listened. She'd become one of the most popular brand ambassadors, doing everything from social platforms to speaking engagements and consulting services. I'd heard that her income last year had been somewhere in the high five figures, maybe even low six—more than I'd made when I'd been the lead on a popular television series. She was also a big advocate for animal rights and no-kill shelters. She'd gotten her Ragdoll cat, Serendipity, from a shelter. The cat was featured prominently on her blog, and from what I could tell, accompanied her everywhere. I had no doubt she'd be bringing it to the fundraiser.

Charisma didn't hesitate but reached out and grabbed my hand. "I feel as if I know you, Shell—may I call you Shell?" At my nod she continued, "I was a big fan of your show, *Spy Anyone*. I just loved you and Gary Presser playing that husband-and-wife team! I cried for days when they canceled it."

"So did Gary," I said with a chuckle. "It's nice to meet you in person, Ms. Walters. We do so appreciate you agreeing to help with our fundraiser, and at the last minute too."

She laid her hand on my arm. "Call me Charisma, Shell. And I am so glad I was able to rearrange my schedule. Once your mother told me the event was also including cat adoptions to celebrate National Adopt a Cat Month, well, that really resonated with me. I had to be in." She turned to my mother and added, "I forgot to mention that I've already gotten over two thousand responses to the announcement I posted on my blog yesterday."

"That many? So fast?" my mother cried. "That's wonderful."

"Actually that's a small response compared to other events I've helped with," said Charisma. "Of course, most of them aren't so last-minute, but I expect we'll hit fifty thousand at least by Saturday. Lots of people who can't attend are asking where to send donations."

"That is good news," I said. "Every little bit helps."

Charisma leaned in a bit closer to me and said, "Tell me the truth, Shell. Have you and Gary Presser left Hollywood for good to run that pet shop, or do the two of you intend to go back to acting at some point?"

I saw my mother out of the corner of my eye and noted the innocent expression on her face. "I can't speak for Gary, but I'm perfectly happy here in Fox Hollow."

Charisma clucked her tongue. "That's a shame, if you don't mind my saying so. A real loss for Hollywood. I was just wondering because . . . well, you know . . . your former director and fiancé is in town." One of her perfectly arched eyebrows inched upward. "You do know he's in town?"

My mother stepped forward and said smoothly, "That's what I stopped by your shop to tell you earlier, dear. Patrick decided to come out here and lend his support to the fundraiser. Wasn't that sweet of him?"

"Oh, yes. To be sure. Wonderfully sweet," I replied through clenched teeth.

"So he will be at the fundraiser," said Charisma. "I look forward to meeting him . . . and Gary as well." Her eyes sparkled. "It's a regular reunion of the *Spy Anyone* troupe, and it will make a wonderful article for my blog! In addition to my coverage of the fundraiser, of course," she added quickly.

I looked at Charisma. "I really don't know how much of a reunion it will be. Gary turned down his offer of starring in a *Spy Anyone* spin-off and I hadn't heard a word from him since I left LA—that is, until today. I happened to run into him when I picked up the menu from Louise."

"You got the final menu? Wonderful." My mother clapped her hands and completely ignored my comment about Patrick. "I'm dying to see it."

"As am I," cooed Charisma. "Especially since Chef Reynaldo Venery is the one preparing it. I have to be honest, the fact Venery is also involved with this fundraiser was another big draw for me. I've sampled his cooking when he was an unknown and more recently when I did an article on that show for my blog last year. The attendees have no idea what a magical taste treat awaits them. Would it be alright if I took a quick peek?" She made a crossing motion over her heart. "I promise not to reveal anything beforehand."

"I'm sure you wouldn't, but I'm not sure that this is the final menu."

"It's not?" My mother threw me a puzzled look. "But I thought it was finally approved?"

"Venery approved it," I said. "But Louise has some . . . concerns."

The puzzled look morphed into a near-scowl. "Concerns? What sort of concerns?"

I glanced at Charisma out of the corner of my eye. She was watching us intently. I shifted my weight from one foot to the other and said in a low tone, "I'd much rather discuss this in private, Mother."

My mother's lips puckered. "Oh really, Shell. Charisma is the soul of discretion. Anything you have to say you can tell me in front of her."

I hesitated, and Charisma wagged a finger in the air. "No, no, it's fine, Clarissa. I really should be going anyway. There's still a lot I have to do on my end before Saturday night." She fixed me with another dazzling smile. "It was lovely meeting you, Shell. I can't tell you how much I'm looking forward to Saturday night, and meeting Gary Presser and Patrick Hanratty." She started to leave, paused, turned around and added, "I forgot to mention that I'll be bringing Serendipity to the event as well. Clarissa mentioned your cats will be acting as goodwill ambassadors. I think Serendipity would also do a wonderful job in that arena, don't you? My little darling has a lot of fans via my blog. I'm sure they will be thrilled to see her in that role."

I shot my mother a sideways glance but she was studiously avoiding looking in my direction. "I'm sure Serendipity would make a fine addition to our feline ambassadors," I said. "You do realize that the cats will be roaming around the lobby unsupervised, mingling with the patrons?"

"Oh, of course," Charisma said. She gave a dismissive wave. "Serendipity is wonderful around people. She has such charm. I'm sure she'll be a great asset."

"I'm sure," I murmured as Charisma sailed out of the cattery and my mother edged up beside me. She gave me a poke in the ribs and said, "So? What do you think of Charisma? Isn't she something?"

"I think her name definitely suits her," I said. "She's got an intense personality."

"That most likely comes from years of running her PR firm. Intensity is what one needs for a good social media coordinator," declared my mother. "I was lucky that she managed to rearrange her schedule. She's quite busy, you know."

"According to her, she was 'in' the minute she found out about the cat adoptions," I said. "It also sounded to me like she was even more 'in' when she found out about Gary and Patrick being there."

My mother arched a brow. "If I didn't know better, Crishell, I'd say you were jealous."

I sighed. "I've told you before, Mother, there is nothing romantic between me and Gary. As for Patrick, that ship sailed long ago."

"Maybe for you," my mother said. "He's no longer with Greta, you know. He only did what he did in a moment of weakness. You and he weren't getting along, and she put the moves on him."

"And who told you that, Patrick?"

"He's told me many things, including what a fool he was to ever let you go. I know, I know—" She waved her hand before I could speak. "You have no interest in Patrick anymore. You're seeing that detective, Josh. I can't blame you for that, dear. Patrick hurt you, and Josh is a hunk. But just because you're no longer interested in Patrick doesn't mean other women wouldn't be. For that matter, she sounded excited about meeting Gary too. And since your friend Olive isn't wearing an engagement ring, I consider both of them to be single and available." My mother took a deep breath, then fisted a hand on her hip. "Now, what's all this nonsense about the menu, and why didn't you want to discuss it in front of Charisma?"

"I just didn't think it was a good idea to publicize the fact that Louise and Venery haven't exactly been getting along this past week," I said. "Louise is at her wit's end, and after what I witnessed today, I'm inclined to take her side."

Both my mother's eyebrows rose. "What you witnessed?"

"Let's just say that Chef Venery's reputation is well deserved."

"His reputation? What about his reputation?"

I sighed. "Sit down, Mother. It's a long story."

• • •

Fortunately it didn't take much convincing on my part once my mother saw the menu. She wholeheartedly agreed it was much too fancy for the Fox Hollow crowd and assured me she'd have a word with Venery as soon as she got home. I shot Louise off a quick text, telling her my mother was on the job!

As we were preparing to leave, Marianne returned with Ms. Dalton. From the expression on the older woman's face, I gathered she hadn't been too impressed with the dog. "I've seen all the cats, and Apollo was the only one I liked," I heard her say. "Don't you have any others?"

"There are some rescues arriving tomorrow," Marianne said. "They were dropped off at the shelter in Porterville, but they're almost full up so we offered to take them. We want to bring a few of them to our fundraiser Saturday."

Her eyes widened. "Oh, the murder mystery dinner? I saw the poster at the library. My neighbor wants me to go with her, but I wasn't sure . . . but if you'll have different cats there, then I think I'll go after all."

She turned on her heel and flounced off. We watched her go, and then Marianne reached up and swiped at her brow. "Boy, that woman is a piece of work. She'd never have been able to manage Apollo."

"Oh, gosh, no," I said. "If you ask me, she's looking for a pet that will take care of her, not the other way around."

"I think you're right about that, Shell." Marianne tossed me a troubled look. "I hope I'm not jinxing anything, but I've got a bad feeling that all the drama Saturday night won't be onstage."

And while I didn't say anything aloud, deep down I had a feeling that Marianne's prediction wasn't all that far off.

Chapter Six

I went back to the pet shop and found both Gary and Robbie knee-deep in customers. Since no one else was in the shop, I decided to go into my office and do a bit of research on Reynaldo Venery. Leila's claim that the man was a ladies' man had definitely piqued my curiosity, and I was eager to learn a bit more about the man Patrick was so desperate to employ. I made my way back to the office, where I found Purrday sound asleep on the floor beside my desk. "Hey, Sleepyhead. Did you have a nice snooze?" I asked the cat as I draped my jacket over the back of my chair. "Feel up to helping me do some research on Venery?"

Purrday raised his head, opened his mouth in a large, unlovely cat yawn, and rolled over on his side. "Fine," I said as I settled into my chair and opened up my laptop. "Be that way. I'll just do all the work myself." I paused. "If the princess were here, I bet she'd help."

Mention of Purrday's favorite playmate, however, didn't serve to motivate him. Instead he rolled over on his other side.

I called up my favorite search engine and typed in "Reynaldo Venery," then hit enter. Ten whole pages of references came up. I clicked on the one for LinkedIn and was immediately taken to his profile. Reynaldo Venery was listed as Executive Chef for *Culinary Surprise*. Under "Summary" he'd written:

> My passion for food is overshadowed by my relentless commitment to my clients, students, & being the best. I sincerely love giving myself in entirety when I approach every challenge that life has to offer. I am an excellent team player and leader who has the intuition and foresight to see a goal and follow through it to its entirety.

A blue box directly above the summary invited me to click on Reynaldo Venery's full profile. I did so. The man had an impressive résumé. He'd graduated from New York City's Culinary Institute and apprenticed at several restaurants around the country before returning to New York. His big break came when he was tapped to take over the head chef position at Manero's Steak House. He turned that restaurant into a three-star Michelin eatery, and when it closed its doors, he relocated to Connecticut and became one of the three rotating chefs in NCBC's top-rated *Culinary Surprise*. The article ended with, *"Culinary Surprise is just the beginning. Venery is definitely on his way to bigger and better things."* Could that be a hint as to him signing on with Patrick?

Next I put "Venery—Business Ventures" into the search engine. Several hits came up, but none that looked particularly interesting. One dealt with Venery's being offered a contract to advertise a brand of barbecue sauce, another a new brand of salad dressing. I clicked on another article, a recent interview with Venery in a North Carolina food magazine. As with the profile, the teaser came at the very end: *Rumor has it Venery is currently being wooed by Hollywood for a show of his own, and is supposedly in talks with several producers.*

Several producers? Did Patrick have competition? That might explain his sense of urgency where Venery was concerned. I didn't think the man would be above playing one producer against another to get the best deal possible. Patrick might want Venery, but I also knew that he was no one's fool. That attitude could explain the dagger look Venery had been giving him. I had the feeling Venery wasn't used to not getting his way.

Next I typed in "Reynaldo Venery—romances." My jaw dropped when over two hundred hits came up. I didn't have time to scroll through all of them, so I just selected the top ones. Leila hadn't exaggerated. Venery's name had been linked with a popular movie actress, a Broadway star, a pop singer and two famous models, just to name a few. One of the models had just celebrated her nineteenth birthday. I shook my head at that one. There was no accounting for taste, was there? Darn, maybe Venery being interested in that young receptionist wasn't such a stretch after all. I jumped to the next page, but before I could dig into it my cell buzzed with an incoming text. I grabbed my jacket, fished the phone out of my pocket and saw I had a text from Louise. *Success!* followed by a string of smiley emojis. I smiled, thinking that my mother certainly hadn't wasted any time. I dialed the inn's number and asked to be connected to Louise. When she came on the line she didn't waste any time with preamble. "Shell, I can't believe it. I don't know what your mother said to him, but Venery apologized not only to me but to my staff as well. It was a reluctant apology, but an apology nonetheless. And my original menu is back in place. I don't know how to thank you."

"You don't have to thank me. It was all Mother's doing. I was just the messenger."

"Regardless, nothing would have been accomplished if you hadn't spoken to her," Louise said warmly. "I'd love to show my appreciation. Why don't you bring a friend and come to the inn for dinner tonight? On the house." She paused and then added, "By way of apology, Venery consented to cook some special dishes tonight."

"Well, when you put it that way, I think Gary might enjoy sampling some of Chef Venery's cuisine," I said with a laugh. "We close tonight at six, so maybe seven thirty?"

"Wonderful! I'll have a table ready and waiting for you."

I hung up and heard the sound of a throat clearing. I glanced up and saw Gary lounging in the doorway. I pointed an accusing finger at him. "How long have you been standing there?" I asked.

"Long enough to hear you talk about sampling Venery's cuisine at seven thirty." He walked inside the office and shut the door behind him. "I take it Clarissa was successful in getting our temperamental chef to change his menu?"

"She was. Louise is so grateful that she offered me and a companion dinner on the house tonight. Since Venery is making some special dishes for the menu tonight, I immediately thought of you."

"Aw, that's so sweet," Gary said. "But I'm not sure I'm the right choice to accompany you."

I stared at him. "You don't want to go? Since you said you're a fan of that show, I thought you'd be thrilled to get an advance sample of Venery's cooking—or do you already have dinner plans with Olivia?"

"Nope, she's teaching a class tonight. I'm free as the proverbial bird. And for the record, I do want to go . . . but I'm willing to sacrifice my own desires for the greater good."

Now I frowned. "And what is that supposed to mean?" Suddenly I sat straight up. "You're not suggesting I should take Mother?"

He rolled his eyes. "No, I was thinking more along the lines of an old friend and a golden opportunity." When I didn't respond he made an impatient gesture with his hand. "Patrick. I'm talking about Patrick."

"You think I should invite Patrick to dinner?" I gave my head an emphatic shake. "Absolutely not. That's not a good idea."

"Why not? He said he wanted your take on Venery, right? It seems to me this is a good opportunity for the two of you to have a heart-to-heart."

I flopped back in my chair. "I can't believe you'd suggest that! A heart-to-heart over what? Why he dumped me?"

"Well, you have to admit the two of you didn't exactly part amicably."

I thrust my lower lip out. "I caught him in bed with Greta Olson. Of course we didn't have an amicable parting. He cheated on me."

"And he regretted it. Come on, Shell. Deep down it bothers you, I know it does. You might not want to be with Patrick anymore, but I'm betting you regret how things ended between you."

I sighed. If I were to be completely honest, I'd known for weeks before I'd found Patrick and Greta together that something wasn't right between us, and hadn't been for a while. We'd grown apart, and it was probably a good thing it had all gone down before we actually married. I'd been angry, yes—but more at myself than at Patrick. "Sometimes it really irks me how well you know me, Presser," I muttered. "All right, I'll give him a call and extend the invitation. I admit, I'm curious to know if Patrick was aware of Venery's other offers."

Gary leaned closer and peered intently at my forehead. "I can see the wheels turning already. You'll be glad you did this, trust me."

"Uh-huh." I made a motion of throwing the pencil at him. "Go on, get out of here before I change my mind."

Gary went back outside and I picked up my phone and once again punched in the inn's number. When the operator answered I asked to be connected to Patrick Hanratty's room. He answered on the first ring. "Patrick, it's Shell," I said briskly. "Louise has offered me and a guest dinner tonight at the inn at seven thirty. I thought maybe you'd like to accompany me."

A long moment of silence and then, "Sorry, but I'm a bit confused. Earlier you turned me down for lunch. You said that it wasn't a good idea. And now out of the blue you want to have dinner with me?"

I bit down hard on my bottom lip before I answered. "I know, but I've given the matter some thought since then. You mentioned you were interested in my opinion about Venery. I thought we might discuss that over dinner."

A long pause and then, "I appreciate the gesture, Shell, but I'm not sure I can do tonight."

Annoyance, sharp and swift, flooded through me. "You know, Patrick, it wasn't exactly easy for me to make this offer. I guess your earlier speech about wanting us to be friends was just a lot of bull."

"It was not," he cried. "It's just . . . I've got a lot going on right now."

"Fine," I said coldly. "If you don't want to, you don't want to."

"I do want to." His words came out in a rush. "I meant every word I said to you earlier. It would please me immensely for us to be friends, and I do want to hear what you have to say about Venery." He blew out a breath. "I'll meet you in the inn dining room at seven thirty. And Shell? I am looking forward to it."

He disconnected. I hung up the phone, hoping that I hadn't just made a huge mistake.

· · ·

Gary shooed me out of the shop shortly before six, and I raced home with Purrday. Two other cats were waiting anxiously at the back door when we came in, and both meowed loudly and swiveled their heads toward their food bowls. "Yes, I know," I said. "Don't worry. Starvation will be averted."

Princess Fuzzypants and Kahlua both butted their heads against my ankles, then followed me to the cupboard where I kept their food. They watched me intently as I pulled out two cans of chicken and tuna. I held them out, and all three cats licked their lips in unison.

Cats fed, I went into my room and changed out of my work attire. The Fox Hollow Inn's dining room was considered upscale in Fox Hollow, so I decided to dress the part. I rummaged through my closet and pulled out a slinky black dress I'd gotten on sale last week at Taylor's. I'd originally planned to save it for a date with Josh, but what the heck? Now was as good a time as any to debut it. I put the dress on with strappy black sandals, added two-inch gold hoop earrings and a gold bracelet, and brushed my hair until it framed my face like a fluffy golden halo. As I studied my reflection in the mirror, Purrday padded into the room. He hopped up on the bed and looked at me, then raised his paw.

"Ow-orrr."

"Glad you approve, my little fashion consultant." It wasn't the first time Purrday had passed judgment on one of my outfits.

Purrday cocked his head. Was that disapproval I saw in his eyes? "Don't worry," I assured him. "I'm not making up with Patrick. But there's no harm in letting him see what he missed out on, is there?"

Purrday blinked his big blue eye, then hopped off the bed and strolled over to the fleece cat bed in front of the window. He hopped in, turned around twice, and then lay down. A few seconds later I could hear his light snoring. Oh, for the life of a cat! I blew him a kiss and murmured, "Sweet dreams," as I shut the door.

• • •

The inn's parking lot was crowded when I pulled in. News of Venery's being in charge of the kitchen tonight must have spread. I saw an empty spot near the back entrance, parked, and decided to go in that way rather than walk all the way around to the front. I pushed through the door and almost ran straight into the back of a woman with flame red hair who stood right in front of it. She turned around and glared at me. "Sorry," I heard myself murmur, even though I wasn't totally to blame.

She didn't say a word, just turned her back on me, effectively halting any further conversation. I shrugged and started for the main lobby, and as I passed the bank of elevators, one opened and a man hurried out. He was dressed in an expensive-looking three-piece suit that reeked of Brooks Brothers, and even though his tall chef's cap was absent, I recognized Reynaldo Venery. The redhead saw him too, and immediately made a beeline for him. He glanced up, saw her, and his lips drooped downward. He turned quickly and started to move down the corridor, but she caught up to him and grabbed his arm.

"Thirty minutes," I heard her say. "That's all I need. "Or fifteen, whichever you choose. It's up to you."

He looked at her in much the same manner as I'd seen Purrday look at the birds in the backyard. "It's up to me, eh? Then I choose neither."

The redhead didn't seem at all intimidated by Venery's brusque manner. She stood her ground, hands on her curvy hips. "I won't be put off, Rey. You and I both know you want to hear what I have to say, and you sure as heck don't want me to say it in public."

Venery's nostrils flared and his eyes widened, showing the whites. "You are bluffing."

The redhead stood her ground. "Am I?"

His lips pulled back in a snarl and he took a step toward the redhead. Jabbing his finger in the air, he said, "Understand this. I won't be threatened."

"It's not a threat," the redhead said coolly. "It's a promise."

Venery stood erect, feet planted apart. "Then," he said, "I would be very careful about making promises you cannot keep. Because if push comes to shove, I have a few *promises* of my own to make good on." With that, he turned on his heel and practically sprinted down the corridor. The woman stared after him for a second, a startled expression on her face, and then followed him. Hm, I thought. Was this another woman scorned, or was there another angle to this meeting? I hesitated, torn between heading over to the dining room or following Venery and the woman to see how the rest of the drama played out. And while I was debating that, a hand came down on my shoulder and spun me around.

Chapter Seven

I let out an involuntary gasp as I stared into Patrick's eyes. I shoved his hand away and took a step backward. "Geez," I said. "What were you trying to do, give me a heart attack?"

"Not at all," my ex said. "You looked a bit disoriented. I was only trying to help."

I took another step backward. "Well, I'm not disoriented. I was just thinking about something." For some reason, I thought it best not to mention what I'd just seen. "Are you ready for dinner?"

"About that." He hesitated, and I saw uncertainty flicker in those blue eyes. "I'm awfully sorry, Shell. Something really important's come up, and I'm afraid I'm going to have to take a rain check."

I decided to bite the bullet. "Look, Patrick, I did some research and I know about Venery being wooed by other producers. I'll bet Venery has been putting you off, considering those other offers, and you came here to try and convince him to sign on with your show."

"You've really become quite the sleuth, haven't you?" He held up both hands in a gesture of surrender. "Okay, I admit I came here hoping to finally get him to sign the contract. The man's been stonewalling me for weeks. I thought that perhaps I could force his hand, get him to make a decision."

I made a clucking sound with my tongue. "If you really have your heart set on this guy, I don't think force is the right way to go. You might end up pushing him away."

Patrick sighed. "Sometimes I think that wouldn't be such a bad thing, but Venery is popular, and that's what I need right now. At our first meeting he said he loved the show's concept, and I really thought we had a deal. But then he kept hemming and hawing, putting me off. I found out about those other offers, and I confronted him about it. He denied it, but I knew he was lying." His hand came up and he ran it through his thick mass of hair, messing up the ends. "I hired a PI to get intel and I found out that he's been in talks with Teslor Productions."

"Teslor, huh?" I'd heard of that production company. They'd started out shortly before *Spy Anyone* had been canceled. The company was small but was reported to be growing fast. "They're thinking about a cooking reality show too?"

"Yes. The concept is slightly different, but Venery would still be the main focus."

"Well . . . maybe the fact that Venery agreed to meet with you this weekend means he's leaning toward choosing you."

Patrick's shoulders hunched, and he avoided looking directly at me. "Ah, about that . . . that's not exactly true."

My eyes narrowed. "What do you mean? You said that Venery agreed to meet."

"No, I said that Venery told me he would be here this weekend and that it was a good time for a meet. I never said anything was arranged." He blew out a breath. "The truth is, Venery's been avoiding me ever since I arrived. He's refused to see me or take my calls. I finally managed to corner him a few hours ago. I told him I knew about the other offers, and that I'd heard Teslor Productions was in the running. I asked him point-blank if he was meeting with a representative of theirs here and he said point-blank that while he did have some business in Fox Hollow aside from the charity event, he had no negotiations for any kind of television show going on."

I cocked my head at him. "But you don't believe him?"

He shot me an exasperated look. "Of course I don't. I have a feeling that he's meeting with someone from Teslor, possibly even as we speak."

A lightbulb clicked in my mind. "If I recall correctly, the head of Teslor Productions is a woman, right?"

He nodded. "Yes. Tessa Taylor."

I tapped a finger against my cheek. "Would she happen to be about five-three, flame hair, a rather curvaceous figure?"

Patrick's jaw dropped and his eyes popped wide. "How on earth could you know that?"

"I saw her with Venery just a few minutes ago. She wanted to talk to him, but Venery told her to get lost."

Patrick's expression brightened. "He did?"

I nodded. "She wanted a half hour of his time and he essentially told her to take a hike. Then he stalked off toward the elevators, but she was right on his tail."

"Hm." Patrick stroked at his chin. "I'm not surprised. Tessa's quite a go-getter, that's why her company has become so successful. She's got a rep for always getting her man—by any means—which is exactly why I have to stay one step ahead of her."

I frowned. "One step ahead? What does that mean? Patrick, I hope you're not planning on doing anything foolish."

"I like to think I've learned from my mistakes, Shell. My biggest one was letting you go." He held up his hand. "Don't worry, I have no expectations in that area. Just wish me luck."

He leaned forward, gave me a peck on the cheek, then turned on his heel and hurried off down the hall. I started to go after him, then stopped. Keeping Patrick out of trouble wasn't my responsibility anymore. He was a big boy, after all. My stomach growled, reminding me of the reason I was here. I pulled out my phone and hit the speed dial button for Gary. The call went directly to voicemail. "Oh well," I murmured as I slid my phone back into my purse, "there are worse things in life than eating solo."

· · ·

The hostess led me to a beautifully set table in the center of the dining room, then placed a velvet-covered menu as well as a wine list before me. Since I was driving I decided to forgo the wine and studied the menu instead. I was trying to decide between the lobster Newburgh and steak Diane when a waiter came out of the kitchen balancing a tray on which rested a delicious-smelling rack of lamb. I sniffed the air appreciatively as he passed my table and headed for one set far back near a secluded alcove. I recognized the redheaded woman sitting there immediately. Tessa Taylor. Apparently she'd given up on Venery and decided to eat instead. That theory seemed to be confirmed when the waiter set the rack of lamb in front of her. She'd barely taken a bite of her meal when she put down the utensils and reached for her phone, which was lying there on the table. She picked it up and I saw her eyes widen. The next instant she pushed her chair back, snatched up her purse and hurried toward the rear exit. I couldn't help but wonder what had prompted that. A meet with Venery? Or Patrick?

I scraped my own chair back and hurried out the same way as Tessa had. Once in the corridor, I looked around. There was no sign of the redhead, but she couldn't have gone very far. I made a left and moved swiftly down the hallway. No sign of Tessa Taylor. I was about to turn to go back to the dining room when I heard the rumble of voices further down the corridor. One of the voices sounded like Venery's. I looked around and spotted a small alcove partially concealed by a potted plant off to my left. I'd just squeezed into the crevice behind the plant when two figures came into view. They paused, inches from my hiding place. I peeped out from behind the leaves of the plant. One figure stood directly in front of me, and I recognized Venery even before I heard his voice.

"I know you lodged a complaint. Foolish move, my dear. You above all should know what happens to people who cross me," Venery said. "And to people who refuse to help me. Just remember, you have far more to lose than I. And you do owe me, remember?"

The other figure murmured something too low for me to hear. Curiosity burned inside me. The build was slight, so I suspected it was female. Tessa Taylor, perhaps? Or possibly a current or former flame of the chef's?

Venery turned and marched off down the hall. The second figure choked back a sob and moved into the light. I had to choke back a gasp as I recognized Venery's companion. It wasn't Tessa Taylor.

It was Louise Gates.

Chapter Eight

"So how do I look?" I did a pirouette for the two felines sprawled across my comforter. Princess Fuzzypants sat up and waved one paw in the air. "Merow," she said.

I grinned. "Thanks. I think I look pretty good myself. And so do the two of you."

The princess let out a rumbling purr. I'd gotten silk collars for the cats to wear that had "Feline Ambassador" emblazoned in script on them. The princess's was red, Purrday's blue, and Kahlua's white. I looked over at Purrday. "How about you, Purrday? Do you think we look good?"

Purrday raised his head. He closed his good eye, opened it again, then lifted his paw and batted at the collar. He made a murphing sound and rolled over on his side. "Okay, I get it. You don't like your collar. Relax, it's only for a few hours. What do you think of my dress?"

Purrday turned his head and made a motion resembling a shrug. "Merow."

"That's it? Somehow I expected more out of my main furry fashion guru," I said. I paused and did a twirl before my full-length mirror. The dress was one I'd worn once before to an Emmy Awards after-party. It was a deep cobalt-blue with a V neckline and a flared skirt. I especially liked the sheer chiffon sleeves that puckered slightly at the wrist. A matching blue scarf with silver threads running through it was knotted casually around my throat. I picked up my silver evening bag and slipped into my matching shoes. "Come on, let's go find Kahlua and Gary. Josh will be here soon." I wagged my finger at them. "You cats are goodwill ambassadors tonight, remember."

Both Purrday and Princess Fuzzypants let out loud meows. I assumed that meant they were looking forward to their assignment.

Gary was just coming out of his room when the cats and I exited mine. He paused and let out a loud whistle. "Wow, you look fantastic, Shell. Isn't that the dress you wore to the 2022 Emmy Awards? Joshy's eyes are gonna pop out!"

"Thanks for the compliment," I said. I gave him and his black suit a quick once-over. "You look pretty spiffy yourself. Olivia will swoon—and so will the vulture."

"Vulture? What vulture?"

"Oh, nothing important," I said with a dismissive wave of my hand. "I hope Josh gets here soon. I want to try and have a word with Louise before the event begins."

Earlier today I'd done more research on Venery. I'd found an article in *Foodie Magazine* that went into Venery's education and touched on his background, growing up in Georgia. It was at the end of the article, though, that I found something really interesting: a detailed list of all the restaurants Venery'd worked in during his career. One name on the list stood out: Maison Richard in New Orleans.

I remembered Louise had mentioned she'd worked as a sous chef in New Orleans. Was it possible she and Venery had worked at the same restaurant? I struggled to remember the conversation I'd overheard between Venery and Louise last night. Venery had said something about Louise owing him. Why? Was it because of something that had happened at this restaurant? I'd gone on the Maison Richard website and on their "About Us" page found an old photograph that depicted the cooking staff. It was rather grainy, though, and even though I immediately recognized Venery, it was hard to tell if one of the other chefs might be Louise.

The doorbell rang, and I raced down the stairs, cats at my heels, to open the front door. Josh stood there, and I grinned at him. "Why, Detective Bloodgood," I said. "You sure do clean up nice."

He grinned back. "Why, thank you, ma'am." The charcoal gray suit fit across his broad shoulders like it had been molded to his body. The collar of his pure white shirt was a distinct contrast to his almost black hair, and the tie he wore was almost the exact same shade of blue as his eyes. Even his black shoes gleamed. "You look pretty amazing yourself."

I did a twirl. "It must be the dress. Either that or the fact that we haven't seen each other all week."

"That could have something to do with it," he said with a chuckle. "Oh, and by the way, no worries that I'll get pulled away this evening. Amy Riser agreed to fill in for me tonight if I took over her weekend shift next week. Her boyfriend wants to take her on a weekend trip to New York." He shifted his gaze to my feet. "I see your entourage is ready to go."

I looked down and saw Kahlua had joined the other two. "I think they've been looking forward to it all day. Their day wasn't as busy as mine. They got to take catnaps."

Gary came over, hand outstretched. "Hey, Joshy," he said. "Good to see you. Looking forward to tonight? At least you know the dead body won't be a real one."

"That will be a nice change of pace," Josh agreed. "I just hope the weather holds up until after the event is over."

We all looked out the window at the dark clouds looming overhead, a sharp contrast to the earlier sunny sky. "Looks like the weather person might be right for a change," I remarked. "Leila said they were predicting a hurricane for tonight."

"Oh, yeah. With escalating winds. They were starting to kick up when I got here." Josh turned the collar of his coat up. "Let's hope the worst holds off until after midnight. There are varying reports. Some say it will hold off, some say the worst will hit us around nine, and one lone fellow actually thought there was a chance it would pass over."

"I like that guy, whoever he is," I remarked.

"This weather feels more like March than June," Gary said. He pulled his car keys out of his pocket. "Well, I've got to go pick up Olivia. We'll see you at the inn later." He edged closer to me and said in a low tone, "Before I go, want to tell me just who the vulture you mentioned earlier is?"

I grinned at him. "Oh, you'll know it when you see it, trust me."

"You want to be mysterious, huh? Okay, fine. Good luck with Louise, though. I'm curious as to what she'll have to say about what you found out earlier."

"That makes two of us."

Gary gave me a wave, hopped in his car and drove off. I turned the collar of my own coat up. The wind was strong, much stronger than I'd expected, and I looked askance at the trees that surrounded the property. They actually seemed to be bending with the wind. We ran quickly over to Josh's car and got in, me in the front, the cats in the back. As Josh backed out of the driveway, I turned the radio to the local news station. The weather report was just finishing.

". . . that hurricane is still a few hours off, but already the winds have started to kick up in some parts of the state. The National Weather Service has issued a Severe Storm Warning for most parts of the state, and state officials are saying if you don't absolutely have to go out, please stay home."

I shut the radio off. "Darn. I hope that weather report doesn't keep people from coming tonight."

"Not to jinx your fundraiser," said Josh, "but I rather hope the majority of folks take the weather service's advice and stay off the roads. If this storm turns out to be as bad as they predict, I'll probably get called in anyway." He sighed. "I bet Amy is kicking herself for agreeing to sub tonight. Man, am I gonna pay for this."

• • •

Marianne rushed up to us the moment we arrived. "Thank goodness you got here all right. Do you hear that wind? Maybe we should have canceled," she added fretfully.

"There are a lot of varying reports," I said. I gave her arm a reassuring pat. "Maybe Lady Luck will stay with us and the worst will hold off until after the event is over."

The wind chose that moment to let out a fierce howl, and Josh held up his phone. "If you'll excuse me, I just want to call in and make sure everything's going smoothly."

Josh moved off and a short, dark-haired woman approached us. "Hello, I'm Andrea Palmer, the night manager. Ms. Gates wanted me to welcome you and be sure everything was set up according to your specifications."

I bit back a disappointed cry. "Louise isn't here?"

"Oh, Ms. Gates is here, it's just . . ." She lowered her voice and continued, "One of the chefs misplaced Chef Venery's special knife. He doesn't know yet, so she's been tearing apart the kitchen, trying to find it before Venery has a kitten."

I remembered the fit Venery had thrown over the gnocchi and could just imagine what he'd do if his knife were missing. "I completely understand," I said.

Andrea smiled. "Thanks. Now, if you'll follow me . . ."

Marianne and I accompanied Andrea to the Appalachian Room. I blinked in astonishment as I entered. The setting for this particular murder mystery scenario was a fabulous penthouse suite on Manhattan's Upper East Side belonging to a rich financier. Sissy and Roz, the teen volunteers, had gone all out to transform the entire right side of the room into just that. The center of the room held a chaise lounge and some wing chairs, and they'd set them before a mock fireplace, above which hung an oil painting of a white-bearded gentleman who looked a bit ominous himself. I had no idea where they'd gotten the painting from, but it certainly contributed to the mood.

We heard the buzz of a cell phone and Andrea fished hers out of her pocket. She looked at the screen and said, "I'm sorry, I have to go out front. If there's anything else you need, just ask."

Andrea left and Marianne handed me a sheet of paper. "These are the hiding places for the weapons," she said. "I put Sissy in charge and she got a little creative, if you ask me."

I took the paper and ran my finger down the printed list. Sissy had hidden our selection of murder weapons—dagger, lead pipe, revolver and vial of poison—in very strategic places throughout the set. "She did indeed," I agreed. "Did she update the murderer's packet with the weapon of choice?"

"She did," Marianne said with a laugh. "And she was thrilled beyond words that we let her choose the weapon. Or, as she put it, the 'instrument of doom.' She refuses to tell us which one she picked, though. Said that since we're picking out the murderer and victim, something should be a surprise."

"I guess that makes sense." I glanced around at the dining area proper. Louise's staff had done a wonderful job here too. There were tables set for ten arranged in a geometric pattern. Off to the left were two long tables set with silver and gold tablecloths. Three carving stations were positioned in back of each of the tables. The gold table already had several silver chafing dishes set up, from which delicious smells emanated.

Marianne raised her hand, fingers crossed. "Now if that storm can only hold off till after the event ends, we'll be all set."

We made our way back to the room's entrance, where two tables had been set up. One contained a sign-in sheet, the other the clue packets the guests received to aid them in solving the murder. I glanced at my watch. "I guess we should start setting all these out. The guests will be arriving soon."

"That reminds me. I wonder what's keeping your mother . . . and our actors," murmured Marianne. She cast an anxious glance at her own watch. "They were supposed to be here an hour ago to go over the skit and get into their costumes." She gestured toward the rack of clothing, which had been donated by Kandy Korn Costumes. "Good Lord," she cried as the door to the front entrance suddenly banged open. "Was—was that the wind?"

The next moment my mother fairly flew into the lobby, accompanied by Garrett Knute. Even though her French twist was a little undone from the wind, I had to admit my mother looked spectacular in her outfit: black crepe wide-legged pants and a white lace blouse, topped with a black sequined jacket. "It's really starting to get nasty out there," she declared. "No rain yet, but that wind—whew!" She reached up to give her hair a pat. "I must look a fright."

Garrett patted my mother's arm. He looked very dapper in his three-piece gray pinstriped suit, his iron-gray hair slicked back. "Not at all, Clarissa," he said soothingly. "You hardly have a hair out of place."

She beamed at him. "How sweet of you to say. Well, I'll give myself a quick once-over in the ladies' room. Here's hoping the worst of this storm will hold off, or maybe even blow over."

Garrett looked at me, a twinkle in his eye. "I see your goodwill ambassadors are here and ready for duty." I followed his gaze and saw Purrday, Princess Fuzzypants and Kahlua lined up like a reception line. "They don't appear to be bothered by the storm," he observed.

"Purrday and the princess don't seem to mind them. Kahlua usually hides under the bed."

The door opened again and this time Charisma Walters sailed through, a large amber Ragdoll cat clutched tightly in her arms. "Goodness, it seems as if Mother Nature isn't going to let up," she said. "I hope this storm doesn't end up being as bad as all the weather forecasters are predicting. If it is, we may all end up spending the night here." Her gaze dropped downward and the corners of her lips twitched upward. "Ah, and who are these good-looking feline friends?"

I introduced each cat. Charisma smiled and shifted the Ragdoll in her arms. "And this is my baby, Serendipity." She set the cat down. Serendipity's rhinestone collar gleamed in the hall lights. My cats regarded her warily for a moment, and I could have sworn I saw the princess and Kahlua glance down at their own collars. Then Purrday stepped forward and gave a tentative sniff. Serendipity let out a soft meow, then she turned to the other two female cats. "Merow," she said. The princess and Kahlua both stepped forward and gave the newcomer a welcoming sniff.

I looked at Charisma. "Looks like they'll get along."

Charisma laughed. "Of course they will, dear. Serendipity is a very laid-back cat. She gets along with most animals."

Sniffing done, the four cats trotted off in the direction of the cat adoption room. Charisma watched them go then turned to me. "I don't know about you, but this darn storm has me a bit rattled. I could use some liquid nourishment—and I don't mean water."

"I'll show you where it is," Marianne offered. "I could do with some liquid courage myself."

"Thank you—Marianne, right?" said Charisma. She gave a quick glance around. "I thought perhaps Gary Presser would be here . . . and Patrick Hanratty."

"Gary will be here shortly. He's picking up Olivia Niven, my friend and his date," I added. I saw Charisma's lips droop slightly at that. "I have no idea where Patrick is, but I'm sure he'll be here. He promised my mother he'd attend."

"Of course Patrick is coming." We all turned to see my mother come up behind us. "He assured me there was no way he'd miss it—besides, he's staying right here at the inn."

Charisma's eyes lit up. "Is he? How convenient." She took Marianne's arm. "Now, how about that drink?"

The two of them headed for the bar, and I turned to my mother. "I haven't seen the adoption room yet. Marianne said the girls did a great job. Want to come with me?"

My mother sighed. "I suppose I should. So, Crishell, lead the way."

• • •

When I opened the door to the coat-check room just behind the dining area, I let out a little cry. The girls had done a marvelous job transforming the area into a miniature shelter. The cages for the twelve cats and kittens that had been transported here tonight were lined up against the wall, and they'd cordoned off a small area just in case a potential parent might want to play a bit with a potential adoptee. There were catnip toys, a jungle gym for cats, and a long tunnel set up in the designated play area, along with a wide table and three chairs in the other corner for potential parents to fill out the required shelter forms. A shorter table to the left of the entrance had the programs we'd had made up with photos of the cats up for adoption, both here and at the shelter. Another sheeted table had pitchers of water and soda on them, and a large platter of cookies as well. Roz Tidwell was just reaching for a cookie when we walked in. "Hey, Ms. McMillan, nice to see you."

"Hello, Roz. This is my mother, Clarissa McMillan. You and Sissy have done a fabulous job back here."

Sissy was bent over one of the cages, playing with a beautiful all-black cat. As we approached, the cat sat back on her haunches and narrowed her wide eyes, apparently displeased at having her play time interrupted. She let out a soft growl as we approached. "Hey, Dahlia, none of that when a potential owner approaches your cage," Sissy admonished the cat. The cat's response was another growl, and then she turned around twice and flopped over on her side, her back to us. Sissy wiggled her fingers at the cat. "Don't mind Dahlia. She's just annoyed because she can't wander around here like she does at the shelter. She's become quite adept at unlocking her cage. But she won't do any of that tonight," Sissy added quickly. She looked at the cat, who was hunched in the far corner of the cage. "You're a spoiled girl, but best behavior tonight. You want to get adopted, right?" She glanced back at me and her eyes widened. "Shell, did you get another cat?"

I looked down and saw Serendipity making her way tentatively toward Dahlia's cage. She poked her nose through the bars and meowed softly. Dahlia's head swiveled. She saw the cat, and she bared her fangs and let out a sharp hiss. Serendipity immediately moved away from the cage and ambled off toward Purrday, which elicited a sharp meow from Princess Fuzzypants.

"Smart cat," I observed. "She knows when to quit. And she's not mine. This is Serendipity. She belongs to the social media expert, Charisma Walters."

"Oh, right, now I recognize her from the photos on Charisma's blog," said Sissy. "She did say in her post today that she and Serendipity were attending the fundraiser tonight. Do you know she got over forty thousand responses for donations to the shelter?"

"She did mention she'd hoped to get at least fifty thousand," I responded. "She came close."

"Hey, she's not done. Donations are open through tomorrow. She could well pass fifty," said Sissy. She gave me a hopeful look. "Do you think she'll come back here? We'd love to meet her in person."

"I'm sure she will. And I bet she puts photos on her blog, too, of the great job you two did. I do feel bad, though, that you're going to miss the event by volunteering to stay in here."

"Oh, don't worry about us," said Roz. She reached under the table and pulled out a familiar box. "We brought Clue so we can have our own murder mystery party here."

"So what happens now?" asked my mother. "Do your cats and Charisma's stay here?"

"No, they'll go back into the reception area and greet the people as they arrive. Hopefully they'll lead some back here to look at the animals and maybe adopt one or two." I looked at the two teens. "When the skit starts, though, I'll need you girls to make sure the cats all stay in here."

"That's right," my mother agreed. "We don't need any cats prancing into the dining room just as our murder is being committed—although I imagine Shell's cats are used to that sort of thing." She looked down her nose and added, "Purrday in particular."

Purrday raised his head. "Merow."

"No problem," Sissy said. "Roz and I won't let them out of our sight, but we know they'll be good, right, guys?"

Four pair of feline eyes blinked simultaneously.

"Thanks," I said. "I'll be back to get them once the guests start arriving."

Mother and I returned to the lobby, where we found Marianne and Charisma chatting. Each held a drink in her hand. "We still have a little time before the festivities begin," said my mother. "I think I'll get a drink too. This storm isn't doing my nerves any good."

Garrett took her arm. "One would never know you're nervous, my dear. I imagine we can attribute that to your fine ability as an actress. It takes a lot of talent to maintain such a cool exterior."

My mother batted her eyelashes. "Why, thank you, Garrett," she purred. "It's nice to know someone appreciates my artistic abilities."

She linked her arm through Garrett's and the two of them started for the bar. I decided this might be a good time to try and track down Louise. Midway down the hall I caught a glimpse of none other than Chef Reynaldo Venery. He was wearing a white apron over what appeared to be an expensive-looking suit, his white chef's cap perched on his head. He was talking on his cell, and appeared to be pretty calm, so I guessed he still hadn't heard about his knife. I saw a door off to my left and without any hesitation, tried the knob. The door opened and I saw that it was a utility closet. I squeezed myself in between the wall and the vacuum cleaner and closed the door, leaving it open just enough for me to peer out.

Venery was very close to my hiding place now, and to my consternation he stopped dead right in front of it. "I told you, I want nothing to do with that situation," he barked into the phone. "How many ways can I say this? Now, please do not bother me about this again."

He shoved the phone into his pocket with an oath and started to turn in the direction of the kitchen, when suddenly a familiar voice called out, "Venery! Wait!"

I held my breath as the speaker came into view. Patrick! He marched right up to the shorter man and waved his finger under his nose. "Don't walk away from me, Venery. I'm not finished talking to you."

Venery turned his glittering stare on Patrick. "As I told you before, we have nothing to talk about. I'm considering another show, one that appears to be a much better fit for me."

"It's Taylor's show, isn't it?" Patrick spat. "How did she convince you to pick her? Does she have something on you?"

Venery's facial expression didn't change one iota. "What makes you say a thing like that?"

"Because it's been my experience that men like you always have something to hide. And if you do, Venery, I swear I'll find it out. I'll ruin you just like you're going to ruin me."

Something flickered in Venery's eyes: anger? fear? It was gone as quickly as it appeared, and he pulled down hard on the lapels of his jacket. "Don't be ridiculous, Hanratty. There's nothing for you to find. No one forced me to do anything. You have no one to blame for this but yourself."

Patrick's face purpled. He leaned in closer to Venery. "Do you know, right now . . . I could kill you."

"Yeah, well, get in line. There are a lot of people ahead of you for that particular honor." Venery sneered. "Excuse me, I have a dinner to supervise."

Venery stalked off. Patrick scrubbed his hands over his face, then walked off in the same direction. I waited a few moments more for good measure, then emerged from the utility closet. I had to admit Patrick's outburst upset me. I'd never known him to lose his cool like that before. I glanced at my watch again and sighed. No time to hunt down Louise now. Maybe I'd get a chance later. I started to head back to the dining room when Marianne suddenly materialized out of nowhere. "Oh, Shell. It's a disaster!" She waved her arm in a circle and started to talk very fast. "We might as well start packing up everything now. I just got a call from Milton Knapf, the manager of Foxglove Entertainment. He just got off the phone with the state police. It seems the bus carrying our actors was involved in a terrible accident. They're not coming. Face it. Our event is ruined."

Chapter Nine

I thrust out my hand and laid it on Marianne's shoulder. "Calm down, Marianne. Take a deep breath and then tell me exactly what happened. What sort of accident?"

Marianne paused, took a deep breath, let it out. In a slightly calmer tone she said, "A tree, uprooted by this vicious wind, fell on the bus that was carrying them here. Five of the actors were rushed to the hospital. The others seem to be okay—minor injuries—but there's no way they can get here tonight, and Milton has no one else to send." A thin sheen of sweat had broken out on her forehead, and her hand moved up to rub at the back of her neck. "This whole event is ruined. There's no one to put on the skit. We might as well pack up the cats and give everyone their money back."

I nibbled at my lower lip as I thought. "Well, now, wait a minute. Maybe we can still pull this off."

Marianne's expression brightened a bit. "You think so? How?"

"Well, maybe some of the guests would like to become part of the show."

Marianne's face fell. "I doubt that, Shell. The people I talked to are more interested in trying to guess whodunit and win that grand prize of a spa weekend at the Hilton."

"Maybe so, but it doesn't hurt to ask." I looked at my watch. "They should be arriving now. Let's go back outside."

Sure enough, a line was starting to form in front of the reception table. My mother and Garret sat behind the table, checking off names. I saw Leila Simmons just moving away from the table and I hurried over to her. "You were in the Drama Club in college, right?"

"Yeah, and hello to you too." She paused and looked at me intently. "Something's wrong. Is one of the skit actors sick?"

"Worse. We just found out that the bus carrying the actors was in a very bad accident. They're not coming," Marianne blurted out.

"Oh my gosh! Not the accident on Mulholland Bridge? That was a real disaster, from what I heard. Fortunately no one was seriously injured or killed." She glanced around the crowded lobby. "I wouldn't mind taking one of the parts, and I'm sure some of the Fox Hollow Players are here. I'm sure they'd be glad to help out. As a matter of fact, I saw a few of them in the lobby. I'll go ask them right now."

Leila hurried off and I turned to Marianne. "If I remember correctly, there are eight or ten parts that need to be filled." I looked at Marianne. "You have a copy of that skit script, right?"

Marianne nodded. "Yes. I'll go get it."

She hurried out and returned a few minutes later with the scripts. I grabbed one and thumbed quickly through it. "Not too bad," I muttered. "Eight roles in total, four female, four male. And we still have to choose the murderer and victim." I paused. "I'll take the part of the killer."

"You can't," Marianne cried. "As sponsors, we're not allowed to participate, remember? We're tasked with choosing the winners."

"I think considering the circumstances, an exception can be made. I'm sure Mother and Garrett Knute can handle picking the lucky winners," I replied. "Which means you can take on one of the roles too," I added in a pleading tone.

Marianne hesitated, then nodded. "Of course, if it means saving the fundraiser. But I'd prefer a small part."

Leila returned a few moments later with Vi and John Kizis in tow. "Vi and John said they'd be glad to take two of the parts."

John, a tall, heavyset man with black hair, grinned. "In college when we did murder mysteries I always played the victim. Our drama coach said no one could play dead as good as me."

"Okay, you've got it." I dug through the packets, found the one marked *Victim* and pressed it into his hand. He opened it and grinned. "Francis X. Leonard, ruthless businessman. Perfect."

"I'll take whatever you want to give me," said Vi. "As long as I'm not the murderer."

"Don't worry, that part's already taken," I assured her. While Leila, Vi and Marianne flipped through the script, I reached for the packet marked *Murderer*, opened it and quickly scanned the paper inside. "Looks like our killer is Ashley VanHorn, the editor of *Style* magazine. Seems Francis X. was blackmailing her over an illegitimate child."

Leila looked up from the script and said, "I'll take Kara, the ingénue. She's got quite a few lines."

"So does Elena the interior designer," remarked Vi. "I can handle that."

"It's always been a dream of Vi's to be a real actress, like the one she used to idolize, right, dear?" John said. He chuckled. "You used to pore over that newsletter every three months like it was gold."

"Yeah, like you aren't a closet thespian too," Vi shot back. She grinned at me. "He can recite most of Shakespeare's soliloquies in his sleep."

While Vi and John continued their good-natured arguing, I held a script out to Marianne. "That leaves Monique the party planner for you. She doesn't have many lines at all."

"I suppose," sighed Marianne. "Who's left?"

I consulted the character list. "We need to fill the remaining male roles: the lawyer, the stockbroker, and the author."

"I saw Doug Harriman in the parking lot," ventured Vi. "He's with the Fox Hollow Players. I'm sure he'll take one of the roles."

I knew Doug. He was a photographer for the *Fox Hollow Gazette*. Quentin Watson, the editor and owner of the *Gazette*, had tasked him with getting photos of the event. "I'm sure he will," I said. "Especially if he can get some behind-the-scenes photos. That would score him some points with Quentin."

"How about asking your ex," suggested Leila. "I know directing is his forte, but I bet he'd be happy to take one of the male roles."

"Maybe," I said. "I haven't seen him so far though."

Andrea Palmer stuck her head in the doorway. "Sorry to interrupt your meeting, Shell, but your mother asked me to find you and Marianne. Guests are starting to arrive and need to be checked in. She's also a bit concerned because the acting troupe isn't here yet."

I looked at Marianne. "I take it Mother hasn't a clue what happened?"

"Milton couldn't reach her, so he called me. I think your mother probably shut off her phone." Marianne laid her script down. "I'll go and bring her up to date."

Marianne and Andrea hurried off, nearly colliding with Josh. "There you are," he said. "I just got a call from Amy. There was a major accident just off the highway."

"I heard," I said. I quickly filled Josh in on what had happened with the actors' bus, ending with, "Leila suggested that we take on the parts. I don't suppose you'd care to do one?"

"I would," he said, "but I really should be available, just in case things worsen and Amy needs me." He touched my arm. "I'm sorry."

"No need to be," I said. "I understand, but I hope you don't have to leave."

We made our way back to the main lobby. Josh's phone beeped, and as he took the call, I stole a quick glance out the large picture widow. No rain yet, but I could see tree branches swaying and leaves swirling in what looked to be a very blustery wind. No one could predict the weather, but I had to admit it certainly was an appropriate background for tonight's event. I saw Marianne with Doug Harriman, his Nikon slung around his neck. As I passed, she lifted her hand and gave me a thumbs-up.

The line at the reception table stretched midway out into the lobby. Apparently the weather hadn't scared many of the attendees off. I saw Garrett Knute seated behind the table, checking off names. The assistant manager, Andrea, sat beside him, handing out tickets and smiling and chatting with the guests. Charisma Walters stood off to one side, deep in conversation with Marianne and my mother. I walked right over to them and my mother threw out her arms dramatically. "Marianne just told us about the accident," she cried. "What a terrible thing to happen."

"We're trying to recruit volunteers to take on the parts so we don't have to cancel," I said. "In true showbiz tradition, the show will go on."

"Wonderful," said Charisma. "So I take it you've been successful with your recast?"

"Almost. We still have two male parts to cast. Vi, Marianne, Leila and I are taking over the female roles."

"Crishell! You and Marianne absolutely cannot do that," my mother cried. "None of the sponsors are allowed to participate!" She waved one arm dramatically in the air.

I started to protest when Charisma cut in. "Look, if it will help, I'd be happy to take one of the parts. I was quite the thespian in college."

"Are you certain you want to do that?" asked my mother. "After all, you came here to review and publicize the event, not get commandeered into service."

"Trust me, Clarissa, it's no trouble. I would love to do this," Charisma said. Her face glowed just like a kid at Christmas. "The experience will make a tremendous article for the blog—an inside look at how a murder mystery dinner comes together."

"You can choose between my role and Marianne's," I said. "Marianne's part only has a few lines. Mine is meatier and . . ." I leaned over and whispered in Charisma's ear, "She's the killer."

Charisma's eyes glowed even brighter. "I'll take your part, Shell." She lowered her voice and added, "I've always wanted to be a killer."

"Great. Then here you go. The coatroom in back of the dining area is where the actors are gathering." I handed over my play packet. Charisma opened it and read the sheet of paper within. "Got it," she said. "This will be . . . interesting."

Charisma moved off and my mother looked at me. "That was very nice of her," she said. "So . . . all the parts are filled?"

"There are still two male roles," I said. "I'm sure when Gary gets here, he'll take one. But unless we can fill the other . . ."

"Say no more. Consider it filled."

My mother and I both whirled around and saw Patrick standing behind us. My first thought was that Charisma would be sorry she missed him. He did look handsome in his black suit and white shirt. I noted he had his favorite pair of cuff links, gold with a blue lion insignia.

My mother reached out and grabbed his hand. "Of course we can count on Patrick to help save the day," she crooned.

Patrick leaned over and kissed my mother on the cheek. "No problem, Clarissa. I know how important this fundraiser is to you." He turned to me. "So? Where do I report for duty?"

"The coat-check room just off the dining area," I said. "Leila will give you the script. If you get there before Gary, you can have your pick."

"Well, then, I'll have to hustle." He touched two fingers to his forehead and started off. My mother looked fondly after him. "You can always depend on Patrick to come through when the chips are down," she said. "And I should get back to the reception table. In spite of the weather, it appears as if everyone's shown up."

My mother left and I squared my shoulders. I wanted to get this event underway as soon as possible, and to do that I had to speak to Louise. But first I needed to round up the cats and get them back to the adoption room. I saw a young couple fawning over Princess Fuzzypants, who was stretched out on the floor at their feet in all her catly glory. The couple turned out to be newlyweds and were definitely interested in adopting a cat. I sent them along to the cat room, then with the princess in tow went to track down the others. I found Kahlua charming an elderly couple. Unfortunately, they already had three cats and weren't interested in adopting a fourth. I was looking around for Purrday and Serendipity when a woman sidled up to me and touched my arm. "Hello, Ms. McMillan."

I looked blank for a moment, and then recognition set in. "Ms. Dalton," I said. "I'm sorry, for a moment I didn't recognize you." With her hair curled and makeup on, dressed in a champagne-colored blouse and black maxi skirt, Doris Dalton looked entirely different than she had at the shelter.

"I know." She let out a nervous giggle and did a little twirl. "When I looked in the mirror I hardly recognized myself either." She twirled her ticket in her hand. "I'm at table thirteen. I hope that's a lucky number. Maybe I'll be the one to guess the killer's identity." She gave a quick look around. "We only just got here. That storm is really starting to kick up. Do you think I'll have time before the show starts to look at the cats?"

"I think so," I said. "Best to go now, because we plan on starting the event shortly."

Ms. Dalton walked off, and I was about to continue my search for the remaining cats when a familiar voice called out, "Hey, we made it." I turned and saw Gary and Olivia heading toward us. I hurried forward and threw my arms around Olivia. "Boy, am I glad to see the two of you," I said.

"You should be," said Gary. "It's really getting nasty out there. To be honest, I actually considered turning around."

"I'm glad you didn't," I said. "We have a bit of a . . . situation." I explained about the accident and what had happened to the acting troupe. When I finished, Gary said promptly, "Say no more. I'll be glad to do the remaining part."

I squeezed his hand. "You ham," I said. "I knew I could count on you." I looked at Olivia. "What about you, Olivia? Marianne really doesn't want to participate. Do you think you could do the party planner role? She only has about a dozen lines."

"I hate to be a spoilsport," said Olivia. "But storms scare the bejesus out of me. One peal of thunder and I'd scream like a victim in a horror movie. Sorry."

Gary put his arm around Olivia. "I'll walk you to your table on my way to the coatroom."

Gary and Olivia walked off. I was about to do the same when someone touched my arm. I turned and saw Andrea looking at me. "Did I hear you say you're looking for someone to do one of the skit parts?" As I nodded she went on, "The receptionist, Summer, was in the Drama Club in college. She might be willing to help out. She's on her break right now. I think she might have gone to the cat room."

"I'm headed there right now. Thanks, Andrea." The woman left and I made my way to the cat adoption room with the princess and Kahlua bringing up the rear. When we entered I saw a large crowd clustered around the cat cages, and I spotted Purrday and Serendipity right in the thick of the crowd, weaving in and out and offering meows of encouragement. Relieved, I glanced around the room. I didn't see Summer, but I did see someone who surprised me—Tessa Taylor. The woman was in a skintight blue dress and standing in front of the black cat's cage, but she didn't seem very interested in Dahlia. From the way she was craning her neck to and fro, I got the impression she was looking for someone. Venery? Patrick?

After a few moments, she walked away from the cage and out the rear entrance. I considered following her but then I spotted Summer over in the far corner, in front of one of the kitten cages. She was deep in conversation with another woman whose back was to me. Summer's brows were drawn together, and she was gesturing with her hands. She looked upset, and for a moment I debated interrupting them. Then her companion turned, and I recognized Doris Dalton. The woman said something to Summer and then turned and walked off in the opposite direction. Summer started to move away as well, but I hurried forward and touched her arm.

"Summer, right?" At her nod I said, "Is everything all right? You look kind of upset."

She hesitated, then shook her head. "No, not really."

"Are you sure? It looked as if you were having a rather unpleasant conversation."

"Oh . . . her." Summer gave her head a shake. "She was asking me questions about the cats. I tried to explain to her that I don't work at the shelter, but . . ." She shrugged. "She was pretty insistent. She finally gave up and said she'd find someone else."

Summer started to move off, but I touched her arm again. "I heard you were in the Drama Club in college."

Summer looked a little surprised. "Why, yes, I was. Why?"

I explained our predicament. Summer listened, and when I finished she shook her head. "I'd like to help," she said, "but I'm on duty tonight. I really shouldn't even be here now."

"I'm sure Andrea can get one of the other girls to cover for you," I said in a pleading tone. "As a matter of fact, I'm positive she would. She was the one who suggested you for a part."

"She did?" Summer's lips twitched upward. "Well, when you put it like that . . . if you're sure I won't get in trouble . . . I'm in." She glanced at her watch and tapped at the face with a red-tipped nail. "I just need to make a phone call first."

Summer moved off and I texted Marianne that Summer would be replacing her. She responded with a jumping-for-joy emoji. I decided now was as good a time as any to track down Louise. I hoped she'd been successful locating Venery's knife. As I rounded the corner I saw her. She had on a black maxi dress, diamond earrings twinkling in her ears. A large diamond brooch in the shape of a flower was pinned to the bodice of the gown. She stood in front of her office, her shoulders hunched, her back to me. She appeared to be speaking very softly into her cell phone. As I drew nearer I heard her say, "I know, I know. I have to take care of him, but I'm not sure just how to do it."

Chapter Ten

For a second I just stood there, stunned. Who was Louise talking to, and who was the "him" she had to take care of? Could it be Venery?

Louise glanced up, saw me, and whispered something too low for me to hear into her phone before she jammed it into the pocket of her dress. She forced a smile to her lips and walked toward me. "Shell, lovely to see you. I'm sorry I wasn't around earlier, but I had some things I had to take care of. I hope everything was to your liking?"

"Your staff did a wonderful job, Louise," I said. "Andrea told me about Venery's missing knife. Were you able to find it?"

Louise's nose wrinkled. "No. It's as if the thing vanished into thin air. To be honest, it wouldn't surprise me if he hid the darn thing himself so he can make a scene later." She glanced upward as the wind howled again. "I do think it might be a wise idea to get the party started, though."

"My thoughts exactly," I said. I filled her in on the accident. "Fortunately we found other people willing to take on the roles, so the show will go on, as they say. But I think because of the weather we should try and make it an early night."

She sighed. "I'll find his nibs and tell him to get the appetizers moving," she said. "All things considered, I don't think he'll put up too much of a fuss—at least I hope not. The man has to have some sense."

She started to move away but I caught her arm. "Speaking of Venery, there's something I wanted to ask you. You mentioned you worked in New Orleans as a chef?"

Louise nodded. "Yes. But that was ages ago. Why?"

"Well, I happened to come across an article about Venery and it mentioned he also worked as a chef in New Orleans, at Maison Richard. So I was wondering . . ."

"If I might have worked with him there?" Louise barked out a laugh. "Shell, there are hundreds of restaurants in that city. And I can assure you, I never worked with a chef named Reynaldo Venery." The wind let out another loud howl. "I think I should try and get things moving. Please excuse me."

She hurried off before I could say another word. I still had the feeling Louise was better acquainted with the volatile chef than she let on, but right now I had to put that aside. I slipped into the main dining room. My mother and Garrett Knute were seated at a table right in front and I hurried over. "Louise is going to have the kitchen start serving appetizers," I said to my mother. "I think this might be a good time to give your welcome speech."

There was another loud peal of thunder and my mother rose to her feet. "I think you're right," she said.

My mother made her way to the dais and I slipped back outside and hurried over to the coatroom. I took one look around and said, "Where's Summer? And Patrick?"

"We were hoping you knew," Leila said. "Neither one has shown up yet." She worried at her lower lip. "So what now? Should we cancel the skit?"

I set my jaw. "No, absolutely not. What part was left for Patrick?"

"The stockbroker," said Gary. "It's only a few lines, though. We could either cut it or I could do both."

"Or me," volunteered John. "I can do two roles."

"No, doing that might confuse the audience. Since neither is the victim or killer, we'll just cut those two parts and hope for the best," I said. "Mother was just about to give her speech, and then they'll start serving the appetizer. That's our cue to start the skit."

I left them donning costumes and slipped in the back of the Appalachian Room to listen to the rest of my mother's speech. As usual, she sounded poised and confident as only Clarissa McMillan could. "I want to thank everyone for coming out tonight. Let's not forget the reason we're gathered here on this dark and stormy night is not only to have some fun playing detective, but to view the shelter's selection of adoptable cats and celebrate National Adopt a Cat Month." When the applause died down she continued, "One last note . . . our food tonight was prepared under the careful supervision of one of the premier chefs in this area. Many of you know him from the cable show *Culinary Surprise*. He wanted his role in this kept low-key, but I think he also deserves a round of applause . . . Chef Reynaldo Venery."

I noticed Venery for the first time. He'd been standing over by the carving stations, and the expression on his face was anything but welcoming. The moment my mother mentioned his name, however, the frown disappeared, replaced by a dazzling smile. He came forward, smiling and bowing. He looked out over the audience and said, "Thank you, everyone. It was my pleasure to help out with the festivities tonight, particularly in light of the fact that it helps support such a worthy cause, finding homes for homeless animals. I trust you will find everything to your liking and . . ."

Venery's voice trailed off and for a fleeting second his expression seemed to darken. The thundercloud look was gone as quickly as it appeared, though, and he cleared his throat and coughed lightly. "Forgive me. I think I'm just a bit overcome. Once again, it has been a pleasure, and bon appetite!"

With that, Venery turned to my mother, gave her a wide smile, and then stalked off toward the kitchen. I turned my head and looked in the same direction that Venery had, fully expecting to see either Patrick or maybe even Tessa Taylor, but all I saw were people seated at their tables, eating and chatting away. I frowned. Something—or someone—had definitely upset the chef, but as to who or what it had been, I hadn't a clue.

• • •

"Someone will be murdered here tonight."

Leila, a long blonde wig covering her dark hair, picked up a large candle and positioned it so it lit her face from below, giving it an eerie cast. She raised her arm and looked out over the audience. "Each of you has known this person in some way. Your connection is in the packet you received tonight. There are weapons hidden throughout this room. Only one is the murder weapon. The others can be used as bargaining chips to barter for information. If you are approached by a player with a weapon, you are obliged to share your information with him or her.

And now, we join a cocktail party given by the fabulously wealthy businessman Francis X. Leonard. Leonard has secrets, but so do his guests. As I said before, someone will meet a tragic end tonight. It is your job to find out whodunit, and why."

Leila blew out the candle, and for a moment the room was in darkness. Then the lights came back on, revealing John, with a white wig, goatee and a very loud jacket seated in a wing chair. Leila went over to him, threw her head back and laughed. She laid one hand on his arm. "Delightful party, Francis X. I didn't realize you had so many friends."

"I didn't either," John, in character as Francis X., said gruffly. "I have a feeling all the vultures are here tonight to hear my big announcement. I fear most of them will not be pleased."

"Really, Francis X.?" Leila batted her heavily made up eyes at him. "Tell me more."

"Yes, Francis. Do tell more," said Charisma. I would have hardly recognized her in that platinum blonde wig and low-cut blouse. If she had a beauty mark, she could easily have passed as a Marilyn Monroe look-alike. My gaze fell on the vase on the small table near Charisma. I knew in a short while, when the lights went off again at a signal from me, she'd take the pearl-handled revolver hidden inside the vase and shoot poor Francis X. with a bullet right through the heart. John's packet had contained a small vial of fake blood that would be used to effect the "fatal wound."

Gary, in his part as the author, rose from his chair and towered over John. "Tell the truth, Francis X.," he hissed. "You're afraid, aren't you? Of what I might put in my newest novel, with the lead character based on you. You're worried what secrets I'll reveal."

John laughed loudly. "Worried? Afraid? Not me. If anyone should be those things, it's you."

Outside the wind was howling so loudly John had to almost shout to make his voice heard over the din. Suddenly we heard a loud crack of thunder and then a crash that shook the building. Several people in the audience screamed. From my position at the rear of the room I had a good view of all the tables. I saw Tessa Taylor get up and glide noiselessly outside. As the door to the main lobby opened, I saw a shadowy figure hurry down the hall. Whoever it was moved too fast for me to discern if it were male or female.

Suddenly there was another loud crash of thunder and all the lights went out, leaving the room in total blackness. I frowned. I hadn't given the signal, so the power outage had to be a result of the storm. I started to inch my way slowly forward, blinking as my eyes gradually became accustomed to the darkness. I saw a few figures moving around on the stage, but I couldn't discern just who they were. Suddenly there came a loud agonized wail, more like a yowl. Suddenly all the lights came back on. Gary, Doug and Leila were on the stage and they all exchanged puzzled glances, before we heard another loud wail, this time from the hallway. "That sounds like a cat," someone yelled out. The side door to the room suddenly banged open and a dark furry form streaked inside and whizzed past us. I sucked in a breath as I recognized Dahlia. Somehow the cat had gotten out of her cage!

The audience, who'd been pretty silent up till now, started to murmur.

"Is this part of the show?" I heard someone say.

"Maybe," someone else answered. "They are showcasing cats, after all."

Dahlia, meantime, had jumped up on the lectern and stood there, her back arched, tail erect. Her green eyes seemed to glow. "Fft," she said, peeling back her lips and exposing her sharp white teeth. I moved forward and reached for her, but Dahlia was too fast for me. She eluded my grasp and sped back out the side entrance. I didn't hesitate but went right into the hallway after her. No sign of her. I turned left and went around the corner, and then I saw her. She was on her hind legs, pawing almost frantically at a door at the very end of the hall. I moved cautiously forward and said in a soothing tone, "Here, Dahlia. Everything's going to be all right."

The cat turned its head to look at me, and then let out another loud wail. She pawed again at the door, her nails scraping against the metal. I inched closer. "What's wrong, Dahlia? Is something in there?"

Dahlia threw back her head and let out another bloodcurdling wail. "Ow-*orrrr*!"

A knot started to form in my stomach, and I felt the hairs at the back of my neck start to rise. I stepped forward and gripped the door handle. It swung inward at my touch, and Dahlia darted inside ahead of me. I stepped inside and paused, letting my eyes adjust to the darkness. I felt along the wall and my fingers found a light switch. I flicked it on and the room was instantly flooded with bright light. I gave a quick look around. The room appeared to be some sort of storage area. There was steel shelving on the walls, filled to the brim with boxes. I noticed a pile of boxes scattered in the middle of the tiled floor, and as I drew closer, something else: a man's shoe sticking out from under them.

"Oh, no," I murmured. Dahlia chose that moment to leap on top of the pile of boxes. She stood there for a moment, back arched, and then she jumped off. Her motion caused the boxes to tumble sideways, revealing what lay underneath: Chef Reynaldo Venery, a silver knife handle buried almost to its hilt in his chest.

Chapter Eleven

My breath caught in my throat; you would think I'd be used to this by now. Even though there could be no doubt Venery was dead, I stepped over to the body, knelt beside it. I reached out, placed two fingers against his neck. Still warm. He hadn't been dead long.

Dahlia sat on her haunches by Venery's feet, shivering. I reached down, picked the cat up and cradled her against my chest. She purred softly as I stroked her back. Still holding the cat, I leaned forward for a closer look at the knife sticking out of his chest. Silver, with a leaf pattern. It appeared Venery had been killed with his own knife.

Being careful not to touch anything, I backed out of the room, Dahlia still in my arms. As I entered the hallway I saw Gary heading in my direction. "There you are," he said. He looked at Dahlia and said, "I see you found the source of that yowling."

"That's not all I found," I said. I inclined my head toward the storeroom. "It seems the play's opening line was prophetic."

"The opening . . ." He stopped speaking, eyes wide. "No! You found a body?"

"Yep. Venery. Someone put a knife through his heart."

Gary let out a low whistle. "Oh, boy. Well, so much for Josh having a quiet evening. We need to tell him about this right away."

"I agree, but we also have to be discreet," I said. "Josh might want to keep this quiet for now. People will start to panic if they think there's a murderer among them. Why don't you go and get Josh and bring him back here. I'll stay here with Dahlia."

Gary moved off and I started to pace back and forth in front of the storage area. Dahlia whimpered, and I cradled the cat closer. "It's all right, Dahlia," I crooned. "You did a good thing, leading me here." The cat looked up and blinked at me, then burrowed her head in my chest. I stroked her gently. "Yes, I know you're scared. But once Josh comes and I explain what happened, I'll take you back to your cage where you can rest."

The cat leaned her head against me and I continued to pace. My thoughts traveled to Venery and the speech he'd given. The man had certainly looked upset about something, but what? Or who? I mentally ran through all the people I knew had some sort of negative interaction with the man. There was Tessa Taylor, Louise . . . and Patrick. I'd heard him threaten Venery earlier. Had he made good on it? Patrick had also accused Tessa Taylor of having something on Venery. Had Tessa confronted the chef, and had the confrontation escalated into murder? I'd learned from past experience anything was possible.

I'd also overheard Louise saying earlier that she had to "take care" of someone but was unsure how. Had she been talking about Venery? Had she found his missing knife and decided that might be the best way to take care of business? I recalled the look that had crossed Venery's face when he was giving his speech earlier. Something—or someone—had rattled him. He'd told Patrick there was a long line of people who wanted to kill him. Maybe one of them were here tonight. But finding out who would be like looking for a needle in a haystack.

"Shell!"

I looked up and saw both Josh and Gary approaching. "Gary filled me in on your discovery," Josh said. His lips set in a grim line. "Show me."

We all went into the storage area. Josh knelt beside the body and after a few minutes rose to a standing position and looked at me over his shoulder. "You didn't touch anything, right?"

I shook my head. "Only the pulse at his neck. The body's pretty warm, so I don't think he's been dead very long." I nodded toward the murder weapon. "That knife in his chest . . . according to Louise, Venery owned a knife just like it. He was very protective of it, called it his lucky charm. It went missing earlier, and Louise was trying to locate it before Venery found out." I let out a breath. "I suppose it could be possible he caught the thief, and Venery got stabbed in a scuffle."

Josh didn't answer, just rubbed at the back of his neck as he stared at the body. Finally he said, "I need to get this area secure immediately. I also have to ensure that no one leaves the premises." He pulled his phone out of his pocket. "I'm going to call and see if I can get backup sent out here. This storm won't exactly make that easy." He paused. "Louise has a security team here at the inn, doesn't she?"

I nodded. "Yes, but I'm not sure just how many men are on it, or how many are here tonight."

"I saw her talking with your mother when I went to get Josh. I can go get her, if you want," offered Gary.

"Okay, but don't say anything about Venery. Just tell her I have a few questions I'd appreciate her answering," said Josh. Gary nodded and dashed off. Once he'd gone, Josh slipped his arm around my shoulders. "You okay?"

I gave him a thin smile. "Of course. It's not exactly the first time this has happened to me." I paused and then added, "There are a few things I need to tell you, Josh. I think they're important."

I told him about the interactions I'd noticed between Tessa, Patrick, Louise and Venery. I also mentioned Venery's strange reaction at the end of his speech. "Something got to him," I finished. "But I didn't see Tessa, Patrick or Louise in the immediate vicinity, so I have no idea what—or who—could have upset him."

"That's my job to find out," Josh said grimly. "And I have a feeling it won't be easy."

"There's something else," I began, but I stopped speaking as Gary came marching forward, Louise in tow. She marched right up to Josh. "Gary tells me you have some questions about the inn's security? Is there a problem?"

"You could say that. Chef Venery's been murdered," replied Josh.

"*What!*" Louise's eyes bugged, and her cheeks paled. Her hand came up, touched the side of her face. "Mur—murdered? He's dead? Are you sure?"

Josh nodded. "Yes. I need your help, Ms. Gates." He waved his arm at the storage room. "I need this room cordoned off and someone stationed here to make sure no one goes in or out until I can get back up here. Unfortunately, because of the storm, I'm not sure just when or if my backup will get here. How many men are on your security team?"

"Ten, but only six are here tonight," said Louise. "The captain is here, though, and I'm sure he'll cooperate fully."

"Good. Right now we need to cordon off this area, station someone here to make sure no one goes in or out. How many exits are there besides the main one?"

"There are four exits altogether, and they're all protected with security cameras and alarms."

"Good. I'll need the footage pulled on each one, and have a man stationed at each exit until backup arrives."

"I'll contact the captain at once," said Louise. She pulled out her cell phone then paused. "Are you sure I shouldn't make some sort of announcement about this?"

"Absolutely not." Josh shook his head. "I don't want news of Venery's murder getting out, at least not until backup gets here. People might panic and want to leave, and in this storm I don't need people driving off and getting into accidents. I'd rather they stay here, where they're safe and dry. Also, the killer probably thinks Venery's body is well hidden. We don't want to tip him—or her—off."

"I agree," I said. "The murder mystery skit will help to keep people occupied." I looked at Louise. "Why don't you go make a brief announcement that the cat's been found, everything's under control and the skit will continue shortly. Gary, you go get everyone else ready to go. And I'll take Dahlia here back to the cat adoption room."

Josh looked at Gary. "I saw Al Linden sitting at one of the tables. Think you could discreetly get him to come back here?"

Al Linden was the county assistant coroner. Gary nodded. "Can do."

"Great. Okay, everyone, you all know what to do. And remember do not mention anything about Venery's death to anyone until I give the go-ahead." He looked at Louise. "It's okay to tell your security team, but if anyone on your kitchen staff asks about him, just say you have no idea where the man is. We've got to keep this under wraps as long as we can."

"Of course," Louise murmured. She paused and then said, "If you don't mind my asking, Detective, how . . . how did Chef Venery die?"

Josh looked her right in the eyes. "I'm sorry, Ms. Gates, but that information is confidential, at least for now."

Louise nodded. "Sure. I understand." She gave another glance at the storage room door as Josh put his phone to his ear. "This is Detective Bloodgood. I've got a one-eight-seven over at the Fox Hollow Inn . . ."

• • •

"Oh, thank goodness. You found her."

I walked into the cat adoption room, Dahlia in my arms, and was greeted by Marianne. "I've been helping the girls look for her too. Where did you finally find her?"

"She'd gone into one of the storage areas," I said. "It took a bit of coaxing to get her, but I finally succeeded." I looked at the cat in my arms. "You're a good girl, Dahlia," I murmured.

Marianne sniffed. "Good? That cat is a little terror."

Dahlia's head swiveled in Marianne's direction and she let out a sharp meow.

I laughed. "She disagrees with you, Marianne."

A chorus of meows sounded, and we turned to see my three cats lined up in a row. Purrday lifted his paw, pointed at Dahlia. "Merow," he said again.

Sissy laughed. "Looks like you've been outvoted." The teen took Dahlia out of my arms. "You should be named Houdini," she said to the cat. Then she tossed me a sheepish grin. "There was a woman in here looking at the cats. She really liked Dahlia and she kept sticking her fingers in between the bars of the cage. She might have loosened the catch. I should have checked it more thoroughly, but I was too eager to get back to the game."

"It was an accident," I said. "Don't beat yourself up over it."

"I'll try not to." Sissy put Dahlia back inside the cage and fastened the latch. The cat let out a loud meow of protest. Sissy shook her finger at her. "Sorry you can't roam around like you do at the shelter, Queen Dahlia. Now, you stay in your cage like a good girl the rest of the night."

Marianne looked at me. "Is everything all right?" she asked.

I started. "Of course. I found Dahlia. Why wouldn't it be?"

Marianne peered more closely at me. "I don't know. You just look kind of upset."

"Do I? It's been a long night. Say, did Summer ever show up?"

"Not that I know of. Everyone thinks that once the cat's found the skit will continue, although . . ." Marianne waved her cell in the air. "I've been checking the weather reports. A lot of the roads are getting flooded out. We may have to call it a short night, otherwise people might not be able to get home." She sighed. "Truthfully . . . I'm a bit out of the mood to solve a murder, and from the snatches of conversation I overheard, a lot of people are starting to feel the same way." There was another loud crash of thunder, and Marianne jumped. She put her hand over her heart. "As much as I hate to call off the fundraiser, I'm tempted to tell your mother we should pack it all in right now."

"You can't do that," I cried and then added, "Think about it, Marianne. If it is that bad out, people will be safer to stay here. For all we know, the storm could let up a bit."

"Maybe," Marianne said doubtfully.

I squeezed her arm. "I know that's the right thing to do. Why don't you go on back outside and see what's happening with the skit?"

Marianne left and I went to find my cats. The three of them, and Serendipity, were all parked around Dahlia's cage. "Dahlia's fine," I told them. "She did have a harrowing experience though. Maybe someday she'll tell you about it, but for now she's got to stay mum."

Princess Fuzzypants sat back on her haunches and pawed at the air. "Merow," she said.

I smiled at the cat. "Yes, I know you and Purrday both have experience in that area. But like I said, we don't want to upset the natives so . . . keep it on the QT. Okay?"

Both the princess and Purrday let out loud meows. Kahlua and Serendipity just looked bored. I chuckled. People might think I was daft, talking to the cats as if they understood me but . . . somehow I had the feeling that they did. I leaned over and said, "I think right now the best place for you guys is right here. If anything changes, I'll come back and get you."

All four cats meowed and then returned to sprawling around Dahlia's cage. I left and saw Sissy and Roz sitting at the table in the front of the room. "I doubt anyone will be looking at the cats anymore tonight," I told them. "If you want to get a head start on packing up, it's fine with me."

"We'll wait a little bit. You never know. There have been a few people not interested in solving the murder mystery who have come in and out," said Sissy.

"We're used to doing this. It won't take long to get everything in order." Roz gestured at the game board on the table. "Besides, we're in the middle of a great game of Clue. Which I plan on winning."

"Think again," crowed Sissy. "I'm this close to solving it." She held up her hand with two fingers nearly touching.

I left them hunched over the Clue board and went back to the dining room. I opened the door a crack and peered in. I saw that Gary had gotten everyone together and they'd resumed the skit, but had moved ahead to the questioning portion. John lay sprawled across the makeshift stage, fake blood on his shirt. I shut the door, deciding things were pretty much well in hand there, and went back down to the storage area. The door was shut and a large man wearing dark trousers and a dark shirt with *Security* emblazoned on the sleeve rose from a chair positioned in front of the door. He held up his hand as I approached. "Sorry, ma'am," he said. "This area is off-limits."

"It's all right," I said. "I just wanted to check with Detective Bloodgood. I'm Shell McMillan. I found the body."

The guard shot me a doubtful look. "Wait here." He opened the door and disappeared inside and returned a few moments later. "Detective Bloodgood said you can go in," he mumbled.

I nodded and went into the storeroom. Al Linden was just rising from a kneeling position beside the body. He looked at Josh and said, "I've done all I can do here. Of course, once I get him on my table I can be more thorough." He reached up to scratch behind one ear. "From my preliminary examination I'd say the murder occurred here. The body doesn't appear to have been moved. A more thorough exam should confirm that."

"Any estimate as to the time of death?" asked Josh.

"It was fairly recent. I'd estimate somewhere between nine and nine thirty, give or take."

"That's right around the time the lights went out," I said. Both Josh and Al looked up, saw me standing there. Al shot me a smile. "Well, hello, Shell. Keeping your record intact, I see."

I made a face. "It's not exactly a record I try to maintain." I switched my gaze to Josh and said, "The skit's been resumed. Marianne was starting to panic. She wanted Mother to call the evening to a halt, but I managed to talk her down."

"Good," Josh said. "Backup's on the way, but there's no telling how long it will take them to get here. At least we know the killer is still in the building. I reviewed the security footage and it appears no one's gone in or out of the building or the parking lot for the past two hours." He paused. "Have you seen Patrick Hanratty? Leila told me that he and the receptionist, Summer, were supposed to take part in the skit but neither of them showed up."

I shook my head. "I haven't seen either one since they agreed to participate."

"I see," Josh said. "Did Patrick and this Summer know each other?"

"I don't think so. I did see Patrick flirting with her the other day but . . . that's typical modus operandi for Patrick. I also noticed Venery giving both of them dagger looks that day," I added.

Josh raised an eyebrow. "You think that's significant?"

"Could be. I did some research on Venery. It appears he's quite something with the ladies—and he likes a lot of them young."

"So you think that young receptionist and Venery might have been involved? And that was why Venery gave them a dagger look?"

"It's possible. Then again, Venery might have been annoyed because he didn't expect Patrick to be here. Apparently they were in negotiations for a cooking reality show and Venery was avoiding giving Patrick an answer. Patrick thought that Tessa Taylor was here to convince Venery to do her show. Tessa Taylor owns a production company, and from what I understand was also courting Venery."

Josh's phone buzzed and he went to answer it. Al picked up his bag and said, "I'm glad I'm not a detective. This all sounds pretty complicated." He sighed. "Well, so much for a relaxing evening with my wife. I'd best get back to the table, where I will studiously avoid the pointed questions my wife and the others are sure to ask."

Al left and Josh came over to me. "That was Amy. Most of the main roads are flooded out. The back road out here is still okay, but it's only a matter of time before that floods too, so it looks as if we'll all be here for quite a while."

I grimaced. "So we're all stranded here with a killer on the loose. That thought is a bit unsettling, to say the least."

"I know. I'm just praying the backup gets here soon." His phone rang. "Maybe that's them now." He put his cell to his ear and moved away.

I left the storage room and started to walk back to the dining area. I was halfway there when I heard a loud clap of thunder. Suddenly there was a tremendous gust of wind and the front door banged open. A tall figure swaddled in a black cloak stood on the threshold. I let out a shriek as the figure raised its arm and pointed a finger straight at me!

Chapter Twelve

"Whoa, Shell? Calm down. It's only me."

I sucked in a breath as the figure lowered the cloak hood to reveal Detective Amy Riser. She gave her head a brisk shake and water dropped from her black bangs onto the floor. "Sorry if I startled you," she added. She gave a quick look around. "Where's Josh?"

"Back in the storage area with the body." The folds of Amy's cloak flapped open and I took note of her muddy boots and saw that the hems of her jeans were soaked. "I'm glad you made it here okay."

"Yeah, well, it wasn't easy," she answered. "Roads are flooding fast, and that wind is a killer. I've never seen so many reports of power outages. You're lucky you've got power here."

"The inn has a good backup generator," I said. "The power did go out briefly, though. We think that's when the murder occurred."

Before Amy could comment two police officers appeared in the doorway behind her. I recognized Denny Miller, a policeman who'd briefly dated Leila. The other officer I'd never seen before. Denny looked at Amy and said, "I called Josh to let him know we were here. He said he'd meet us in the lobby—oh, there he is."

We all turned as Josh approached. "Boy, am I glad to see you guys," he said. "I appreciate you coming. I know it couldn't have been easy navigating roads in this mess."

"You're right about that," Denny said. "We had to come in the back way. Good thing Harris, here, drives a Hummer."

"Yeah, well, a dead body trumps flooded roads," said Amy. She gestured toward the two men. "You know Dennis Miller, and this is Morgan Harris, one of the new recruits. I tried to get two other men, but . . ." She spread her hands. "There are accidents galore, and everyone else is tied up."

"I appreciate any help at all, considering the circumstances," said Josh. "We have the inn's security team on board also. Let me bring you guys up to speed." He motioned to the far corner of the lobby. "We can talk over there." He turned to me, and I noticed that he'd put on what I referred to as his cop face. "You'll be okay, right, Shell?"

I nodded. "Yes. I'll just go back to the dining room and see how everyone's doing. I noticed that they've progressed to the question-and-answer portion of the show."

"Tell them they don't have to rush," said Josh. He gave my arm a squeeze then turned to Amy and said, "We also have two persons who are MIA who may or may not be connected to the murder."

As he, Amy and the two officers moved over to a far corner of the lobby, I turned in the direction of the Appalachian Room but stopped when I saw a door at the far end of the hall open. Andrea Palmer stepped through and went over to sit behind the reception desk. I changed course and walked over to her. She seemed absorbed in something on the computer screen but glanced up as I approached. She offered me a faint smile. "Hello, Shell. Is there something I can do for you?"

"I was just wondering if Mrs. Gates is anywhere around," I said. "I had a few matters to discuss with her."

"She developed a splitting migraine and went to her office to lie down," said Andrea. "Frankly, with all the agita she's had this past week, I'm shocked she didn't get a migraine every day. Anyway, I told her to take as long as she needed, I could handle things."

I wondered if Louise really had a migraine, or if it was just a convenient way of hiding out. Aloud I said, "I hope she feels better. I also need to speak to Patrick Hanratty. He was supposed to take part in the murder mystery program but he never showed up. He'd mentioned earlier that he didn't feel well, so I'd just like to make sure he's okay."

"Of course. I can ring his room, see if he answers." Andrea turned back to the computer and her fingers flew across the keyboard. She looked at the screen and frowned. "That's odd. He was in 406, one of our Executive Suites, but according to this, Mr. Hanratty checked out earlier today."

My jaw dropped. "Checked out? Are you sure?"

She tapped some more on the keyboard, then gave a brisk nod. "Yes. It's right here. He checked out at three thirty this afternoon. Oh, wait." She leaned over, peered more closely at the screen. "It says on his final bill that his luggage is in our west storage area. There's no notation that he picked it up, so he must still be around here somewhere." She reached out and gripped the phone. "Do you want me to get in touch with security, have them take a look around the premises?"

"No, no, that's not necessary." I started to move away, then stopped and looked back at Andrea. "Just out of curiosity, where is the west storage area?"

"It's at the opposite end of that hall. It's not a large area. We use it to keep small supplies, and guests' luggage if they have lag time between checkout time and their flights home."

"I see. Oh, and one last thing. Have you seen Summer? She was supposed to take part in the play as well but she didn't show up either."

Andrea's lips twisted into a tight expression. "I'm sorry to say that doesn't surprise me. That girl is a bit flighty, if you ask me. She's also deathly afraid of storms. Wouldn't surprise me one bit if she was holed up somewhere, waiting for it all to blow over."

Andrea turned back to the computer and I moved away from the desk, deep in thought. Patrick hadn't mentioned checking out earlier when he'd volunteered his services as an actor. Had he done so because he'd intended all along to murder Venery? I couldn't believe that, but I figured Josh and Amy might. There had to be some sort of reasonable explanation. I had to find my ex and find out just what that might be. I actually hoped that I'd find him holed up with Summer.

I returned to the Appalachian Room, and the first thing I noticed was that my mother wasn't seated at her table. I went over and slid into her empty chair. Garrett turned toward me and smiled. "Ah, Shell, there you are. That show was great. They're doing Q and A with the suspects now."

I glanced over at the stage then turned back to Garrett. "Do you know where my mother is?" I asked.

"With Josh. He motioned to her from the doorway a few minutes ago. Something about a police fundraiser?" He chuckled. "You know your mother and fundraisers—oh, look. Your friend Olivia is asking a question."

Olivia had risen from her seat, notepad in hand. "I have a question for Ashley VanHorn," she said, turning toward Charisma. "Just what did you mean when you told Francis X. Leonard that the past has a way of catching up? Was there a hidden meaning in that statement?"

Before Charisma could answer, the side door to the room opened and my mother walked in, Josh and Amy behind her. My mother stepped right over to the podium and tapped on the mike. "Attention, everyone," she said. "I'm so sorry to interrupt, but I'm afraid I have some disturbing news." You could have heard a pin drop as she continued, "I've just been informed that the storm has worsened and the main road's flooded out. Our police department has requested everyone's cooperation in staying put tonight until the weather lets up."

A murmur of concern went up from the audience, and my mother held up her hand. "I know, I know. Hard as it is to believe, it appears the weather bureau was spot on with their prediction. Trust me, you all are a lot safer in here than you would be out on the roads."

"Are you telling us we might have to stay here all night?" a woman in the audience asked.

"We're hoping not, but we can't rule out that possibility," my mother answered. "Fortunately, we have good company and good food in here to keep us occupied until the winds die down. Barring a real emergency, I want everyone to sit tight here. This storm isn't anything to fool with."

Everyone started to murmur again. Olivia called out, "What about the murder mystery play? Will that continue?"

I saw my mother glance over at Josh, who gave an imperceptible nod. "Yes, the production will continue," she said. "And don't forget, whoever is first to guess both the correct killer and their motive will win a fabulous spa weekend at the Hilton." My mother stepped away from the podium and left the room, followed by Josh and Amy.

The audience applauded, and then Olivia stood up and faced the makeshift stage. "Ms. VanHorn," she addressed Charisma. "I believe you owe me an answer to my earlier question?"

I got up and went back into the hallway. I didn't see Josh or Amy but my mother was standing there, looking at her cell phone. She looked up as I approached and shot me an accusing glare. "Really, Crishell? Another one?"

I shifted my weight from one foot to the other. "I gather Josh filled you in on the latest development?"

"Venery's murder? Yes, he did." She arched her brow at me. "Tell me you and Gary and those cats of yours aren't going to investigate this."

"There's no need for us to get involved, Mother," I said in a soothing tone. "Josh and Amy are both here, so the investigation is in very capable hands."

"Hmpf. I hope so," my mother grumbled.

"I was wondering about something though," I said. "Did Patrick mention to you that he'd checked out of the inn?"

My mother's eyes widened. "Patrick checked out? No, he didn't say a word to me. Why?"

I shrugged. "It just seems a bit odd, that's all. And he never showed up to participate in the play."

"I did notice that," my mother admitted. "I just assumed he'd changed his mind. He's not an actor, after all." Her eyes narrowed. "Crishell, you can't think . . . you can't possibly think that Patrick had something to do with Venery's death!"

I paused, unsure of just how much to reveal to my mother. I wasn't sure if Patrick might have confided in her about his proposed series and interest in Venery. Finally I said, "I don't know, Mother. Right now I don't think anything. But it's just odd that he's nowhere to be found."

"Well, I know Patrick well enough to know he's not a killer," my mother snapped, "And you should know that too, Crishell. Whatever happened between the two of you, you've got to know Patrick would never do anything like that." Her phone beeped. She glanced at the screen and then said, "Sorry, dear. I have to take this."

My mother moved off, cell to her ear, and I was about to return to the dining area when the door opened and Gary appeared. "Is the Q and A over already?" I asked.

He nodded. "Yep. Everyone is busy writing down their guesses. I thought I'd find you and see what's up."

"Plenty. For one thing, it seems that Patrick checked out of his room earlier today."

Gary's eyes widened. "You're kidding."

"I wish I were," I said grimly. "I'm pretty sure that won't help his case. Where in the world could he be?"

"The logical answer would be he's hiding somewhere, riding out the storm to make good his escape."

I made a face. "That sounds like something Josh would say."

Gary grinned. "Maybe Joshy's rubbed off on me. Hey, don't get me wrong. I like Patrick. I can't see him as a killer. But to a cop, his actions would seem suspicious, especially in light of what transpired between him and Venery."

"Patrick's not the only one who had issues with Venery," I said. "I heard a pretty good argument between Venery and that Tessa Taylor the other day." I tapped at my chin with my forefinger. "And then there's Louise."

"Louise Gates? Why, because of the difficulties she had with Venery over the menu?"

"People have been killed for less," I said. "But I have a feeling there might be more to Venery and Louise's relationship than meets the eye."

"You're talking about what you discovered about New Orleans, right?" said Gary. "Did you get a chance to ask Louise about it?"

"Yes. She denied it. She said she never worked with a chef named

Reynaldo Venery."

Gary studied me for a long moment before he said, "And you didn't believe her."

I let out a giant sigh. "No. I did not."

The door to the Appalachian Room opened and from inside I heard my mother's voice over the microphone. "Thank you, everyone. There will be an intermission while the committee reviews the questionnaires and chooses the winner. In the meantime, please enjoy the selection of desserts provided by the inn."

Someone from the audience shouted out, "Will Chef Venery be preparing his famous cherries jubilee?"

"I'm afraid Chef Venery is busy with other matters at the moment," my mother answered. "But rest assured, the selection of desserts was approved by him and are delectable."

"Nice save, Clarissa," Gary mumbled under his breath. He jerked his thumb toward the dining area. "Don't you have to help select the winner as one of the sponsors?"

"My mother, Garrett and Marianne are on the job. They won't miss me." I pulled Gary over to a small alcove. "What are the most common motives for murder?"

"What is this, a quiz?"

"Sort of. I'm trying to get some perspective on who our killer might be."

"Well, then." Gary pressed his back into the wall. "Money, sex and power—not necessarily in that order."

"Right. Let's start with the money angle. Who stood to profit from Venery's death?"

"Hm." Gary put a finger to his lips. "Not Patrick, not if Venery wasn't going to do his show. Or that Tessa Taylor either, if the same applied."

"Patrick thought Tessa might have had something on Venery, something she was using as leverage to force him to do her show over his."

"If that's the case, it would make more sense for Venery to have murdered Tessa, not the other way around."

I wrinkled my nose. "That's true. And I hate to say it, but I still think that Louise and Venery have some sort of a past. From that brief snatch of conversation I overheard, it sounded like Venery might have been holding something over Louise's head."

"Now that would be a motive for murder," observed Gary. "Depending, of course, on how serious the thing he was holding over her was." He scrubbed at the back of his neck. "What about the sex motivation?"

"You think Venery and Louise had an affair?"

"I guess that might be possible, but I was thinking more along the lines of Venery and Tessa Taylor. They could have had a recent affair that went wrong. Maybe they argued and she killed him, a crime of passion. Or—" He held up his hand before I could interject, "What about that girl Summer? You said Venery liked 'em young, right? Maybe they had a fling, and Summer thought it was more serious than that. They have an argument, and she kills him, maybe even in self-defense."

"That could make sense," I said thoughtfully. "Summer would have had access to the kitchen and the murder weapon."

"Although, if Summer did take the knife, it could indicate premeditation," said Gary. "She might have planned to kill the old boy, not off him in a crime of passion." He lifted his hand, started to tick off on his fingers. "So, we've got four suspects with a possible motive: Patrick, Tessa Taylor, Louise Gates, and the receptionist Summer—maybe. Opportunity: any of them, I guess, when the lights went out. We don't know for sure where any of them were. As for means, well . . . I'm guessing that both Louise and Summer would have had access to the kitchen and the knife. Patrick and Tessa are question marks in that area, although you know the old saying, where there's a will, there's a way."

"True, but . . . something else strange happened. At the end of Venery's little speech, he looked out into the audience and I could tell he saw something—or someone—that rattled him. I looked around, but I didn't see any of our suspects." I ran my hand through my hair. "Mother was concerned that you and I would get involved in investigating Venery's death. I have to admit, this is one time I'd be glad to back off and leave the detecting to Josh and his team," I said.

"Me too," agreed Gary. "But I've got the feeling that Patrick is going to end up getting pegged as suspect numero uno."

"I have the same feeling. And I also think it's going to be up to us to get him off," I finished.

Chapter Thirteen

We returned to the small room just off the main hallway where the committee consisting of my mother, Garret and Marianne were grouped around a small table that was littered with papers. "We're all in agreement, then," my mother was saying as Gary and I stepped inside. She glanced up and pinned me with a steely gaze. "Well, Gary and Crishell. How nice of you to show up."

"We figured you guys could handle picking the winner," I said. I slid into the seat opposite my mother. "So, who won the Grand Prize?"

"It's probably best you weren't judging," said Marianne. "Olivia Niven won. She correctly guessed Ashley VanHorn as the killer, and she came closest to the motive—emotional blackmail."

"Good for her," I said. I looked over my shoulder at Gary. "Maybe she's picked up some of your detective skills after all."

"Yours too," Gary said gallantly. He turned to Marianne. "What was the actual motive?"

"It was blackmail, but over a stolen design. Olivia guessed he was blackmailing her over an indiscretion in her past. Some people had the blackmail part right, but not the killer, so, Olivia wins hands down. She got both components correct."

"It was harder to pick the two runners-up," said my mother. "But we did finally choose two people who had the killer correct." She started to scrape back her chair. "I suppose I should make an announcement."

"I'd take your time," said Gary. "I peeped into the dining room and everyone seems to be having a good time gobbling down all those desserts. And since it doesn't look as if anyone will be going anywhere anytime soon . . . I'd stretch it out a bit."

My mother sat back down. "I suppose you're right." She gave me a hard look. "And what have the two of you been up to?"

"Oh, this and that. Mainly chatting about how well the fundraiser's been going, in spite of the storm," I said innocently.

The door opened and Charisma walked in. She'd shed her Marilyn Monroe wig, beauty mark and low-cut dress and was back in her simple black sheath, not a hair out of place. "I've been mingling with the crowd, getting quotes for my blog," she said brightly. "Most of them are having such a good time, they're hardly aware of the raging storm—except when that wind lets out a howl," she added. She shot me an anxious look. "I'd really like to go back to the cat room and check on Serendipity," she said. "She usually does well in storms but this one is a real doozy."

"I saw your cat when I brought Dahlia back to the room," I said. "She's fine. She's with my cats."

Charisma let out a relieved sigh. "Good, but I'd feel better if I could see her." She laid her hand on my arm. "Would you mind taking a walk with me back there?"

"Of course not." I turned to the others. "I'll be back in a little while."

Garrett Knute smiled. "We'll be here."

Charisma and I moved out into the hall and started walking in the direction of the cat room. "All things considered," Charisma said, "I think you can chalk this fundraiser up as a success."

"It seemed as if everyone did enjoy the skit," I said. "Even though it was an abbreviated version."

"They didn't know that," Charisma said and chuckled. "Your friend Olivia seems as if she's a pretty good detective. She asked some very insightful questions." She paused and then added, "I was a bit disappointed that Patrick Hanratty never showed up, though. You don't think he could have left in this storm?"

"I doubt it," I said. "I'm sure he's around somewhere."

"Oh, good," she breathed. I thought she sounded relieved. "Then I still have a chance to meet him. I know my readers would be very interested in reading an interview with him. I get quite a few requests for celebrity interviews."

"Do your readers often suggest topics for your blog?"

"More than you'd think," Charisma responded with a rueful smile. "I get quite a few that are really good ideas, and more that are outlandish, like interviewing certain political figures, and some convicted criminals. You'd be surprised."

"I'm from Hollywood, remember," I said with a smile. "Nothing really surprises me."

"No, I suppose not," Charisma said thoughtfully. She was silent for a few moments before she added, "I have to admit, I was very disappointed that I haven't gotten a chance to interview Chef Venery. Every time I try to broach the subject with Ms. Gates, she just says he's very preoccupied."

I swallowed. "Well, I imagine that it is rather time-consuming, executing a dinner like this."

"Oh, piffle. Venery's done this hundreds of times. He's a pro." She lowered her voice. "I think the man is deliberately avoiding anyone connected with the press, and I know why!"

I looked at her. "You do?"

She nodded. "I have to be honest, Shell. I told you that once I found out Venery was involved in this fundraiser it was the driving force behind my acceptance. I was hoping to get a juicy story out of this experience—one that might even open up a brand-new career for me."

I stopped in my tracks. "You've got my attention, Charisma. What juicy story were you hoping to get out of Venery?"

"Well . . ." Charisma glanced around, then dragged me over to a tiny alcove off the main hallway. "You have to promise not to repeat what I'm about to tell you," she said as she reached into the pocket of her dress and pulled out her cell phone. "I got this in my email a few weeks ago."

She held the phone out to me. I took it and read the email, which had been sent from an account called anonymousfriend:

> Dear Ms. Walters:
> What celebrity chef is headed to Fox Hollow under the guise of helping out a local charity, but is really coming here for another reason? This local event is nothing more than a smokescreen for his real mission— to make sure a particular skeleton stays buried in his closet.
> A Friend

"A few days after I received that, the announcement was made about Venery being the chef for this fundraiser. That lightbulb clicked in my brain! Who else could this be?" Charisma reached out to retrieve her phone, and she looked at the screen. "Venery has some sort of secret, one that he doesn't want to get out. And if I could be the one to uncover it . . . why, the sky would be the limit."

My thoughts were whirling. If this tip were on the level, it might explain a great many things. I struggled to recall the conversations I'd overheard recently. Venery had mentioned Louise owing him something. Could it have to do with this so-called skeleton he wanted to remain buried?

Then there was Tessa Taylor. She'd told Venery that what she had to say he wouldn't want made public. Venery'd accused her of bluffing, but she'd stood firm. Was she privy to the chef's secret?

Charisma waved her hand in front of my face. "Shell? Are you okay? You look like you zoned out for a moment."

I shook my head and smiled. "No, no, I'm fine. I was just . . . surprised by that email."

"I have to admit, I'm not. A man as disagreeable as Rey Venery is bound to have a few enemies, and more than one secret he wouldn't want to get out. I'm sure his climb up the culinary ladder wasn't without some hitches. Think about it, Shell. Venery is exactly the type of man who'd have a humdinger of a secret."

Silently I agreed with Charisma. Venery had most likely been a man of many secrets—and one had gotten him killed.

• • •

The cats were all doing fine in the coatroom. They'd moved away from Dahlia's cage and were now scattered around the room. Kahlua was perched atop a cat tower, taking a snooze, while Serendipity lounged below, chewing on a catnip mouse. Purrday and the princess were over by the card table, where Sissy and Roz sat, still engrossed in their game of Clue. Charisma fussed over Serendipity for a few minutes, but it seemed to me the cat was more interested in her catnip mouse than her human.

Charisma apparently realized the same thing, because she gave the cat a pat on the head and straightened. "It seems Serendipity is doing fine here," she observed. "So I think that perhaps I'll just pay a little visit to the kitchen, see if I can catch Chef Venery off guard."

I started. "Are you sure you want to do that, Charisma? I've seen the man throw a temper fit. It's not pretty."

Charisma waved her hand. "I've seen it as well, when I visited the set of *Culinary Surprise* to interview Venery and the other chefs. The man was rude and condescending, not only to me but to his fellow chefs. The man's a toad, everyone knows that. But maybe, if I play my cards right, I can get some sort of hint as to his real purpose in being here in Fox Hollow."

"You really think he'd let anything slip to you?"

Charisma shot me a knowing smile. "Trust me, Shell, I know how to play dirty. Venery wouldn't be the first person I've gotten something out of." She wiggled her fingers. "I'll see you back at the Appalachian Room." She turned and blew a kiss Serendipity's way. "And I'll see you later, my little love bug."

Charisma swept out. I considered following her, but I knew I wouldn't be able to deter her from getting into that kitchen. I started to send a text to Louise, then stopped. If she really did have a headache, she wouldn't be answering her phone. Instead I sent it to Gary: *Can you intercept Charisma Walters? She's on her way to the kitchen. Wants to interview Venery. Can u think of something to distract her?*

A moment later I got an answer from Gary: *On my way.*

"Well, she said she wanted to spend some quality time with Gary and Patrick. I hate to stick her on Gary, but desperate times and all that," I muttered.

I decided to swing by the kitchen just in case Gary needed help deterring Charisma. I said a quick goodbye to my cats and to Sissy and Roz and left. Midway down the hall, I had the sensation that I was being followed. I whirled around, nearly colliding with Purrday and Princess Fuzzypants.

I bent down and gave each cat a scratch behind their ears. "You two are bored, aren't you," I said. "Okay, you can come with me. The way things are going tonight, I just might need your protection."

Purrday and the princess both let out loud meows. We continued down the hall and I was just about to turn down the corridor that led past the kitchen when I caught a flicker of movement out of the corner of my eye. I turned in time to see a figure melt into the shadows at the far end of the hall. Whoever it was had moved too quickly for me to get a good look, but my first impression was that it had been a man. Patrick?

I looked down at the two cats. Both of them were standing still, their tails sticking straight up in back of them, the hair on their backs furrowed. "I wasn't imagining it," I said. "You guys saw it too."

Without giving it another thought, I moved swiftly down the corridor in the direction I'd seen the shadowy figure disappear. I was so fixed upon finding them that I failed to see the raised portion of floor until it was too late. The toe of my shoe struck it and I went sprawling across the floor.

"Great," I grumbled. I raised myself to a sitting position and flexed my legs. The only thing injured appeared to be my pride. As I struggled to a standing position, my eye fell upon a scrap of paper underneath a small table about a foot away from me. I reached for it, turning it over in my hand. It was pale blue with a navy border around the edge, and I recognized it immediately as inn stationery, the kind they had in the reception area and in the rooms. The top half of the sheet that had the inn's name emblazoned across it had been torn off, leaving a ragged edge. There was writing on the paper in pencil, a childish scrawl. I hesitated only briefly before unfolding the note and scanning the printed words. The message was short and to the point:

Admit the truth or suffer the consequences.

Chapter Fourteen

I stood rooted to the spot and read the note again. It most definitely sounded like a threat to me, but for whom had it been intended? I peered more closely at the note. There was a smudge mark in front of the first word, as if something had been erased. I squinted at it, trying to discern what it might be. It looked like a single letter, maybe an *R*, but I wasn't entirely certain.

"Shell?"

I whirled around, still clutching the note, and saw Gary coming toward me. "Wh-what are you doing here?" I asked. I craned my neck to and fro. "Where's Charisma? Don't tell me she got into the kitchen?"

He grinned at me. "Almost. When we got there she was just about to enter."

I looked at him questioningly. "We?"

"I took Doug Harriman with me. He convinced her to give him an interview for the *Gazette* on being a famous blogger. She was a bit reluctant at first, but once Doug told her she'd have the front page, she caved."

"Doug promised her that? But I thought stuff like that was up to Quentin?"

"It is, but Charisma doesn't know that," replied Gary. "Besides, I'm sure Quentin would be thrilled to have a famous influencer like Charisma on the front page."

"That's probably true," I said. "But this is only a temporary fix. Charisma won't give up on trying to talk to Venery."

I explained about the email tip Charisma had received. When I finished, Gary let out a low whistle. "Sounds as if someone was gunning for him, doesn't it," he remarked. "I'm betting the sender of that email might be the one who killed him."

"It's a possibility. Take a look at this." I held out the note I'd found under the table. Gary took it, read it, then handed it back to me.

"Interesting indeed," he commented. "Do you think that note was intended for Venery?"

"It very well could be." I tapped at the paper. "Doesn't it look as if something has been erased right here?"

Gary squinted at the note over my shoulder. "Yeah. A single letter, maybe?" He peered more closely and then added, "I'd say it's a capital *P*."

"A *P*? I thought it looked more like an *R*," I replied. "That would make sense if the note were Venery's, right? Seeing as his first name was Reynaldo." I flicked at the paper with my nail. "This was written on inn stationery," I said. "I recognize it."

"So do I. It's all over the place in the inn, especially in the lobby. Anyone can grab a sheet." Gary looked at the note again. "From the way the note is worded, it sounds as if the recipient is the one with some sort of secret the writer wants him to admit. Tessa could have written this to Venery, or maybe Venery wrote this to Louise. It could go either way." He paused and then added gently, "It's also possible that the note could have been written either by or to Patrick. There might have been more going on between them than he admitted to you, and I still think that erased letter looks more like a *P*. Maybe Venery found out something to use to get him off his back once and for all."

"Or maybe that letter is an *R*, and the writer knows about whatever skeleton Venery is supposed to have in his closet," I said.

"I think it's time we filled Josh in on all this," Gary said. "Maybe the police can track down the sender somehow."

"*Ow-orrr!*"

I'd completely forgotten about the cats and now two furry forms, one white, one red, streaked past us down the long hall like cats on steroid catnip.

I was already halfway down the hall. "Come on, Gary, we have to get them. Whenever those two get together they end up getting into trouble."

We raced down the hall, and when we turned the corner saw the cats in front of a door in the middle of the hallway. Both of them were on their hind legs, scratching at it.

"What are they doing?" asked Gary.

"Your guess is as good as mine," I replied. I approached the cats cautiously. Princess Fuzzypants turned her head and let out a loud meow. Purrday followed suit. Then they continued their furious scratching.

"Something has them riled up," said Gary. "And I for one don't think it's just catnip. You know they have good instincts. Maybe we should just take a quick look in that room, just to make sure all is well."

I hesitated, then pushed open the door. The cats immediately sped into the room, Gary and I right behind them. I felt on the wall, found a light switch and turned it on. Harsh fluorescent light flooded the room, which I could tell at first glance must be the west storage area Andrea had referred to. Floor-to-ceiling steel shelves occupied most of the room, and they were filled with various sundries and supplies. I noticed a set of black luggage off in the far corner that looked familiar to me.

I touched Gary's arm and pointed to the luggage. "That looks like Patrick's luggage," I said. "Andrea said it was stored in the west storage room, so that must be what this is."

"Ow-*orrr*!"

Another mournful wail, and two furry forms shot out from the far corner of the room and right past us. Purrday leapt up on a low shelf, stretched out full-length, and started to growl. The princess spun around in a circle, then gave a giant leap and landed right on top of a shelf that held glass bottles right next to Patrick's luggage.

"Okay, both of you," I said in the sternest voice I could muster. "We have to leave right now!"

The princess looked at me, then let out a sharp meow. Then she leapt through the air and landed square on one of Patrick's suitcases. The zippered compartment on the front was open, and the princess's paw dipped inside.

"Princess Fuzzypants," I cried. "Get your paw out of there right now, or no treats for you tomorrow!"

The cat shot me a baleful look, then slowly removed her paw from the compartment. I saw something glisten on the tip of her nail in the overhead light, and the princess held up her paw. "Meower," she said, almost proudly.

I stepped closer and my breath caught in my throat. I recognized the article at once. It was the diamond brooch that Louise had been wearing earlier. Behind me I heard Gary suck in a breath. "Good God! Are those real diamonds?"

"They certainly look real," I said. I knelt down and reached out, gently stroked the princess's back. "What have you got there, Princess? Let me have it, please."

The cat didn't move a muscle as I reached out and gently disengaged the brooch from her nail. I held it up. "I'm certain this is Louise's. I saw her wearing a brooch like this earlier."

Gary took the brooch from me, turned it over in his hand. The stones twinkled, sending out flashes of light. "I'm betting these are real diamonds," he said. "But if they belong to Louise, what are they doing in Patrick's luggage?"

"Someone must have stashed them here, maybe waiting for the storm to let up and make a getaway," I suggested. I held up my hand. "And no, I don't think it was Patrick, even though he's the obvious choice. I don't think he's even met Louise."

"We need to find him," said Gary. He gestured toward the cats. "Right now I think we should get these two back to the adoption room before they can get into more trouble."

"*Meroo!*"

Gary and I both jumped at the loud wail. I immediately saw what the trouble was. While the two of us had been talking, the princess had stuck her paw back inside the zippered compartment and now couldn't get it out. "*Meroo!*" she wailed again. I knelt beside the cat, gently reached out and thrust my hand inside the compartment. "Take it easy, Princess," I crooned. "I'll have you free in just a minute." As I disengaged her paw from the material, my fingers touched against something hard. I freed her paw, then dipped my hand back in. When I pulled it back out, two more diamonds winked in my palm.

Gary stared at the objects in my hand. "More diamonds? What is it with these cats and diamonds?"

I swallowed. "These look like the studs Louise was wearing earlier," I said. "Think about that note, Gary. What if Venery wrote it to Louise, and she gave him the jewels to buy his silence. Then whoever murdered Venery found them and hid them here until they could make their getaway."

Gary scratched at his head. "That door wasn't locked. Anyone could have come in, slipped the jewels in Patrick's luggage and left. They probably figured no one would be going anywhere in this storm and it was a good place to hide the jewels."

"So the next step should be interrogating Louise, see what she knows about her missing jewels. If someone stole them or if she gave them to someone as payment."

Gary frowned. "If she gave them to a blackmailer, do you really think she'd admit it?"

"She probably wouldn't," I said grimly. "But I'm asking her anyway."

• • •

We took the cats back to the adoption room. "Keep a close eye on them," I said to Sissy and Roz. "Between the two of them and Dahlia, I think we've had enough of cats on the loose for tonight." I glanced over at the corner where both Kahlua and Serendipity lay, snoring peacefully. "Maybe give them some food?"

"I have some leftover turkey from the buffet," Sissy ventured. At the word *turkey*, both Purrday and the princess sat up straight and let out a resounding purr. We left the two cats happily chowing down. Neither seemed a bit tired after all the running around either. Gary looked at his watch. "I probably should go check on Doug and Charisma. Make sure that interview is still going on so Charisma stays away from the kitchen."

"Good idea. And if they're done, offer to be interviewed yourself," I said. "Charisma mentioned she'd love to interview both you and Patrick for her blog. As a matter of fact, she was quite excited about meeting you both."

Gary shot me a suspicious look. "Say, wait a sec. Is Charisma the vulture you referred to earlier?"

I spread my hands. "I can neither confirm nor deny, but if I were you I'd try not to be anywhere alone with her for too long."

"I suppose there are worse fates," Gary grumbled. "At least she's good-looking." He put his hand over his heart. "The sacrifices I make for you," he said.

"I'd do the same for you," I assured him.

He made a face. "Liar."

Gary went off to track down Doug and Charisma and I made my way down the back corridor toward Louise's office. As I approached, I saw a pencil-thin beam of light emanating from underneath the door. As I drew near, however, the light winked out.

Undaunted, I rapped sharply on the door. "Louise, it's Shell I know you don't have a headache. I need to talk to you. Now!"

No answer. I rapped again. "Louise, you can either speak to me or to the police. Which would you prefer?"

I heard the sound of footsteps, then the light winked back on. The door opened and Louise, looking pale and wan, stood there. "Shell," she said. Her hand reached out, grasped my arm, and she fairly pulled me into the room. She closed the door and stood against it, her eyes narrowed. "What do you want?"

"Some answers for starters." I faced her, my hands on my hips, and decided not to beat around the bush. I pointed to her dress. "Where's your diamond flower brooch? I saw it on you earlier this evening, but I didn't notice it on your dress when you were speaking to Detective Bloodgood."

Louise's hand flew to her bosom. "I-I took it off," she stammered. "The clasp is a bit loose, and I was afraid I might lose it. Why?"

I leaned over and pushed her hair back from her ears. "Your diamond earrings are gone. Were the backs loose on them too?"

She drew back as if she'd been stung. "What is this, an inquisition?" she snapped.

I looked her straight in the eye. "Tell me the truth, Louise. Venery was blackmailing you, wasn't he?"

Her eyes darted nervously around the room, almost as if she were looking for a means of escape. "Wh-what makes you think that?" she said at last.

I ignored her question and countered with another of my own. "I found a note in the back hallway. It said, 'Admit the truth or suffer the consequences.' Tell me the truth, Louise. Did Venery send you that note?"

She looked genuinely surprised. "What are you talking about? No one's sent me a note like that," she said.

"Okay, then I have to ask this: Did you write that note and give it to Venery?"

Her eyes popped wide. "Me? Good heavens, no! You believe me, don't you?" she asked anxiously.

"I believe you when you say you didn't write that note, and you didn't receive it either. But now I need you to tell me the truth. You did know Venery from somewhere else, didn't you?" As she opened her mouth, I held up my hand. "Before you answer, I want you to know that I overheard you and Venery talking in the back hallway the other day. I could tell from the conversation that the two of you were more than just acquaintances."

Louise's jaw set, and she clamped her lips together. I leaned forward and said gently, "I heard what he said to you about what happens to people who cross him."

Her head jerked up. "He-he accused me of being behind Clarissa's request that he go back to the original menu," she said weakly. "He wasn't happy. Venery hated being told what to do."

"I'm sure he wasn't, but it's more than that. Have you crossed Venery in the past, Louise?"

Her face turned white and she pressed her fist against her mouth. "Oh, Lord!" She sagged against the door. I reached out and grasped her arm, pulled her up. Then I led her over to her desk. She eased herself into her chair, and I took a seat in one of the high-backed chairs in front of the desk. For a few minutes you could have heard a pin drop in the room. I was just about to say something else when her eyes flew open and she leaned across the desk and fixed me with a stare.

"What's the use of denying it," she whispered. "Yes, it's true. Venery was blackmailing me."

I could feel my heart sink almost all the way down to my toes. "Oh, Louise! Why?" As Louise remained silent a sudden thought occurred to me. I leaned forward and said, "I asked you once before if you'd worked with Reynaldo Venery, and you were very careful to tell me that you'd never worked with anyone by that name," I said. "Venery had a different name when he worked with you at Maison Richard, didn't he?"

She looked startled for a moment, and then she nodded. "Yes. Back then he was Ronald Payson." She massaged her temples lightly with her fingertips as she continued, "I was young, just out of culinary school. Maison Richard was my first big gig. Venery was one of the head chefs. He—he always liked me, always made it a point to flatter me."

"Are you trying to say Venery came on to you?"

"Yes, but it was right around the time I met Bill. Venery stopped when he realized nothing was going to happen between us." She choked back a sob. "Thinking back, that's probably the reason behind why he did what he did."

Louise leaned back in her chair and I could see she was trying to compose herself. Finally she leaned forward and said, "The owners, Henri and Amanda Duval, were two of the nicest people you'd ever hope to meet. Henri was a good bit older than Amanda, but the two of them were very devoted to each other, or at least they were at first. Amanda was a beauty, born of a Sicilian father and a French mother. She had ebony hair, pale white skin, and eyes as blue as the sky. She looked like a princess out of a fairy tale. So of course Venery set his cap for her."

"He had an affair with the boss's wife?"

She nodded. "I found them together one night, in the kitchen after hours. I thought I got out of there unobserved but Venery saw me. The next day he approached me, told me that I'd better keep silent over what I'd seen or he'd see to it that I was fired. Bill was just starting out. Neither of us had much money. We were planning to be married. I needed that job."

"So he's been blackmailing you all those years because you knew he had an affair with the owner's wife?"

Louise shook her head. "Goodness, no. He was blackmailing me because he claimed to have proof my husband murdered Henri Duval."

Chapter Fifteen

I stared at Louise. "Wait . . . what? Your husband murdered your employer?"

"No, but . . ." Louise scrubbed at her face with the back of her hand. "Henri Duval had a terrible allergy to certain types of nuts. He was quite fond of a pesto sauce that contained soy nuts, which were not harmful to him. One evening he wanted that particular sauce for his pasta at dinner. Bill came into the kitchen to see me that night. He'd noticed I was upset earlier and he wanted me to tell him what was wrong. I tried to skirt the issue, but he persisted, so finally I told him Duval had made another pass at me. He was livid, and then Duval happened to pass by and ordered Bill out. Later, when Duval was eating his dinner, he started to choke. Suddenly he grabbed at his throat and collapsed. The coroner said that he died of an allergic reaction.

"The police searched the kitchen and found the soy nuts, but then they also found a container of pine nuts hidden way back in one of the cabinets. They confiscated the sauce and tested it for traces of pine nuts but couldn't find anything. They tested the containers for prints, but so many of us had handled them it was fruitless. After a while they ruled it an accidental death. I thought nothing of it until a week later when Venery came to me. He said that Henri had suspected someone of stealing staples from the kitchen, so he'd installed a security camera a few weeks before. Venery said that he'd gotten to the tapes before the police and watched them. He told me the tape showed that after Henri had told Bill to leave, Bill had grabbed a jar of pine nuts and dumped some into the sauce. I was flabbergasted. I accused him of lying. I told him Bill was angry with Duval, but he was no murderer."

"That sounds pretty convenient," I said. "How would your husband have known about Duval's allergy in the first place?"

Louise flushed. "I-I did mention it to Bill on several different occasions," she said.

"Did you actually see this tape?"

"Oh, yes. Venery insisted on showing it to me. There was a man standing beside the sauce pan and you can see him dumping a jar of pine nuts into it. But you could only catch a glimpse of the man's profile, and the tape was so grainy it was impossible to make a positive identification.

Venery managed to convince me, though, that once the police learned about the tape and Duval's advances toward me, Bill would be suspect number one." She wrung her hands in front of her. "Venery said that he knew someone who could doctor the tape and make the part about Bill adding the nuts go away. He said that maybe someday I might be able to do a favor for him."

"A favor? What sort of favor?"

"He knew that I knew about his affair with Duval's wife. He wanted me to keep quiet about it."

We were both silent for a few seconds and then I said, "You asked Bill about it, right? What did he have to say?"

I could see tears forming in her eyes. "He got very defensive when I asked him about it. He denied it, but there was just something in his manner that made me wonder if maybe he might have done it out of anger. I was so afraid that he might have so . . . I agreed to let Venery doctor the tape."

I laid my hand on top of hers and said gently, "Is it possible the man in the tape could have been Venery?"

"Possible, but at the time I was too upset to think clearly. At the time I couldn't think of a reason why Venery would want to murder Duval. Certainly not because he wanted his wife. That was just a dalliance to him. Then a few weeks later I found out from one of the other cooks that Venery owed Henri a great deal of money, and Henri was pressing to collect it. Venery had no way to repay the debt, and Henri threatened him with prison. He knew about Henri's advances to me, and he saw how angry Bill was that night. I believe that Venery saw his chance and he was the man in the tape. He probably doctored it so that his features were unrecognizable. I thought about confronting him, but then he got an offer to work in New York, so he left. I thought I was off the hook and didn't give it another thought until I saw him in town one day. I nearly didn't recognize him. He'd lost weight, dyed his hair and acquired a goatee. He'd also changed his name to Reynaldo Venery and was now head chef at Antoine's.

"Fortunately a few weeks later Bill got an offer to manage the inn here in Fox Hollow. We moved here and I got a job working in the kitchen. When the opportunity came to buy it, we did. I was just starting to get my life back on track after Bill's heart attack and losing him when who shows up here but Venery, all primed to appear at your mother's benefit. He said that he needed some fast cash and his assets were all tied up. He reminded me of what he'd done for Bill and he said that even though Bill was dead I owed him. That was when I accused him of killing Duval, and setting Bill up as a patsy."

"What did he have to say to that?"

"He neither confirmed nor denied it, he just laughed at me. He was a famous chef, he said. Who would the public believe, him or a little nobody like me. After all, I had no proof." Louise spread her hands. "So what could I do? He could reveal the truth and sully my late husband's good name. Furthermore, he'd tell everyone that I knew Bill had killed Duval, which would make me an accomplice after the fact. He took great pleasure in telling me there are no statutes of limitations on murder, and I could possibly go to jail. He demanded an answer from me, tonight. He said he had to have it now, or else he was going to call the New Orleans police and give them the tape that he'd kept all these years. I told him that I'd give him the money on one condition—that he turn over the tape to me. Surprisingly, he agreed."

"So you gave him the diamond earrings and brooch as payment?"

She nodded. "They're worth quite a bit of money. They were last appraised at fifty thousand each. I told him that was all I had, and he said he hoped it was enough. I was to leave the jewelry in a box in the storage area and he would leave the tape in an envelope there. I did so shortly before the skit started."

"A box in the storage area? The west storage area?"

"No, the main one. He was very specific."

"Why all the subterfuge? Why not do it face-to-face?"

"I wanted to, but he was afraid someone would see us. He was looking out for me, he said, and I should learn to appreciate it. Anyway, I went to the storage area and found a small box on one of the bottom shelves. When I opened it, there was a manilla envelope inside. I took the envelope, put the jewels in its place and left."

"So he did leave you the tape."

"Not exactly. He left *a* tape."

Louise opened the middle drawer of the desk, pulled out an envelope and pushed it across the desk to me. "It's blank," she said tonelessly. "He tricked me. When I saw that I was furious. I was going to go back to the storage area, see if he were there and confront him, but it was just then that the tree hit the generator and the power went out. After that, well . . . I had other things on my mind."

"So you were here, in your office, between eight thirty and nine thirty tonight? Alone?"

"No. Andrea came in and we were going over next week's menu together. I wanted to get rid of her at first so I could find him, but then I figured I needed to calm down. She left a few minutes before nine, but before I could leave my cousin Harold called. He told me he and his family are coming to Fox Hollow next week and wanted to know if I could put them up here. I was on the phone with him until right before the lights went out."

"One last question, Louise. Is there anyone else here, besides you, who would know Venery was formerly known as Ronald Payson, or about that incident with Duval?"

Louise gave her head an emphatic shake. "No one that I know of."

I nodded and laid my hand gently on her arm. "Louise, you have to tell all this to Detective Bloodgood."

She sighed. "I know." She looked at me and let out a bitter laugh. "The only bright spot in all this—if you can call it that—is that Reynaldo Venery is someone I never have to worry about ever again."

I called Josh and told him that Louise wanted to see him, and he said that he'd go to her office pronto. I waited until he arrived and then I left after giving Louise an encouraging smile. I'd believed every word she'd said, and as far as I was concerned, as long as the phone records could prove Louise had been on the phone with her cousin, she was off the suspect list. I had the feeling Josh would feel the same way.

And then there were two—Tessa Taylor and Patrick. And possibly Summer. Any of them could have taken the jewels from Venery's dead body and stashed them in Patrick's luggage for safekeeping. And as much as I hated to admit it, any of them could also have gotten access to the knife and killed Venery. They all had means and opportunity. But which of them had the best motive?

I pulled the note out of my pocket and looked at it again. I still couldn't decipher the partially erased letter, but the thought occurred to me that if it were either an *R* or a *P*, the note could quite possibly have been intended for Venery, since his real name was Ronald Payson.

"Shell!"

I turned around and saw Gary striding toward me. "Doug's really charming the heck out of Charisma," he announced. "She was giggling like a schoolgirl. When I left I noticed her looking at his ring finger."

I chuckled. "After this he might want to start wearing his wedding ring." I twirled the note in my hand. "I just had a very interesting conversation with Louise. Turns out Venery was blackmailing her, but he didn't write her this note." I filled Gary in on Louise's story, ending with, "More than ever I think this note was intended for Venery. And I think the person also knew Venery once went under the name of Ronald Payson."

Gary held up his phone. "I did some investigating too. It seems Tessa Taylor's company is in big trouble, according to the *Hollywood Explorer*. She might have to file for bankruptcy."

"Which would explain why she was so desperate to get Venery for her show. But killing him wouldn't solve her problem, so why would she?"

"There could be another reason. She might have done it in the heat of passion. We haven't ruled out her being one of Venery's conquests."

"True, and I hate to rule her out, because if we do, then we're down to two suspects, Patrick and Summer."

"Or"—Gary stuck a finger up in the air—"another unidentified party from Venery's past who held a grudge against him." His eyes slitted and he was quiet for a few minutes. "Doug's camera," he blurted.

"What about Doug's camera?"

"He didn't have it on him. Charisma noticed it right away and he said he'd left it in the coatroom. He said the lighting was better in the dining area and he'd take a photo of her and her cat to accompany his article later. But . . ." The finger went up in the air again. "He was snapping photos all night. I distinctly remember seeing him snapping photos of Venery when he was giving his little speech. You said that Venery saw something that seemed to upset him, right? Well, maybe Doug caught something on film."

"It's worth a shot," I said, and made a beeline for the Appalachian Room, Gary at my heels. We slipped inside the empty coatroom and I spotted Doug's camera almost immediately. Gary leaned over my shoulder as I clicked away, looking at all the photographs on the digital screen.

"I think he must have taken a photo a minute," I said. "There are some pretty good shots of the cats here. I think Marianne will want copies."

I kept clicking until I came to the photos featuring Venery on the dais. In the beginning shots, the man looked affable, but then his face morphed into an almost stricken expression. It had only been for a fleeting moment, but Doug had managed to capture it. I clicked to the next photo after Venery's face changed expression. It was a shot of a table near the open door to the hallway. Nothing unusual there. All the people in the photo seemed to be listening intently to Venery's speech.

"Wait." Gary leaned over my shoulder. "Stop."

I glanced up. "What?"

"Don't you see it?" He pointed at the photo. "There, in the hallway."

I peered more closely at the photo. There was someone standing in the background, but the image was too grainy to make out who. "That's the hallway that leads to the kitchen area," I murmured.

"Maybe we should show this to Josh," suggested Gary. "He could send it to one of his techs to enhance."

"That would take too long." I pushed back my chair. "I've got a better idea. Follow me."

I pulled the media card out of the camera after noting the photo's number and then the two of us made our way back to the cat adoption room. Sissy and Roz were concentrating deeply over the Clue board when we entered. "Who's winning?" Gary called out.

Roz gave us a broad smile. "Me, of course. I should have this game wrapped up in about ten minutes."

"Then I want a rematch," groused Sissy. She looked at me. "That storm still sounds bad, so I take it no one can leave yet."

"Not yet. Sissy, did you happen to bring either your tablet or your laptop with you tonight?"

"I brought my laptop. Why?"

"You've got photography programs on it, right?"

"Well, sure. Photoshop, Acorn, Gimp—"

I held up my hand. "Thanks, you don't have to go through the whole list. Do you think you could tear yourself away from Clue for a few minutes to help me with something?"

Sissy glanced over at Roz, who waved her hand. "Go on. I need a bathroom break anyway." She waggled an eyebrow at the other girl. "You're only delaying the inevitable defeat."

Sissy made a face at her friend, then reached beneath the table, pulled out a large tote bag, and whipped out her laptop. She typed in her password and a moment later said, "Okay, it's all booted up. What do you need, Ms. McMillan?"

I held out the media card. "I need photograph number one hundred ninety enhanced. Can one of those programs do that?"

"Should be able to." Sissy took the card and slipped it into her laptop.

A few minutes later the photographs started popping up on her screen. "One hundred ninety, you said?" She scrolled to the photograph and let out a whistle. "Man, that's one bad photo," she said. "Who took this? The lighting's off, the background's way too dark . . ."

"Never mind who took it, or pointing out the flaws," I cut in. "Can you make it any clearer?"

Sissy set her jaw. "I'm sure gonna try."

Sissy downloaded the photo to her laptop and handed me back the card. Gary and I stepped off to one side while Sissy started tapping away on the keyboard. Roz came back, saw Sissy on the computer, rolled her eyes, and then picked up a bag of cat food. "Might as well make sure the cats have enough to eat. She's got that look on her face," Roz remarked. "Whatever she's doing is gonna take a while." She left and Gary and I flopped into the other two chairs across from Sissy. About twenty minutes later the teen looked up, a satisfied smile on her face. "It's not perfect, but it's a big improvement. Want to see?"

Without waiting for us to answer, Sissy flipped her laptop around so we could view the screen. Both Gary and I sucked in a breath. The photo was still pretty grainy, but the composition was much better and more in focus.

"Could you make the face of that figure in the doorway any clearer?" I asked.

Sissy frowned. "If I had Topaz Sharpen or Lightroom, I probably could. With the programs I do have this is about as good as it's gonna get."

Both Gary and I leaned over the teen's shoulder. "What about his arm?" I asked. "Can you enlarge it a bit, make it clearer?"

Sissy tapped at the keyboard again and the figure's arm came into focus. I tapped at the screen. "Enlarge that part, right there," I said. Sissy worked for a few moments and then the figure's hand came into focus, and I sucked in a breath as I recognized a gold cuff link with a lion embossed on it. Patrick's cuff links.

Gary set his lips and pointed to the screen. "Can you zoom in on that object sticking out of his pocket?"

"Sure." She bent over the keyboard and a few moments later the pocket came into focus. Now it was clear that the object sticking out of Patrick's pocket was a knife handle, and even though the image was still grainy, you could see the faint impression of something embossed on the handle.

"Oh, Patrick," I murmured. "What have you done?"

Chapter Sixteen

Gary slipped his arm around my shoulders. "Take it easy, Shell. We don't know that he's done anything . . . yet," he said.

"Right," I said between clenched teeth. I looked at the photo again, then turned back to Sissy. I gestured with my hand. "See that tiny bit of writing in the lower right corner?"

The teen peered at the screen. "Looks like a time stamp. Want me to enlarge that?"

"If you could."

"Piece of cake." A few seconds later the time stamp came up on the screen, clear as a bell. Nine fifteen. Well within the time frame of the murder.

I looked at Sissy. "I think that'll be all, Sissy. Thanks for helping out. Would it be possible for you to send that enhanced photo to my phone?"

"No problem." She tapped away, then leaned back with a smile. "Done."

"Thanks. Oh, and please, not a word of this to anyone, not even Roz, okay?"

The teen grinned as she closed her laptop. "Sure, Ms. McMillan. I can keep a secret."

We left the room, and once we were back in the hallway, Gary said, "Calm down, Shell. That photo was still pretty blurry. We can't make out the guy's face. It might not be Patrick."

"Those cuff links weren't blurry, Gary. Those are Patrick's cuff links, and he did have a black suit on tonight. And," I added over the catch in my throat, "that was a knife sticking out of his pocket."

"Once again, it's a very grainy image, but . . ." Gary reached up and dragged his hand along the back of his neck. "It did look like a knife, I'll admit. But it doesn't have to be the same one that was sticking out of Venery's chest. And if it is, well, maybe he took it to screw with his head, or to use to barter to get him to do his show."

I sighed. "I suppose I should tell Josh about this."

"What we really need to do is find Patrick and hear his side of the story. But seeing as that's not possible, I agree. Josh should know."

We retraced our steps to the coatroom, where I put the media card back in Doug's camera. Then we continued on to Louise's office and found Josh just exiting. I ran right over to him. "She told you everything?"

He nodded. "It's quite a tale, but I believe her. As long as her alibi checks out, Louise is in the clear as far as I'm concerned."

I breathed a sigh of relief. "Good." I looked at Josh expectantly. "It won't be necessary for you to put the details of Louise's past relationship with Venery in your report, will it?"

"I told Louise I would respect her privacy, and I meant it. I interviewed her alone, so there are no other witnesses to the conversation. Anything Louise felt she had to do with Venery will remain her secret."

"Good." Then I reached out and squeezed Josh's hand. "You know, sometimes you're not such a bad guy."

He gave me a lopsided grin. "You might want to bear that thought in mind throughout the rest of my investigation. With Louise out of the running, our suspect pool is narrowed down considerably."

I bit down hard on my lower lip. This was going to be harder than I'd thought. I shot Gary a sideways glance. He gave me an encouraging nod, so I blurted out, "Gary and I found something you should see in one of the photos Doug Harriman took."

I pulled out my phone and called up the photo Sissy had sent me. Josh took the phone and stared at it for a few moments, then looked at me. "It's a pretty grainy photo, but it looks like a man slinking down that back hallway. Isn't that the one that leads to the kitchen area?" I nodded and his gaze dropped to the lower corner of the photo. "Nine fifteen. Around the estimated time of Venery's death." Now he shifted his gaze to me. "You know who that is, don't you, Shell?"

"I can't be certain, but . . . Sissy enlarged the photo a bit for us, and the cuff links on the guy's sleeve look like the ones Patrick had specially made for himself."

Josh's jaw set. He tapped at the photo. "I imagine she also enlarged this object in his jacket pocket?"

I swallowed. "It appears to be a knife, but we couldn't tell for certain if it was the murder weapon."

Josh looked at the photo for a long moment, then handed me back my phone. "Can you forward that photo to my phone? I want to get some techs on enhancing that right away."

"Sure." I sent the photo and then said, "If it is Patrick, I'm sure there's a reasonable explanation."

Josh shook his head. "I'm not going to lie to you, Shell. It doesn't look good for your ex and neither does this disappearing act of his."

"For that matter, Tessa Taylor and Summer are MIA as well," I pointed out.

"Yes, but we don't have a photo that shows either of them possibly in possession of the murder weapon." He said in a softer tone, "I'm trying to keep an open mind, Shell, believe me, but even you have to admit Patrick's in real trouble."

I hated to admit it, but Josh was right. How in the world was Patrick ever going to explain this? Unless, of course, there was no explanation and he had killed Venery. But deep in my heart of hearts, I doubted that. Aloud I said, with far more confidence than I felt, "I'm sure once we find Patrick he'll be able to explain everything."

Josh's expression was grim. "I hope so."

Amy Riser came up to us. "That murder skit calmed everything down for a while, but now the natives are getting restless again. Most of them are asking about Venery. It appears the guy had a lot of fans in the audience who'd love to meet him." She clucked her tongue. "We can't hope to keep this quiet much longer."

"I know," Josh said. "I was hoping that I'd have the opportunity to interview two more persons of interest before an announcement had to be made." He was silent for several seconds, then he cleared his throat and turned to Amy. "I'm organizing an all-out search for Patrick Hanratty. His luggage is still here, so unless he snuck out of here and went out on foot in this storm, he's around here somewhere. Grab Denny and Morgan and fill them in. Make discreet inquiries and don't leave any place in this inn untouched. If he's here, we're going to find him. Tessa Taylor and that girl Summer too. They've both been MIA since before that murder skit started. We need to find all of them and get their stories."

Amy nodded, closed her notebook and hurried off. "I should join them," Josh said. He leaned over and gave me a peck on the cheek. "I'll talk to you later."

Josh walked off and Gary laid his hand on my shoulder. "Guess we might as well go back to the Appalachian Room and see what's happening there," he said. "I should congratulate Liv on her win, too."

"You go on," I said. "I want to go to the ladies' room and freshen up."

Gary left and I crossed the hall and pushed through the door to the ladies' room. I walked over to the sink and looked at my reflection. "There's got to be a reasonable explanation for all this," I said. "There's got to be, or my name isn't—"

"Shell McMillan," said a voice behind me. "I need to speak with you. I think you'll be very interested in what I have to say."

I whirled around and almost fell over when I saw the speaker. "Tessa Taylor," I cried. "Where have you been?"

The redhead gave me a measured stare. "If it weren't for this darn storm I would have blown out of here hours ago, trust me. I've just been keeping a low profile. Very low."

Well, that was an understatement. "You said you needed to speak with me?"

"I've heard you're in pretty tight with the law enforcement around here. Also that you're a bit of a sleuth yourself. Considering the circumstances . . . I thought you'd be the best person to approach."

My eyes narrowed. "I take it you know what happened to Venery?"

She nodded. "I was supposed to meet him in the storage area around nine fifteen. I was a bit late arriving. I walked in, saw the shoe under the boxes, and moved in for a closer look. I couldn't get out of there fast enough." She held up her hands, and I saw she wore white gloves. "I didn't touch anything other than the box, and I had these on the whole time."

I remembered the shadowy figure I'd seen in the hall. That must have been Tessa. I decided to cut right to the chase. "Were you blackmailing Venery, or vice versa?"

Her eyes widened. "Blackmail? Goodness, no. Whatever gave you that idea?"

"I overheard your argument with Venery last night. I also found a note in the hallway near Venery's body. It said, 'Admit the truth or suffer the consequences.' I have to ask, did you either write or receive that note?"

Tessa's eyes widened again. "No on both counts, but it might explain why Rey was so frantic to see me." She leaned one hip against the sink. "It all started a few months ago, when I learned Venery was being wooed by a few producers to star in a reality cooking show. I'll admit my production company has been having a rather rough time of late, so I decided to go after Venery myself. That man is—was—a master at playing hardball. One minute he was assuring me that we had his business, the next he was telling me about what a great deal other production companies were offering him. I knew he was engaged in talks with Patrick, and I went to his TV station to have a chat with him, to convince him to sign with us. I arrived early, and he was just finishing up filming a segment of *Culinary Surprise*. The station manager's secretary told me to wait in Rey's office.

While I was waiting, I guess you could say I engaged in a little . . . snooping."

"Snooping?"

Both of her well-shaped eyebrows went up "You know snooping, like any good amateur sleuth does. You walk into an empty office, there are papers strewn all over the desktop, and you glance at them, casually. Well, there was a pile of papers on the edge of the desk and I accidentally knocked them over. When I bent to pick them up I saw an envelope addressed to Ronald Payson, care of Reynaldo Venery. I got curious so I opened it. There was a letter inside, written on pink stationery. It was dated a few weeks ago and there was just one line, written in what looked like a childish scrawl. It said, 'She could use your help.' Under that were two initials, LL."

"She could use your help?" I frowned. "That's cryptic, to say the least."

"That's what I thought," Tessa agreed. "I looked at the postmark on the envelope. It was sent from Fox Hollow. I'd barely replaced it in the pile when Rey came in. He didn't say anything, but I think he was certain I'd been going through his papers. Needless to say, the meeting was cut very short." She folded her arms over her chest. "I confess, finding that note piqued my curiosity. I started to do a little digging. I admit that I thought that if I could get something on him, I could persuade him to sign with my company."

"And what did you find out?"

She shrugged. "Not much. I learned that Ronald Payson was a former chef in New Orleans, and that he'd worked at several restaurants in Georgia and Louisiana. I thought maybe there was some dirt to be had from that angle, but I came up empty." Her smile was thin. "I guess I'm not much of a detective after all. I couldn't find a connection."

I breathed a silent sigh of relief. Louise's secret was still safe. "You should have looked under Reynaldo Venery, not Ronald Payson," I said. "I started to do some research as well, and found an article on a broken engagement between him and someone named Lina Lawley."

"Lina Lawley, eh? That name seems familiar," remarked Tessa. "What did you find out?"

"Nothing," I said. "I got interrupted and never resumed my search."

"I wish I'd known that," murmured Tessa. "Things might have turned out differently. As it happened, I'd seen Patrick a few days before, and he was bragging about having the inside track with Venery. I figured there had to be some connection between this Ronald Payson and Venery, so I called him and told him I knew all about his secret."

"In other words, you tried to bluff him."

"Exactly. He called it, and that's when I asked him point-blank who was the mystery woman who needed his help."

"How did he react?"

"He was cool as a cucumber. Said that he didn't know what I was talking about, and that if anyone needed his help, he'd certainly be there. Then he hung up on me." Her lips twisted into a rueful grin. "I tracked him down here and tried to bluff it out again, but he was having none of it. He told me that unless I could offer him something concrete, he'd have no problem suing me for defamation of character."

"Why did he want to meet with you tonight?"

Her shoulders hunched. "I have no idea. He left me a voicemail message that he needed to discuss that important matter with me. I was hoping that maybe he'd changed his mind about signing on with Patrick, because it was evident the two of them were at odds."

"You said he wanted to meet with you at nine fifteen?"

"Yes. I'd gone back to the pet room for another look at the cats. I'm actually thinking of getting one, and they were all so cute! I especially liked that all-black one."

"Dahlia," I murmured. I remembered Sissy mentioning a woman had been in looking at the cat. It must have been Tessa.

"Is that the cat's name? Dahlia? Very chic. I like it," murmured Tessa. "Anyway, I kind of lost track of time and when I looked at my watch it was almost nine thirty. I hightailed it down to the storage area, but . . ." She spread her hands. "You know the rest."

"I suppose I do," I said. "You found Venery's body and instead of notifying anyone, left it for someone else to do."

"That I did," Tessa said. "I figured I'd get blamed, especially in light of the fact Venery and I have been at odds."

"That's true." I paused for a moment. "Did you hear something?"

Tessa frowned. "Like what?"

I gestured toward the bathroom door. "I thought I heard a door creak."

Tessa shook her head. "I didn't hear anything, but this is an old building. Everything creaks and shakes."

We were both silent for several minutes and then I asked, "Did you send an anonymous email to Charisma Walters with a tip about Venery being in Fox Hollow to cover up a secret?"

Tessa's brow puckered. "Me? Heck, no. I've heard of Charisma Walters. She's a popular influencer. But I assure you, I have never emailed her."

She started for the door but I called out, "One last thing. When you went to the storage area to meet Venery, did you see anyone else around?"

She looked me straight in the eye and said, "You mean did I see Patrick, right? No, I did not, but that doesn't exonerate him. He's become a rather desperate man lately. Desperate people sometimes commit desperate acts. I can see you still care about him, although I don't know why you should."

"Thanks for the unsolicited advice," I remarked. "Now let me give you some. You should tell what you just told me to Detective Bloodgood. It will look much better if you go to him, rather than let him or one of the other police officers track you down."

"I suppose you're right," Tessa admitted. "Better sooner than later I suppose. Wish me luck." With that, she turned and strode out of the ladies' room. I leaned against the sink, trying to process everything she'd just told me. Venery certainly had been a man of secrets. He definitely had something to hide, but what could that be?

I drummed my fingers on the table and closed my eyes, thinking. Tessa had found a letter on Venery's desk postmarked Fox Hollow. Inside was a note that said 'she needs your help,' signed by someone with the initials LL. Venery had volunteered to help out at our murder mystery dinner because he had important business to take care of in Fox Hollow, and he'd said as much to Patrick. So . . . did this important business of Venery's have to do with the "she" who needed his help?

I pulled out my phone and dialed the reception desk. Andrea answered. "Andrea, it's Shell McMillan. I was just wondering . . . what is Louise's maiden name?"

"Frawley. Why?"

"Oh, just a bet I had with someone. I thought it started with an *L*. Thanks."

I hung up feeling relieved that the LL who'd sent that note wasn't Louise. But who might it be? On a hunch I called up the search engine again and this time typed in "Reynaldo Venery—broken romances with women initials LL," and hit go. A few seconds later I was rewarded with a story from the *New Orleans Sun-Times* twenty years ago. The headline read: *No Wedding Bells for Lina.*

New Orleans, LA: It looks as if there won't be wedding bells ringing in St. Louis Cathedral for Lina Lawley and her fiancé, Reynaldo Venery. According to our sources, Lawley and Venery were seen outside Antoine's having one humdinger of a battle. Lawley took off her four-carat diamond ring and threw it at Venery's head before storming off in a huff. Neither Lawley nor Venery could be reached for comment.

I felt a rush of elation. LL could well be Lina Lawley. I needed to know more about her. I typed her name into the search bar, but before I could hit enter, I paused, listening. I could have sworn I heard the bathroom door creak. I whirled around, but no one was there. I turned back to my phone, my finger poised over the enter button, and I heard it again. This time I whirled around just in time to see the door swing shut.

I slid my phone back into my pocket and crossed to the door. I jerked it open and peered into the hallway.

No one was there.

"I didn't imagine it," I muttered. Someone had been spying on me, but why? I moved further into the apparently deserted hallway. Suddenly I tensed as all the hairs on the back of my neck stood up. I was assailed by the feeling that I wasn't alone.

"Who's there?" I called out bravely. "Gary? Is that you? Tessa? Patrick?" My spine was tingling but still I moved forward, inching slowly down the corridor. Still no one. I paused to scratch at the back of my head. "I guess my imagination is getting carried away," I murmured. I started to turn back when I caught a flash of black out of the corner of my eye. The next second I felt something hard whack me on the back of my head. I saw flashing lights dance before my eyes and then . . . blackness.

Chapter Seventeen

I felt a dull roar in my ears, but that was nothing compared to the throbbing sensation that ran up the side of my neck and radiated into my head. I tried to will away the pain, but after a few seconds it was evident that wasn't working. What I needed was aspirin, maybe a whole bottle. I winked one eye open, slowly, and was greeted by abject, total darkness. I opened my other eye and tiny bright specs of light danced dangerously near the edge of my vision. I closed both eyes and leaned back, willing myself to take slow, deep breaths. After a few minutes I slowly opened both eyes. No specs of light. Well, that was a plus, anyway.

"Where the heck am I?" I muttered. I lifted my arm, started to feel around. Hard floor, maybe concrete? I struggled to a sitting position and sat for a few moments, rubbing at the back of my head with my fingertips. "Ouch." There was a good-sized lump there. What had happened? Oh, yes, I remembered now. I'd seen the ladies' room door close and had gone to investigate. Someone had whacked me but good on the back of the head and had brought me . . . where?

Out of the corner of my eye I could discern a faint glow. The feeble light was coming from somewhere, but I was at a loss to determine just what the source was. I exhaled a deep breath and blinked, and after a few moments I could make out a mop propped up against the wall, and racks of steel shelving lining another. I felt around, and my questing fingers came in contact with a large box. I stuck my hand inside and felt something squishy. I pulled the object out and almost laughed out loud. A roll of toilet paper! I was probably in another of the inn's storage areas. I waited a few minutes, then slowly and carefully got to my feet. I was a bit wobbly but otherwise all right.

"Uh-ohhhhh."

I almost toppled over again. Every nerve, every muscle in my body tensed. Where had that groan come from? Slowly, very slowly, I put one foot in front of the other and inched forward. A few seconds later my foot came in contact with . . . something. I poked at it with the toe of my shoe.

"Uh-ohhhh."

I bent over carefully, because my equilibrium was still in a very tenuous state, for a closer look. A man's body was sprawled out on his side on the floor. This body, though, wasn't dead, not if the groans emanating from it were any indication. "Ohhh," he man said again. "My head feels like it's gonna explode."

I froze at the familiar voice and then, throwing any semblance of caution to the wind, reached out and rolled the body over. Patrick blinked, and then stared up at me. "Shell? Is that you?" I didn't answer, just slipped my hand underneath his head and felt around. "Ouch!" he cried. "Be careful, won't you?"

"You've got an even bigger lump there than I have," I answered. "Think you can sit up?"

He nodded, and I helped him to a sitting position. He reached up and rubbed lightly at the back of his neck. "I feel like I got run over with a Mack truck," he said. "Where in blazes are we?"

"Somewhere with a cold, hard floor, probably a storage area. It's hard to tell in this dim light." I shoved my hand into my pocket, then grimaced. "Whoever hit me took my phone."

Patrick felt in his pocket. "Mine too," he said. "Great. Can't even call for help. Although I do have this." He pulled out a lighter. "Good thing I didn't quit smoking entirely. This should give us some more light, at least enough to find a light switch."

Patrick flipped the switch on the lighter and held it up. I could see that the steel shelving I'd noticed before held an assortment of cleaning products, as well as boxes of tissues and a couple dozen rolls of paper towels. He focused the light over toward the center of the room, and I could make out several pieces of furniture—bedposts, some love seats, a couch—and several paintings stacked in a corner. I could also make out, in the far corner, the outline of a stairway.

"This must be where Sissy and Roz got the furniture to make up the set for the skit," I said. I gestured toward the stairs. "We've got to be in the basement. That dim light is probably filtering down from upstairs."

"I can see that," Patrick growled irritably. "But how did we get here?"

"No doubt the person who knocked us out brought us here. At least whoever it is didn't kill us too," I said. "Can you shine the light over to the left? I thought I saw a light switch on that wall."

"Sure." He complied and sure enough I was right. There was a light switch. I went over and flipped it, and the room was immediately filled with harsh fluorescent light.

"Yow." Patrick put up his hand to shield his eyes. "I think the dim light was better."

I looked down at the dirty floor and out of the corner of my eye thought I saw something skitter underneath the shelving. I shuddered. "I think you're right," I said. "What you don't see doesn't bother you, but I think this area could benefit from a once-over by my cats."

"In other words, this room is a cat-astrophe?" Patrick started to laugh at his own joke, then stopped. "Sorry. It hurts to laugh. It hurts to talk. It hurts to do anything, actually."

"Then don't make any more jokes," I advised. "You never were a comedian."

He winced. "Thanks for the compliment. I'm trying to be upbeat about all this." He let out a breath. "Who would have wanted to knock both of us out and put us down here anyway?"

"That's what we've got to figure out. Do you remember where you were when you got knocked out?"

He bent his head, rubbed lightly at his forehead with the tips of his fingers. "Yes. I was in the back hallway, behind the Appalachian Room."

"Near the kitchen?"

He nodded. "I believe so." Suddenly his eyes narrowed. "You said too."

"What?"

"Sorry, I'm still a bit fuzzy." He gave his head a shake. "Before, you said at least whoever knocked us out didn't kill us too. Does that mean someone is dead?"

"Yes." I cleared my throat. "Venery."

He blinked once, twice. "What?"

"Venery is dead. He was apparently killed during that brief blackout. Someone shoved a knife through his heart."

"Oh my God," Patrick cried. His hand went to his left pocket and then he took a step back. "With a knife, you said?"

"Yes." I paused and then added, "The murder weapon matches the description of a knife Venery owned, a family heirloom that apparently went missing during the benefit. Silver, with a leaf design on the handle."

"Oh, no." Patrick let out a moan, staggered backward and sank to the floor. He stayed like that for a few moments before he raised his gaze to meet mine. "I had that knife in my possession," he said flatly.

I nodded. "I know."

He stared at me. "What, have you turned psychic? How could you possibly know that?"

"Long story short, you are in the background of one of the photos

Doug Harriman shot for the *Gazette*." I pointed to his sleeve. "We enhanced the photo, and while your face isn't clear, your lion cuff links are. And there's a knife handle clearly visible sticking out of your jacket pocket."

"Stupid, stupid, stupid." Patrick sucked in his breath, let it out in a soft whoosh. "I knew how much he prized that knife. It sounds silly, I know, but I thought maybe if I had it, I could bargain with him, make him see signing on to do my show was the best choice—the only choice—to make."

"So you stole his knife intending to use it as leverage?"

"Yes." He ran his free hand through his hair. "I wasn't thinking clearly. I was angry at him, and I might have wanted to kill him, but I swear to you I didn't do it."

I laid my hand on his shoulder. "You're a lot of things, Patrick, but you're no murderer. I'd stake my own life on that. I do think, though, that someone wants the police to think that you are."

Patrick snapped his fingers. "It has to be the person who assaulted me. They took the knife and killed Venery, and are hoping I get framed for his murder." He let out a loan moan. "And I haven't helped the situation. That argument I had with Venery in the lobby, when I threatened to kill him?" He compressed his lips into a straight line. "How I wish I could take that back. As a matter of fact, there are a lot of things I wish I could do over."

He stared at me so intently I felt my cheeks start to flame. "Unfortunately, none of us can go back in time," I said. "And to be honest, I wouldn't want to."

"Touché," he murmured. We sat in silence a few seconds and then Patrick said, "Be honest with me, Shell. Am I the main suspect?"

"I think you already know the answer to that."

"Hm, yes, I suppose I do."

For the next few minutes the silence in the room was so thick you could cut it with a knife. Finally I said, "Why don't you tell me what you remember. Starting with how you just happened to get your hands on that knife."

Patrick scrubbed his hand across his jaw. "I checked out and had my luggage put in storage, then I went straight to the kitchen. I'd seen where Venery used to put it on the set of his show, usually in a canister or a little-used drawer, so I had a good idea where to look for it. Once I'd found it, I hid it under one of the floorboards all the way back in the kitchen. I waited until Venery was giving his little speech and all the chefs were busy with prepping the appetizers before I slipped in to retrieve it."

"So you never intended to participate in the murder skit, did you?"

"Actually, I did. Shortly before I volunteered I'd sent Venery a text, telling him that I had something of his that he'd want, and that he should meet me to discuss. He sent me back a text, 'Storage area main floor nine o'clock,' which was around the time the skit would be starting." He flashed me a guilty look. "I had no choice but to blow off the skit. I went there at the appointed time and was just about to enter when I heard voices inside."

"Voices?"

Patrick nodded. "Yes. One was definitely Venery's. The other one was low-pitched, I couldn't make it out. Anyway, I hesitated. I didn't know what to do. I walked down the hall a little bit, and then I thought I heard a floorboard creak behind me. I started to turn and then, wham! I saw stars! Next thing I know, I'm waking up here, with you."

I frowned. "You say you heard voices. You're certain you couldn't identify the second voice? Or at least discern if it were male or female?"

He shook his head. "Nope, sorry. And to be truthful, I wasn't trying to eavesdrop. By that time I was starting to doubt the wisdom of my actions. I was considering sneaking the knife back into the kitchen and texting Venery to just forget the whole thing, but before I could make up my mind I got conked but good on my noodle."

"Seems like Venery had quite a few secret meetings going in that storeroom," I remarked. "Tessa Taylor also got a message from Venery. He wanted to meet her in that storage area too, but at nine fifteen. She was late getting there, but when she arrived he was already dead. She found his body underneath a pile of boxes, but instead of reporting it she left it for someone else to find."

"She's lying!" Patrick roared. Then he sat back and clapped a hand to his head. "Ouch, that hurt. She's lying," he said in a calmer tone. "It must have been her I heard arguing with Venery in there! She must have seen me take the knife and figured I'd make the perfect patsy."

"She couldn't have. Remember, I said she was late for the appointment. Tessa was in the cat room looking at the cats up until nine thirty. Both Sissy and Roz saw her there. It couldn't have been her that you heard," I responded. "And even if she didn't have an alibi, she's only about five three or five four, right? It would be a stretch for anyone to think that a petite woman like Tessa Taylor could knock a big guy like you out, let alone drag you all the way down to this basement."

"She would have been high on adrenaline. That can give people superhuman strength." He balled one hand into a fist and pounded it into the palm of the other. "If not Tessa, then who?"

"That seems to be the million-dollar question. Did Venery ever mention just exactly what his business was that brought him to Fox Hollow?"

Patrick shook his head. "I tried to find out, but he was quite mum on the subject."

"I may have a few thoughts on that," I said, "but right now we need to get out of here. Feel strong enough to walk?"

"Absolutely."

I helped Patrick to his feet and then we started up the stairway. Once we were at the door, however, we found that escape wasn't as easy as all that. The door was locked, presumably from the outside. "Great," Patrick muttered. "So what now? We start banging on the door and yelling?"

I balled my hand into a fist. "Correct."

The two of us pounded on the door and shouted at the tops of our lungs, but after ten minutes of that all we had were sore throats. We were no closer to freedom than before. "Let's go back downstairs and give it a more thorough look. There might be another door we overlooked."

We made our way back down the stairs. When we reached the bottom I stopped short, causing Patrick to bump into me. "Hey, what's the idea?" he cried. "Why'd you stop?"

"Listen," I commanded, putting my hand to my ear. "Do you hear that?"

Patrick frowned. "I don't hear anything."

"I do. It sounds like scratching!"

We were both silent for several seconds, listening, and then Patrick gave a nod. "You're right. But where is it coming from?"

"Over there, I think," I said. "Behind the boiler."

I moved forward cautiously and peeped around the boiler. I started as three eyes blinked back at me. Then two furry forms moved from behind the boiler into the room. "Purrday?" I cried. "And Princess Fuzzypants?"

Patrick was at my elbow almost immediately. "Your cat is here, and with a friend? How on earth did they manage that?"

"If you knew them, you'd understand," I said fondly. "It's hard to explain, but you can trust Purrday and his partner in crime, Princess Fuzzypants, to come to the rescue."

The princess gave a loud meow, and Purrday puffed out his chest.

Patrick scratched at his head. "I guess we should be grateful your cats seem to be explorers," he remarked. "They certainly give new meaning to that old adage about cats being curious."

"Well, they didn't materialize down here out of thin air." I looked at the cats. "Purrday, Princess, show us how you got down here."

The cats trotted a few steps back into the shadows, then Purrday paused and glanced over his shoulder. I tugged at Patrick's arm. "Come on. They want us to follow them."

Patrick cast me a doubtful look. "Behind the boiler? Really?"

"There's a tiny corridor back here that might lead somewhere. It's pretty narrow, but I think we can navigate it." I made a shooing motion at the cats. "Go on, kids. We're right behind you."

Purrday and the princess weaved around the boiler and Patrick and I followed. We had to practically hug the wall, but I was just thankful there were no low-lying pipes to conk me in the head. Midway down the cats veered off to a shadowed area. "Give me your lighter. Looks like there might be a connecting room here," I announced. The cats darted forward and I followed without any hesitation. It turned out to be another corridor, only this one was a bit wider and a few yards down illuminated by a pencil-thin beam of light. Purrday and the princess scampered forward, and as I drew closer I could see there was another flight of stairs leading up. "Success," I cried, and then Patrick bumped into me again.

"You really have to stop doing that, Shell," he said.

"Sorry, but look! Our freedom awaits."

By now the cats were halfway up the staircase. Patrick and I quickly followed. When we reached the top I said over my shoulder, "I'm stopping to take a quick look."

"Fine," said Patrick from behind me. "What do you see?"

"Looks like another storage area."

I stepped forward into the room, Patrick right behind me. It was indeed another storage area. Lit by a dim light overhead, this one contained stacks of folding chairs and tables propped up against the wall. At the far end of the room was another steel rack with boxes scattered on it, and a door right next to it that was slightly ajar. "This must be how the cats got in," I said. I bent down and scooped Purrday up. "This is one time your wandering habits came in handy," I said, giving the cat a fierce hug.

Princess Fuzzypants rubbed against my ankles and I looked down at her with a smile. "You too, of course."

Purrday's tongue darted out and swiped across my cheek, and then he started wriggling. I set him down, but instead of heading toward the door, he turned and started pawing at the steel shelving. "Purrday," I commanded. "Get away from there."

My cat turned. If ever a cat could bestow a defiant look, Purrday was doing exactly that now. He narrowed his eyes at me, turned, and swiped at a large box on the bottom shelf of the rack.

"Purrday, you get away from that right now—"

I stopped speaking as the box toppled over. It flew open, and nestled inside was a pair of pointy-toed black heels. But that wasn't what made me gasp.

It was the fact that the tips of the shoes had tiny red flecks scattered over them. Flecks that looked suspiciously like . . . blood.

Chapter Eighteen

I stared at the shoes, my thoughts in a whirl. If that was flecks of blood on the tips, was it Venery's blood? Had the killer switched shoes and hidden these here? What's more, how had he—or more likely she—known to do so?

I was jolted out of my reverie by something brushing against my hand, and then I heard Patrick's voice in my ear. "Shell, are you all right? What are you looking at?"

I stepped back and pointed at the box. "These," I said.

Patrick peered over my shoulder. "Good God! Is that—is that blood?"

"Looks like it," I said grimly.

"Dear Lord! Do you think the killer wore these?"

Patrick bent over and his hand started to dip inside the box, but I grabbed his wrist. "Don't touch them," I cautioned. "You might destroy any prints that might be on them. You don't want to get your prints on them either . . . just in case." I bent down and grasped the box. "The sooner we show Josh, the better," I said.

Purrday was already standing half in, half out of the doorway. "Merow," he said, and then trotted out into the hallway. I followed, with Patrick bringing up the rear. Once in the hallway I gave a quick glance around. Judging from the numbered doors, we were probably somewhere on the first floor. "This way," I said, motioning for Patrick to follow me. Purrday had already set off at a fast clip down the long hallway. A few minutes later we emerged into the main lobby. Andrea was still behind the reception desk. She glanced up from the computer and saw me. "Ms. McMillan, there you are. Detective Bloodgood was looking for you and so was your mother." Her gaze swept over both me and Patrick. "I see you found Mr. Hanratty," she remarked.

"Yes, I did. Do you know where Detective Bloodgood is?"

"I think he went back to the Appalachian Room."

"Thanks."

With Patrick and both cats at my heels, I headed straight for the Appalachian Room. As I approached I could hear the strains of a popular Katy Perry tune. Patrick moved forward and opened the door, and we all trooped inside. I noticed that the set had been dismantled and the tables pushed back. A large stereo system had been set up on the raised dais, and a young man I recognized as one of Louise's sous chefs was filling the role of DJ. The dance floor was crowded with couples gyrating to the beat of "Roar" and everyone appeared to be having a good time. I craned my neck, looking around. Josh was nowhere to be seen, but I caught sight of Amy Riser over at the other end of the room. Her arms were folded across her chest but her foot was tapping on the parquet floor, keeping time to the music. She caught sight of me and immediately started to push her way through the crowd.

"Shell! We've been looking everywhere for you." Her gaze shifted to Patrick, but before she could say anything I cut in.

"Detective Amy Riser, this is Patrick Hanratty," I said. I looked her right in the eyes. "Someone knocked the both of us out and put us in the basement."

"What?" Both Amy's eyebrows went straight up and then she narrowed her eyes at Patrick. "Is that right?"

Patrick drew himself up to his full height. "It is, and we might still be down there if not for Shell's cats." He inclined his head toward the two cats, who were both seated comfortably at my feet, their tails wrapped around their forepaws. "The basement door was locked from the outside. Fortunately these two clever felines managed to find another exit."

At those words of praise, Purrday sat up a bit straighter and his tail curled. "Merow," he said. I could swear his chest puffed out at least an inch. The princess blinked her big eyes and let out a resounding purr.

Amy looked at the cats and a ghost of a smile flitted across her face for a brief instant before she turned her attention back to Patrick. "If I could have a word with you in private, Mr. Hanratty," she said. "There are some details about this evening that need clarification."

I touched Amy's arm. "I told Patrick what happened," I said in a low tone.

Amy's expression clearly reflected her disapproval. She clucked her tongue. "You shouldn't have done that," she chided.

"Probably not, but I did anyway. For what it's worth, Patrick told me what happened and I believe him," I said.

Amy shot me a look that clearly said *no surprise there*. "I would still like to hear the details from Mr. Hanratty himself," she said.

Patrick shot Amy an affable smile. "Certainly. Detective Riser, correct? But before we begin, might I ask if I'm being formally charged with anything? Because if so, I will need to place a quick call to my attorney."

Amy returned Patrick's smile with a slightly frozen one of her own. "Not at this time, Mr. Hanratty. You're not being taken into police custody. Right now you're merely a person of interest, although we would ask that you not leave Fox Hollow while the investigation is going on."

"That's rather a moot point considering the weather, don't you think, Detective?" responded Patrick. "I will tell you what I told Shell. I had nothing to do with Venery's—"

"Mr. Hanratty!" Amy cut him off before he could finish the sentence. Leaning into Patrick, she added in a low tone, "We aren't making a public statement of what happened earlier at this time. So if you wouldn't mind zipping your lip and following me?"

I looked at Patrick. "Do you want me to go with you?"

He reached out and patted my hand. "Thanks, Shell, but I think I can handle myself. After all, I have truth on my side." He reached up and gingerly touched the back of his head. "And a lump the size of a melon and a splitting headache to verify my tale." He looked significantly at the box I still had tucked under one arm. "Shouldn't you be trying to find your boyfriend?"

Patrick gave my arm a quick squeeze as he brushed past me to follow Amy. I squared my shoulders and headed further into the Appalachian Room, cats in tow. I spotted Gary over in a far corner, fiddling with his phone. He glanced up, saw me, and immediately made a beeline for me.

"There you are, thank goodness," Gary cried. "What happened? When you didn't come back after half an hour I sent Leila to the bathroom to get you. When she came back and said you weren't there, well, I told Josh."

"Amy said he'd been looking for me," I said. "I ran into Tessa Taylor in the ladies' room. She told me her story, and I advised her to tell Josh."

Gary raised one eyebrow. "Her story? I assume it's about Venery."

I repeated what Tessa had told me, ending with, "I'm glad she took my advice. Honestly, I thought she might chicken out."

Gary nodded. "Okay, but . . . that didn't take two hours. Where were you the rest of the time."

"I spent most of it unconscious down in the inn basement," I replied. Gary gasped and I went on, "After Tessa left, I was trying to look up something on my phone when I thought I saw someone else leave. When I went to investigate, I got conked on the head. I woke up down in the basement—with Patrick."

Gary's jaw dropped. "Patrick! He was hiding in the basement all this time?"

"Not hiding, exactly. Someone knocked him out too. Most likely the same someone who murdered Venery."

"Merow!"

I looked down at the two cats at my feet. "Fortunately, Purrday and the princess managed to rescue us—again."

Gary put a finger to his lips. "So I take it Patrick told you he didn't kill Venery. What about the knife we saw in the photo?"

"Patrick admitted he did take the knife. It was just as you figured. He thought he could us it as leverage to convince Venery to do his show. Whoever knocked Patrick out must have taken the knife and used it to kill Venery."

Gary rubbed thoughtfully at his chin. "Did Patrick say when all this happened?"

"He got a text from Venery telling him to meet him in that storage area at nine o'clock. He went there but he heard Venery talking to someone so he didn't go in. He was trying to decide on his next move when he was knocked out."

"And put in the basement. Convenient," remarked Gary.

I ignored his last remark and went on, "According to Tessa, she'd also gotten a text from Venery asking to meet at nine fifteen. She was looking at the cats, though, so didn't get there until shortly after nine thirty. She discovered the body but hightailed it out of there. And she told me that she didn't see Patrick anywhere in the area."

Gary dragged his hand along the back of his neck. "There's still the matter of Patrick having that knife. And we only have Patrick's word that he heard Venery talking with someone else."

"Patrick's lied to me before, but I don't think he is now," I said. "It's possible that Venery sent whoever it was on their way, and the killer saw Patrick and the knife in his pocket and decided to take the opportunity to kill Venery and frame either Patrick or Tessa for his death."

"Don't get me wrong, Shell," said Gary. "I hate to think of Patrick as a killer, but it doesn't look good for him." He held up his fingers and started to tick off. "He had motive, he had opportunity, and he had means—possession of the murder weapon. And he wouldn't be the first person to knock themselves out to get an alibi."

I made an exasperated sound. "You're giving Patrick too much credit. He's not that devious, or inventive."

"Well, they'd better get some sort of a break in this case and soon," Gary said. He pulled out his phone and tapped on the screen. "The most recent weather report doesn't have this storm blowing over until at least two in the morning. They can't keep this quiet much longer."

"I know." I was silent a moment and then added, "One thing I'm almost positive of, though. I think there's a good chance Venery's killer is a woman," I said.

"What makes you so sure?" asked Gary.

"This, for one thing." I took the box I'd been carrying under my arm and set it on a nearby vacant table. "I found this in the basement." I lifted the flaps of the box and tilted it so Gary could peer inside. "It certainly looks like blood to me, what do you think?"

Gary leaned in for a closer look. Finally he said, "They do look suspicious, but we don't know for sure those red flecks are blood, or Venery's blood. It could be something else." He took another look at the shoes. "These look gigantic. A size ten at least, maybe bigger, so you could rule out women with small feet, like Tessa Taylor."

"Yes, I noticed her feet were small." I craned my neck around. "Where's Doug? We need to look at his camera again. Maybe he took one of whoever was wearing these." I let out a breath. "Oh, and I forgot to mention something. That research I was doing right before I got knocked out. It just so happens—"

I didn't get to finish my sentence, though, because Josh appeared just then. He grabbed me in a gigantic bear hug. "Shell, where were you? I've been going nuts looking for you ever since I talked to Tessa Taylor."

I pushed myself out of his embrace—a trifle reluctantly, I might add. "Long story short, I investigated a noise, got conked on the head and ended up in the basement." I looked fondly at the two cats. "We might still be there if not for Purrday and the princess."

Josh frowned. "We?"

"She found Patrick in the basement, who had also been conked on the head," put in Gary. "Detective Riser is talking with him now."

Josh's eyes narrowed into slits. "You found Hanratty?" he asked me.

"Yes. And you might as well know I believe his story about being knocked out. And I also found these hidden in the basement." I pushed the box into his hands. "It's possible whoever killed Venery was wearing them."

Josh peered inside, then shot me a puzzled glance. "A pair of shoes?"

"Look at the tips," I said. "It could be Venery's blood."

Josh stood a few moments just staring at the shoes. At last he spoke. "Where did you say you found these?"

"Actually Purrday found them. They were on the bottom of a supply shelf in the basement," I replied. "Someone didn't want them found, probably the same someone who wanted Patrick and myself out of the way." I rubbed at my chin with the back of my hand. "One thing I think we're overlooking. The killer has to be somewhat familiar with the inn. They knew how to access the basement, and they knew where that storage closet was to hide the shoes."

Josh frowned. "So now you're suggesting that Venery was killed by an employee of the inn?"

"No, just by someone who took the time to familiarize themselves with where things were. Or . . . ." I snapped my fingers. "Maybe that person is the killer's accomplice."

"Now you think more than one person is involved in this?" Josh rubbed at the back of his neck, something I knew he did when he felt frustrated.

"I don't know, I'm just throwing out possibilities," I answered.

He cocked his head at me. "It sounds to me like you have a suspect in mind."

"I do, but it's no one I can put a name to . . . yet," I said with a sigh. "Did Tessa tell you about the note she found in Venery's office."

"The one signed LL? She did. You think this woman, whoever she is, might have come here tonight intending to kill Venery?"

"It's a possibility. Something Venery saw when he gave his speech rattled him. Maybe it was this LL."

"Okay." Josh's lips thinned to a straight line. "I'll have Amy check the guest roster, see if there's anyone with those initials on it."

"If she was intending to confront Venery, she could have bought the tickets under an assumed name," I pointed out. "You need to single out females who aren't local. And what tables were in Venery's line of vision? She might have been at one of them." My gaze traveled to the box containing the shoes. "I still think finding the owner of these shoes is key to solving this whole puzzle."

"Maybe," Josh answered grudgingly. "After all, we don't know those flecks of red are blood, let alone Venery's. It could be paint, for all we know. And we won't be able to get these to the lab until tomorrow morning the earliest."

I wrinkled my nose. "Paint? Doubtful. I haven't seen anything here in the inn painted this bright a shade of red."

"What about nail polish?" suggested Gary.

"Wait!" I grabbed Gary's arm. "Summer had red polish on, and it was bright red, like what's on the shoes. I noticed it earlier when I was with her." I let go of Gary's arm and started to pace back and forth. "As an inn employee, she'd be familiar with the layout. And we haven't seen her since before the murder skit started. She said she had to make a phone call and that was it. Andrea said she was deathly afraid of storms, thought she might be holed up somewhere riding it out, but what if she had another reason to vanish?"

"Vanish? I haven't vanished. I'm right here," said a voice behind me.

Chapter Nineteen

We all turned around. Summer stood in the back doorway, hands on her hips. Her head was tilted and her glare was almost defiant as she addressed me. "Where could I have possibly gone?" she asked. "No one can go anywhere, not in this storm. Not without an ark, anyway."

"Quite true," I admitted. "You can't blame us, though, for thinking you just vanished into thin air. None of us have seen you for quite a while, and you did blow off being in the murder skit."

She had the grace to look a bit ashamed. "Yeah, I'm sorry about that," she mumbled. "I had every intention of helping you guys out, but I remembered I promised to call a friend of mine who's going through a rather rough breakup. There's a room on the first floor that we keep available in case an employee needs some downtime or takes ill. I went there for some privacy. After I was done talking I guess I felt drained. The bed looked so inviting, I thought well, I'll just close my eyes for a few seconds to get my energy back. I stretched out and I must have fallen asleep. When I saw what time it was I came straight here."

Gary and I exchanged a glance, and out of the corner of my eye I saw a vein bulge slightly in Josh's neck. "You've been asleep all this time?" he asked, not bothering to hide the note of doubt in his voice.

Summer nodded. "Yes. I've been pulling quite a few double shifts, trying to save up some money for furniture for my new apartment. I guess it all finally caught up with me." She raised her hand to her lips to stifle a yawn, then added, "I'm sorry that I disappointed you. Were you able to put the play on anyway?"

"Yes, we did," I answered. "There was a blackout in the middle of it, though, thanks to this storm. Fortunately the inn has a good generator and the power was only out for a few minutes."

"A blackout, huh? Well, I believe it. That wind sounds positively evil, and you can hear those huge raindrops pelting against the windows." Her shoulders hunched in a shudder. "I hate storms. I'm glad I was able to sleep through most of this one."

"Andrea mentioned you were deathly afraid of storms. She said you might be holed up in one of the rooms," I said.

Summer's nose wrinkled at mention of Andrea's name. "Yeah, she doesn't like me much. She thinks I'm lazy, but I'm not."

"I'm sure you're not," I said. "You were very helpful when I came to the inn looking for Mrs. Gates the other day."

Summer's face brightened a bit. "I do try my best. Ms. Gates knows that."

"Yes, she mentioned you were a very loyal employee," I said. "She even remarked on how you managed to handle difficult guests—like Chef Venery, for example."

"Chef Venery? That guy is a real piece of work," Summer said. "First day he checked in he hit on me and a couple of the maids. I tried to stay clear of him. The guy isn't exactly a big hit around here." She let out a sigh. "I guess I should get back to the reception area. I'm sure Andrea will have a few words for me."

"I'm sure she'll understand," I said. "And she might not dislike you as much as you think. She was the one who suggested you might take part in the murder skit."

Summer looked surprised. "Hmp. You don't say."

"Was there anyone hanging around the hallway when you went to that room?" asked Gary.

Summer frowned. "Not that I noticed. I didn't see anyone."

"Hm. What number was the room again?" he asked.

"One thirty. It's all the way at the end of the hall, by the supply closet. When the inn isn't fully booked, it's left unlocked. The staff uses it as a 'rest and recharge' room." Her eyes narrowed. "Why all the questions? Don't you believe me?" she snapped.

"We're just glad you're all right, Summer," I said quickly. I reached out and grasped her hand. "In this storm, you could have gotten knocked unconscious and been lying somewhere with an injury."

She nodded. "I guess so. But as you can see, I'm fine." She pulled her hand free from my grasp. "I'm sorry, but I've really got to go."

With that, she spun on her heel and hurried out the door into the hallway. Gary looked at me and Josh. "So? What do you think of her story?"

"Sounds flimsy to me," Josh responded first. "She holed herself up in a vacant room to talk on the phone and then just decided, in spite of promising to take part in the murder play, to just lie down and nap?" He scratched at his head. "I can see why Andrea Palmer described her as flighty."

"She also said she'd been working double shifts," I pointed out. "So it could be possible."

Josh looked at me. "So you believe that story?"

"Honest? I'm not sure," I admitted.

"She seemed a bit nervous to me," observed Gary. "Like when I asked if anyone could have seen her go in or out of the room. And she definitely didn't like it when you grabbed her hand, Shell."

"I did that to check out her nail polish," I replied. "Definitely the same color as those flecks, but her nails looked pretty smooth. I didn't notice any chips or flaking."

"Maybe she spent some of that time in the room redoing her manicure," Gary suggested. "Although while you were checking out her nails, I was looking at her feet. They looked too small to me to be a fit for those shoes."

I sighed. "I suppose it's possible the shoes have nothing to do with Venery's murder. It just seems so odd."

"Well, I'm going to see how Amy's doing with Hanratty," said Josh. "Right now I'd put Summer at the bottom of the suspect list. I don't particularly believe her story, but I also can't see her as Venery's killer. Mainly because I don't think she has a strong motive. He might have made some passes at her, but she seemed more annoyed than upset over it to me." He went over to me and squeezed my arm. "I know what you're thinking, Shell. I'm just following the evidence. If Hanratty is innocent, he's got nothing to worry about."

Josh left and I looked at Gary. "Maybe Summer had no motive to off Venery, but she might have helped someone who did!"

Gary chuckled. "Let me guess. The mysterious LL?"

"Why not? Think about it. She might be a guest here and handed Summer a sob story. Summer seems like an impressionable young woman to me. Plus, if she's working double shifts she needs money, and maybe this person paid her well to help her."

"That's as good a theory as any, I suppose," said Gary. "So, what's our next step? Or are we going to let Josh and his crew handle it from here on?"

I shook my head. "I can't, not as long as Patrick is still in the forefront. I know, I know," I said as Gary shot me a look. "I didn't expect to feel so concerned for his safety either but . . . you were right. We were in love . . . once . . . and I do regret how it ended. I guess helping to clear his name is my way of making things right."

He grinned. "You're an old softie, Shell McMillan. You know that? Even after the guy cheated on you, you want to help him. If anything, he should be the one making things right."

"That is true, but . . ." I let out a sigh. "I can forgive . . . I suppose, but trust me, I'll never forget what he did." I crooked my finger at him. "Come on. Let's go check out room one thirty. Maybe we'll find something in there that will point us in the right direction." A chorus of meows greeted my announcement. "And yes, you guys can come too."

• • •

Sure enough, room one thirty was right at the end of the hall across from the supply closet, and it wasn't locked. Gary, the cats and I stepped inside and looked around. It wasn't very big, but it was cozy and nicely furnished with a double bed, a dresser with a mirror, and a small desk. A thirty-two-inch TV was mounted on the wall opposite the bed, and the bathroom door was slightly ajar.

Gary pointed to the bed. "The comforter does look rumpled," he said, pointing. "And you can see the slight indentation on the pillow where a head lay."

I sniffed at the air. "Smell that?" I asked.

Gary sniffed. "Perfume. I can't quite place the fragrance though."

"I can. It's L'Air du Temps."

Gary sniffed the air again. "I've definitely smelled this tonight. I think quite a few of the female guests must be wearing it."

"Including my mother. It's one of her favorites." I frowned. "I was standing close to Summer and I didn't smell this or any other perfume on her."

Gary shrugged. "The room is unlocked, remember? Anyone wearing it could have come in here, and it might not even have been tonight. That stuff lingers."

"Or maybe there was someone else in here with Summer tonight," I said.

Gary had been riffling through the desk drawer. Now he stopped and looked over his shoulder at me. "Don't tell me you want to go around sniffing all the female guests?"

"No, of course not," I snapped. "That would be too obvious."

"Ya think?" Gary continued rummaging in the drawer. "Nothing in here," he said. "A couple of pens, a few rubber bands, and a pad of inn stationery."

I crossed the room and leaned over Gary's shoulder. "Looks like there are some sheets missing from the pad," I observed. "I wonder if that mysterious note we found was written here?"

"If so, anyone could have done it." He made a motion of turning a key. "Door unlocked, remember?"

"True. And I guess having it checked for fingerprints wouldn't prove anything. Lord only knows how many people have handled it."

"Including us," said Gary. He glanced down and saw the two cats pawing at something on the rug. He leaned over. "Say there, Purrday. What are you and the princess playing with now?" He gently moved the cats aside, picked up the object and held it up. I stepped forward to look at it. It was just a small scrap of white paper with thin blue lines. It looked as if it had been torn from a notebook. Printed on one side were the initials RSD. On the reverse side were two more letters, *NO*, and then a question mark.

"Talk about odd." I handed the scrap to Gary. "What could that mean?"

He looked at the paper then shrugged. "I have no idea. It just looks like some initials, the word *no* in caps and a question mark. We have no idea how long this paper has been here. It's probably totally unrelated to Venery's death."

"Then again, it might," said a voice from the doorway.

I caught a whiff of L'Air du Temps as the person who stood there walked all the way into the room.

Charisma Walters.

Chapter Twenty

"Charisma," I cried. "What are you doing here?"

She pointed at the scrap of paper in my hand. "Actually . . . I came looking for that," she said.

I held up the paper. "This is yours? What does it mean? Is this some sort of code?"

"In a way." Charisma's gaze skittered away from mine as she added, "I'm afraid I haven't been completely honest with you, Shell." She walked over and sat down on the edge of the bed. "When I showed you that email, I didn't tell you the entire story. I did research Venery's past and I found out all about his former life as Ronald Payson—and the fact that he knew Louise Fletcher, now Louise Gates."

I blew out a breath. "Let me guess. You thought this secret of Venery's might have had something to do with Louise?"

She nodded. "A source of mine, who will remain unnamed, clued me in that there appeared to be some animosity between Venery and Ms. Gates. I've been digging around, trying to find out just what it might be, but so far I haven't had any luck."

"And you thought Louise might be the mysterious LL?"

"I considered it. Her maiden name is Frawley, but did you know her middle name is Lana?"

Gary and I exchanged a look and then I said, "No, I didn't know that. I do know she has a past with Venery, but I don't believe that she is this LL." Both Purrday and the princess let out loud meows. "And they don't either," I added.

"I don't think so either," admitted Charisma. "But I had no other leads, until I happened to go to the ladies' room and I overheard your conversation with Tessa Taylor."

"I thought I heard the bathroom door creak," I cried. "That was you?" When she nodded I said, "So then you know Venery is dead."

Charisma had bent down to give the cats a pat on their heads, and now she straightened. "Yes. I have to say, that didn't surprise me. I had a feeling the police were here for more than just warning us about the weather." She crossed her legs at the ankles and looked down at the floor for a few minutes before she continued, "I got the feeling that Tessa Taylor wasn't telling you the entire story, so when it appeared your conversation was ending, I hid in the small alcove across from the bathroom, and when she came out I followed her. She came to this room."

Gary and I exchanged a glance and then he said, "Here? To this room? You're certain?"

Charisma made an impatient gesture with her hand. "Of course I'm certain. I followed her here."

"So she met Summer here?" I asked.

Charisma's brows drew together. "She didn't meet anyone here. She left the door ajar and I peeped in. Tessa Taylor was the only one in the room."

I frowned. If what Charisma said was true, then Summer had lied about taking a nap in this room. Why would she do that? She had to have been somewhere else. Aloud I said, "Okay, so you saw Tessa here? What was she doing?"

"She was on her phone, and she didn't sound happy. I heard her say, 'Renata? Are you sure? Anyway, it doesn't matter now.' Then she listened for a few more seconds and then she said, 'I've got to go.' I managed to duck inside that supply closet a minute before she came out. I saw that scrap of paper on the floor and I assumed she'd dropped it. I barely looked at it when I heard voices in the hallway. I should have just taken the paper, but I didn't think. I shoved the paper into the desk drawer and left. I figured Tessa would be busy with the detective, so I'd just come back and take a closer look at that paper."

Gary reached out to tap at the paper in my hand. "You think these initials could be this Renata Tessa mentioned?"

Charisma shrugged. "Maybe. But then who is LL, and how does she fit into all this?"

"I may be able to answer that." I sat down on the bed next to Charisma. I laid the paper down between us. "Venery has—had—quite a reputation as a ladies' man. I got curious about it so I started doing a little digging. I came across this story that looked interesting, about him and Lina Lawley. Apparently they were engaged, and then Lina broke it off. That happened in New Orleans."

"Oh." Charisma's eyes traveled to the paper. "Do you think that the NO on that paper stands for New Orleans? But why the question mark?"

"That broken engagement happened in New Orleans, but that email you received said Venery came to Fox Hollow specifically to deal with some scandal. It's doubtful the two could be connected," observed Gary. "Maybe that scandal had to do with this Renata."

"And maybe Tessa Taylor isn't as innocent in all this as she'd like everyone to think," added Charisma.

"It seems to me as if there are a lot of different angles to cover," I said. "And unless we can make some sort of a connection, Patrick is going to end up in jail for a crime he didn't commit."

Charisma turned to me. "How about we split the research? I'll start digging into anything *Renata* that could be connected to Venery, and you find out more about his broken engagement to Lina Lawley. Maybe between the two of us we can come up with something that connects them."

"An excellent idea," I said. "Two heads are always better than one—or three in this case," I said with a quick look at Gary.

"Are we going to be doing all this research on our phones?" he asked. "Because my battery is getting low and I didn't bring my charger with me."

"I didn't either," I admitted, and Charisma nodded assent. "I didn't expect we'd end up trapped here," she added. "We shouldn't wear out our phone batteries just in case. But then how are we going to find out anything?"

"Louise must have a computer in her office," suggested Gary. "If we ask she might let us use it."

"Asking Louise might call too much attention," I said. "I'd rather keep this as quiet as possible for now."

Purrday reared up on his hind legs and pawed at the air. "Merow," he said. "Merow."

I snapped my fingers. "You're right, Purrday. Thanks." I turned to the others. "I have an idea," I said. "Follow me."

We all trooped back to the cat adoption area. Sissy and Roz were seated at the table, the Clue board in front of them. They looked up as we entered. "Nothing new, right?" asked Sissy.

"I'm afraid the storm is still going on, so we'll all be here a while longer," I said. Purrday and the princess walked over to where Kahlua lay. The Siamese looked up at them, let out a meow, then stretched. The other two cats flopped down beside her.

"Kahlua seemed a little restless before," said Roz. "I think she actually missed the other two."

Charisma walked over to Serendipity, who was lying on her side, eyes closed. "And how is my little darling?" she crooned. "Taking a catnap?"

Serendipity opened her eyes and let out a loud purr. Charisma gave her a scratch under her chin, and the purr got louder. Kahlua opened her eyes and shot the two of them an accusing stare, as if to say, "How dare you disturb my rest?"

I tore my eyes away from the cats and looked at Sissy. "Would you mind if I borrowed your laptop again?"

She glanced up from the board and gave her head a quick shake. "Heck, no. You know where it is."

I looked at Roz. "I don't suppose you have your tablet with you?" I knew Roz had recently purchased a new tablet, one that came with a keyboard.

"As a matter of fact I do. I brought it just in case I got bored with Clue, but since I've won two games and am on my way to a third victory, I didn't need it," the teen said with a grin. "Why do you need to borrow it?"

"Ms. Walters needs something more substantial than her phone. She's, ah, working on another story for her blog in addition to the fundraiser," I said.

Roz smiled at Charisma, who'd left her cat and now stood beside me. "It would be my honor to loan you my tablet. It's right next to Sissy's laptop."

"Thanks, girls," said Charisma. "I'll be sure to mention both of you and all the great work you've done tonight in my post."

The girls returned to their game and Gary squeezed my arm. "You and Charisma have got this," he said. "I'm going to track down Doug and ask to look over those photos again. Maybe something will jump out at me."

I returned the arm squeeze. "Good luck."

Gary left and Charisma and I made our way to the back table where Sissy's laptop still lay. Sure enough, Roz's tablet was right next to it. Fortunately, the girls didn't have passwords, so we were able to access the internet quickly. I hunkered in front of the laptop while Charisma sat a few feet away on the tablet.

I typed "Lina Lawley—Reynaldo Venery—broken engagement—New Orleans" into the search engine and hit enter. The number of hits it returned was staggering. I found the article that had originally captured my attention: *No Wedding Bells for Lina*. I reread the article, then moved onto the next one, which went into more detail.

Lawley-Venery Nuptials Off

New Orleans, LA: Speculation that New Orleans chef Reynaldo Venery would be the one to finally get Lina

Lawley to the altar died yesterday after the couple had a knock-down, drag-out fight in the square in front of Antoine's, where Venery is head chef. Onlookers described the fight as "vicious," with both Lawley and Venery hurling insult after insult at each other. The altercation ended when Lawley removed her four-carat diamond and threw it at Venery, calling him a "disgusting piece of humanity" and a "lousy lover to boot." As Lawley started to storm off, Venery attempted to stop her, but she twisted away from him, shouting, "It's beyond me how you got into this in the first place."

Neither Lawley nor Venery were available for comment, but Ms. Lawley's agent does confirm the fact that the engagement is off "indefinitely."

I tapped my finger on the table. *Indefinitely.* What did that mean? Had there been a chance of reconciliation? Obviously they'd never done so, but had the door been left open? I called up IMDB, the Internet Movie Database, and keyed in Lina Lawley. The photo that came up showed an extremely pretty blonde woman with big blue eyes, high cheekbones and a wide, generous mouth. I scrolled through the list of credits. It appeared Lina's career had been relegated to small roles in B pictures. I clicked on her bio. She'd been born Louanne Perkins and raised in Estelle, Louisiana, population sixteen thousand. Active in her high school drama club, she'd played the lead in the senior production of *Streetcar Named Desire*, catching the attention of a Hollywood talent scout who was in the audience cheering on his nephew, who was playing Stanley. Afterward he gave Louanne his card and told her that if she was ever serious about a career in show business to give him a call. Encouraged by his comments, Louanne applied to both Yale and Juilliard, but was turned down. She persisted, though, and finally managed to get accepted into Humboldt State's drama program. She dropped out after a year, though, called the agent, and started getting work in commercials. She caught the eye of Derek Vaughn, who cast her in his low-budget film *Motorcycle Blonde*. The film was a flop but Louanne, who by then had changed her name to Lina Lawley, was a bona fide hit.

She appeared in minor roles in three other Vaughn films, which resulted in her getting a popular Los Angeles magazine's award for Starlet of the Year. She appeared in a few more movies in minor roles, and right before her engagement to Venery had been signed to star in a major film. After the fiasco with Venery, however, Lina had suffered a "breakdown" of sorts. She bowed out of the film and announced she was taking a short break from moviemaking. During said break she met and married a Los Angeles restauranteur. Five months later they divorced, and Lina announced she was retiring from show business and never returned to the Hollywood scene.

I paused in my reading. It appeared to be a dead end, and yet my gut was telling me that there was more to the Lawley-Venery breakup than met the eye. Whatever the reason had been, it was certainly well guarded. I looked at Lina's photograph again. Something about it struck me as familiar, but I couldn't think just what that might be. I angled a glance at Charisma. Her brow was furrowed and her lips drooped downward. "Any luck on your end tracking down Renata?" I asked.

Charisma pushed her hand through her hair. "I guess it all depends on what you consider lucky," she said. "I tried a search of Renata and Venery and came up with bupkis, so I decided to just concentrate on the name Renata. There are several restaurants with Renata in their name in the United States, including one fairly prominent one in Oregon. There's also a Renata Battery Company based out of Switzerland."

"Several restaurants, huh? Could one of them have a connection to Venery?"

"I searched them—nothing," Charisma said. "I even searched under Ronald Payson. Dead end there too." She made a face and then continued, "In other interesting trivia, Renata also was, apparently, quite a popular name for baby girls at one time. It's of Latin origin and means reborn, in case you're interested." She sighed. "I know, none of that could possibly connect to Venery. I just thought it was interesting. I've always been fascinated by unusual names and their origins. For example, the word *charisma* refers to someone who possesses a personal magic of leadership that inspires devotion and loyalty. It became popular as a girls name from the ex-Buffy actress, Charisma Carpenter, who was actually named after a perfume. Not to toot my own horn, but I think my parents chose quite an appropriate name for me."

I smothered a smile. I had to agree.

Charisma coughed lightly and then continued, "Then there's Amaya, which is both Japanese and Spanish in origin. It means *mother city* and *night rain*. Then there's also Apricity—"

"All very interesting, I'm sure," I interrupted. Something was pinging at the back of my mind. "Let's get back to Renata. Is there any chance it could be a feminine derivative of Ronald?"

"Oh, wow, I never thought of that," said Charisma. "It could be. After all, Willa is a derivative of William, Josephine from Joseph, Cecilia from Cecil . . ."

I had typed "Renata—feminine of Ronald" into the laptop while Charisma droned on. Now I let out a sharp cry. "Bingo." I turned my laptop so Charisma could see. "Renata is a feminine Latin name meaning *reborn*. It is also a feminine derivative of the boys name Ronald, although not one of the more popular choices."

"Good guess," Charisma said. "But I'm confused. What would that have to do with Venery or with Tessa Taylor?"

"I'm not quite sure . . . yet," I said. "It's just . . ."

I got no further because at that moment the door opened and Patrick came bustling through. "There you are," he said. "I've been looking all over for you." He walked over and plopped down in the chair opposite me. "That Detective Riser is some piece of work."

I gave my ex a quick once-over. "You seem to have survived her grilling well enough," I said.

"Thanks. It wasn't easy." Patrick stretched out his long legs. "You'll be very happy to know that the good detective tried her best, but she could not shake my story. And do you want to know why?" Without waiting for me to answer, he held up a finger. "Because I'm telling the absolute, unvarnished truth, that's why. The only thing I'm guilty of is taking that knife."

I regarded my ex with hooded eyes. "Patrick, you said that before you got knocked out you heard voices coming from the storeroom, correct?" He nodded and I continued, "You knew definitely one belonged to Venery. Think hard. Do you think the second voice could have been female?"

Patrick's lips scrunched up as he thought, and finally he shook his head. "Sorry, Shell. I just can't be certain. Whoever it was spoke too softly."

"Okay. Now, up until you got knocked out, you still had the knife in your possession, correct?"

He patted his jacket. "It was in my jacket pocket before I was knocked out, I'm sure of that."

"Did you see or hear anything before you were knocked out?"

His brows drew together and he was silent for several seconds before he responded. "I did hear a noise behind me, a tapping sound."

"Like the sound of someone walking in high heels would make?"

"Maybe. Anyway, I started to turn, but then I felt a sharp pain in the back of my head and that was it. Darkness."

"And at that point, you'd turned away from the storeroom door, correct?"

He nodded. "Oh, yes. On that point I'm very clear. I'd started to walk down the hall a bit. I was trying to figure out what to do next."

"How far away from the storeroom were you? Were you still close enough that you would have heard the door open?"

He paused then shook his head. "No, I was pretty far down the hall. Plus, I wasn't really paying much attention to my surroundings, as evidenced by the attack on me. Just what are you getting at, Shell?"

I scratched at my head. "I'm not entirely sure yet. But I'm thinking that it's possible more than one person could be involved in this."

Patrick drummed his fingertips on the tabletop. "Venery had a lot of enemies, that's for sure. But to want him dead? It had to be someone with a helluva grudge. Something bigger than signing him to do a reality show."

"I agree." I turned the laptop around so Patrick could see. "Take a look at this. Do you remember that actress?"

Patrick looked at the screen and his eyes widened. "Lina Lawley! That's a blast from the past. I haven't heard her name in ages."

"Did you know she was engaged to Venery?"

Patrick started. "No, I did not. My father probably did, though. He had a gigantic crush on her—he even subscribed to her fan club."

Charisma looked up from her tablet. "She had a fan club?"

"Yep. They send a newsletter every three months from New Orleans. Come to think of it, he hasn't mentioned getting one lately."

"Maybe they stopped sending them," Charisma suggested.

Patrick shook his head. "I doubt that. Even though the woman hasn't been seen in public in years, her fans are all diehards. They hang on to any tidbit they can get, no matter how insignificant." He smiled faintly. "Just ask Shell and Gary about all of their diehard fans, the ones they used to encounter at the conventions we attended when we were making *Spy Anyone*."

"That is true," I agreed. "Those people knew every detail of not only our lives but our character's. They knew things you wouldn't think they'd know."

Patrick smiled, reminiscing. "I remember at one of those gatherings they were obsessed with the fact that Gary always knocked on wood before a take. How they found that out I'll never know. It's not the sort of thing one tells in a fan magazine interview. Then at another one they wanted to know if Shell and her sister had ever made up after a recent falling-out. They were actually genuinely concerned . . . what's wrong, Shell?"

I'd scraped my chair back while Patrick was talking and stood up. "It is amazing, isn't it?" I said. "Just what a die-hard fan will fixate on. And for the record, LiAnne and I do speak . . . when necessary." I turned toward the door. "I'll be right back," I said.

"Wait," both Patrick and Charisma called after me. "Where are you going?" Patrick added.

I didn't answer. I was already out the door and halfway down the hall.

Chapter Twenty-one

I hurried down the hall and back into the Appalachian Room, pausing in the doorway to scan the room. The person I was looking for was nowhere to be seen, but I caught sight of Olivia chatting with Leila in the far corner and quickly made my way over there. Olivia turned, caught sight of me, and gave me a big wave. "Shell, there you are!" She held up a long manila envelope. "Guess what! I won the Grand Prize! A spa weekend for two at the Hilton!"

"So I heard," I said. "Gary will be pleased. He loves to go to the spa."

Olivia snorted. "Who said I'm taking him?" she replied. "After all, it's not like we're committed to each other, or going steady or anything like that."

"Uh-oh." I looked at my friend. "Trouble in paradise?"

She sighed. "Not really. I guess since Gary and I haven't seen too much of each other lately, I was hoping he'd pay a bit more attention to me tonight. But I've hardly seen him since he was in the skit. I'm starting to think he's avoiding me."

"I'm sure that's not the case," I said quickly. "I know for a fact he's very fond of you."

"I'm fond of him too," Olivia admitted. "Although sometimes I have to admit I wonder just what he sees in me. After all, he dated some pretty glamorous women when he was in California. He could have his pick of anyone." She paused and then added, "And I saw Charisma Walters giving him the eye."

"Yeah, glamorous women with scarcely a brain in their heads," I said. "Most of those were publicity dates set up by our agent anyway. As for Charisma, I really don't think she's Gary's type. She seemed interested in Patrick too. I think she's just star-struck." I laid my hand on Olivia's arm. "If I were you, I'd really think about inviting him. It would be a good opportunity for the two of you to spend some alone time together."

"Yeah, well, I'll think about it—unless you'd like to go? We haven't spent much girl time together lately either."

I shook my head. "Believe it or not, I've never been a big fan of spas."

Olivia looked me up and down. "No one would know it to look at you. They'd think you spent most of your time there."

"I know you mean that as a compliment, so thanks," I said. I glanced around the room. "I don't see Doug Harriman. I thought he'd be around here, taking pictures for the *Gazette*."

"You'd think so, right?" spoke up Leila. "I haven't seen Doug or his camera in a while, though."

"He's got to be around here somewhere," added Olivia. "He knows he's got to have a good array of photos or old Quentin will have his head."

"True," I agreed. "I'm also looking for Vi Kizis. Have you seen her?"

"Last I saw her and John they were headed for the bar," Leila offered. "John wanted to celebrate winning one of the runner-up prizes."

"I think both he and Vi are getting a bit antsy at not being able to leave too," added Olivia. "As a matter of fact, lots of people are. Did Josh give you any indication as to when it'll be safe for people to venture out?"

"The storm seems to be calming down a bit, but most of the main roads are still flooded out," I said. "They're just trying to prevent any more accidents and people getting hurt."

"I think the crowd would be more amenable to staying if Chef Venery would make an appearance," said Leila. "I hate to say it, but the guy seems to have blown the event off. And from what I've heard, it's not unusual."

I swallowed. "How can you say that? I'll admit Venery is a bit . . . eccentric. And he's got a temper, I witnessed it myself. But I doubt he'd bail on an event he was in charge of—one that was quite good, if I do say so myself."

"It was excellent, but maybe it's a case of sour grapes," ventured Olivia.

I looked at my friend. "What do you mean?"

"Well . . . I overheard some people talking about it. They said Venery had planned a super-elite menu, but he and Louise butted heads over it, and Louise won out. They couldn't see Venery taking that lying down, so they figure his disappearing act is his form of revenge."

"Sounds typical," Leila put in. "It would be just like him to take it out on the poor people who paid good money to taste his food. The guy more than lives up to his reputation as a prima donna." She sighed. "And I suppose my chances of maybe getting an exclusive with him are slim too."

Olivia frowned. "You would want to interview a snake like that?"

Leila shrugged. "The guy's a snake, but he's a popular one. My editor would love it."

Inwardly I couldn't help but feel a bit relieved. If people believed Venery was MIA due to a hissy fit, that was so much the better. "Snake is a pretty accurate description," I said. "I witnessed one of his famous temper tantrums and I can confirm it wasn't pretty."

"Ms. McMillan?"

I turned around and saw Doris Dalton standing behind me. She ventured a shy smile. "I'm sorry, I didn't mean to interrupt you."

"It's fine, Ms. Dalton," I said. "Can I help you with something?"

Her gaze dropped to the floor. "I-I was just wondering . . . are there any cats left to be adopted? Or are they all spoken for?"

For a second I just stared at the woman. She was still interested in cats? "Oh, to be honest I'm not sure," I finally said. "I know quite a few people put in requests for adoption. Was there one in particular you were interested in?"

"Two actually," she said. "One was that buff-colored cat? Jerome, I think was the name on his cage. He looked like a real sweetie. And that all-black cat, the one who got loose during the skit."

"Dahlia?" Wow, she couldn't have chosen two cats farther apart in personality. Jerome was a laid-back snuggle bunny of a cat who'd been rescued from a hoarding situation, while Dahlia was a certified troublemaker. "I don't know about Jerome, but I know there was another person interested in Dahlia."

"Really?" Doris's face fell. "I'd hate to miss out on another pet. It still stings that I lost Apollo." She threw a withering glance in Marianne's direction before shifting her gaze back to me. "I suppose I should go back to the cat room and check it out?"

I nodded. "That sounds like a good idea."

She gave me a pleading glance. "I'd rather not go by myself. I hate to ask but . . . could you come with me?"

I hesitated and glanced over toward the bar area. I didn't see any sign of Vi or John, or Gary or Doug either, so I turned back to Mrs. Dalton and nodded. "Of course."

I waggled my fingers at Leila and Olivia and accompanied Mrs. Dalton out of the room. "I do so appreciate this," the woman said as she fell into step beside me. "I'd have asked my neighbor, the woman I came with, but she's not exactly fond of cats."

"It's no problem," I said. "If you don't mind my asking, which cat are you leaning toward?"

"I'm not sure," she replied. "I'll have to see how they react to me. Do you think maybe I could hold them?"

"You could hold Jerome for sure. Dahlia, that might not be such a good idea right now. Dahlia is much more active than Jerome, and I'm afraid she might get away from you and roam about."

"Get into trouble, you mean," said Doris. She chuckled. "I have a relative who works here and they mentioned how the cat got out of her cage. She did spice up that skit, though."

"She certainly did," I agreed. We walked in an awkward silence for a few moments and then I asked, "Did you enjoy the play?"

Doris stifled a yawn. "Frankly, I thought it was boring. I'm not a professional detective, of course, but I do read a lot of mysteries—some true crime even—and that skit wasn't even remotely close to being a good whodunit. No offense," she added quickly.

"None taken. After all, I didn't write the script." My phone buzzed in the pocket of my dress. I fished it out and saw Gary's name on the screen. "Excuse me just one moment," I said. I moved away from Doris and hit the answer button. "Where are you?" I hissed into the phone. "I thought you were going to talk to Doug and try and get a look at his photos."

"That's the thing," Gary responded. "I'm with Doug right now. We've been looking all over for his camera. It's gone MIA."

Out of the corner of my eye I saw Doris Dalton watching me intently. I tried to keep my tone neutral as I responded, "Are you sure about that? It was there a few hours ago when we replaced the media card."

"I know, but it's not there now. We've turned practically the entire first floor upside down looking for it."

"Well, I'm escorting Doris Dalton to see the cats. As soon as I'm done I'll help you and Doug look. Oh, and by the way, have you seen Vi Kizis anywhere? I need to talk to her."

"No, but if I see her I'll text you. Good luck with that Dalton woman."

I disconnected and went back to Doris. "Problem?" she asked.

"No. I'm just trying to find a friend of mine. Gary said he'd be on the lookout for her."

"Oh," said Doris. "I thought maybe that call was about Chef Venery. I've heard he's missing."

"Missing? Who told you that?" I asked.

Doris shrugged. "Lots of people are speculating about why he hasn't been more visible. I have to admit, I do think it's a bit strange. I've seen his show and it is odd that he's not around to take bows and hear everyone praise his cooking, even if it wasn't the menu he wanted."

If nothing else, tonight had given me a new respect for the power of the Fox Hollow gossip line. "I'm sure everything's fine," I said glibly. "Venery is probably just sulking somewhere. He might not have wanted to throw a hissy fit in front of all these people."

Doris let out a snort. "You've obviously never seen that show. He throws hissy fits all the time. People love stuff like that though. That's probably why the show is number one in its time slot."

I didn't have an answer for that, so we continued onto the cat room in silence. The first thing I noticed when we walked inside was that the table Patrick and Charisma had been sitting at was empty. Sissy and Roz looked up from their game of Clue, and I saw both their eyes pop when they saw Doris Dalton next to me. Sissy immediately rose and hurried forward. "Hello, Ms. McMillan. Is there something we can help you with?"

I nodded at Doris. "Ms. Dalton, here, is interested in seeing two of the cats again. Jerome and . . . Dahlia."

Sissy's eyebrows rose at mention of the lively cat's name. "Dahlia? I think she might be already spoken for. Jerome isn't, though," she added quickly.

Doris Dalton fixed Sissy with a penetrating stare. "But you're not entirely certain that Dahlia is taken?"

"N-no," Sissy stammered. She looked over Doris Dalton's shoulder at me. "Tessa Taylor said she was thinking about filling out an adoption form."

Doris pounced on Sissy's words. "She was thinking about it? But she didn't complete the form?"

The teen tossed me a pleading look. "No, not yet. But she said she'd be back."

"Well, I'm here now and I'm willing to fill out your form immediately," said Doris. "Where is it?"

"I'll get you one. But don't you want to see the cats first?"

Doris's lips compressed to a thin line. "No, I think I'll fill out the form first. Do I have to do a separate one for each cat, or will one suffice?"

Sissy shot me a sidelong glance. "I think Marianne would want separate forms," she squeaked.

"Of course she would." Doris muttered something under her breath, then raised her hand in an impatient gesture. "Fine. Then I'll fill out two."

"Okay." Sissy gestured toward a nearby table. "Have a seat and I'll get them."

Doris stomped over to the table and sat down. She thrust her legs under the table and adjusted her long skirt beneath her, exposing shoes with black rounded tips that seemed well scuffed. She saw me looking and said defensively, "I have bunions. Can't wear those fancy heels. Besides, I spent a fortune on this outfit."

Sissy returned with the forms and Doris busied herself filling them out. I took Sissy's arm and pulled her over to the side. "Where did Charisma and Patrick go?" I asked in a low tone.

"Mr. Hanratty wanted to go to the bar to get a drink, and Charisma went with him," Sissy said.

I frowned. "How long ago did they leave? I was just over at the bar and didn't see them."

"Not long after you did."

I bit back a sigh. In that case, I would surely have seen them. They'd gone somewhere else, but where?

I looked over at Mrs. Dalton, busily scribbling away. "I think she'll be okay. Once she's done, let her see the cats, but don't take Dahlia out of her cage."

"Are you kidding? Marianne would have my head," said Sissy. She glanced over at Doris and added, "I really don't know how serious she is about adopting a cat."

"She seemed serious about wanting to adopt something the other day at the shelter."

"So I heard but . . ." Sissy edged closer to me. "She was in here before, but she spent most of her time talking to that young receptionist instead of looking at the cats."

"Oh, right. Summer." I frowned. "Ms. Dalton did mention a relative who worked here. I wonder if it could be Summer."

Sissy rolled her eyes. "I hope not. Could you imagine having that woman as a relative?"

"Not really," I said with a chuckle. "Anyway, there are a few people I need to find. I'll check in with you later." I inclined my head toward Doris. "If she asks for me, tell her I had to leave."

"No problem. I just hope that Tessa Taylor doesn't come back while she's here."

"If Tessa does come back and things start to get heated between those two, text me," I said. "I'll get Josh or Amy Riser to break up any disagreements."

Sissy grinned. "I half hope she does. I'd love to see Detective Bloodgood take that woman out in cuffs."

Before I left I went to check on my own cats. They, along with Serendipity, were all snoozing near Dahlia's cage. Purrday was snoozing on his side, the princess snuggled up against him. All was quiet now, but I had the feeling their peaceful slumber would soon be interrupted once Doris came to look in on Dahlia. I went back to the main lobby and looked around. There were several groups of people milling around, most with drinks in hand, but John and Vi weren't among them. I went over to the reception desk, expecting to see Summer there, but instead a young girl with curly black hair was seated there, fiddling with the computer. She looked up with a ready smile as I approached. "Can I help—oh my gosh!" She let out a squeal. "You're Shell Marlowe! I used to love you on that spy show!"

"Thanks . . . Simone," I responded, glancing quickly at her name tag. "It's always nice to meet a fan, but since the show ended and I moved here, I go by my real name now, Shell McMillan."

"Oh, right, right," the girl said. "Can I help you with something?"

"Possibly. I was looking for Summer. I thought she'd be working the reception desk."

"Join the club," said Simone, and I could hear the note of bitterness in her tone. "She was only back here about fifteen minutes when she said she had a splitting headache and was going to lie down in one ten, the free room." She glanced around, then leaned over the counter and said in a lower tone, "Ms. Palmer came looking for her too. She's not very happy with Summer today—not that she is any other day," she added.

"Yes, I gathered there was some friction between them."

"There's friction between Summer and a lot of us," responded Simone. "She's got an attitude, you know? Like she thinks she's better than everyone else. To be honest, I'm surprised she's still here, but maybe she won't be, soon."

"What do you mean?"

"Well . . . Ms. Palmer came by a little bit ago and she wasn't happy at all to see me here in place of Summer. It wouldn't surprise me if she went to the free room to have a few words with her." She paused and then added, "There was another woman here a little bit ago. She asked where the other receptionist was. I assume she meant Summer."

"Another woman? What did she look like?"

Simone thought for a moment, then shrugged. "I'm sorry, I'm not that good with faces and I really wasn't paying much attention." The cell phone on the counter beeped, and she shot me an apologetic look. "I'm sorry. I have to take this."

I moved away from the desk, wondering who this other woman might be. Tessa Taylor, perhaps? I was midway across the lobby when another thought occurred to me. I retraced my steps back to the reception desk. Simone was off the phone and back on the computer. She gave me a puzzled glance as I approached. "Was there something else you needed?" she asked.

"Just some clarification. You mentioned the free room for the employees was one ten? I was under the impression it was one thirty?"

"Oh, no, it's one ten. I know that for a fact because I've used it." She tapped at her computer and peered at the screen. "One thirty is one of our regular rooms, which right now is vacant."

"Oh, well, thanks. Sorry for the confusion."

"No problem." She cleared her throat and said in a timid voice, "I hope you don't mind, but I wanted to ask you . . . could I have your autograph?"

I signed the back of a message slip for Simone and told her I'd ask Gary to stop by and do the same. Then I turned and made my way down the long corridor I'd traveled down earlier in the evening. If one thirty wasn't the free room, then it would explain why Summer hadn't been in the room with Tessa Taylor. It could also mean that she had, in fact, been telling the truth about falling asleep. It didn't explain why Tessa Taylor had been in that room, but I couldn't worry about that now. I had to talk to Summer.

I found room one ten without any trouble. It was located in the middle of the corridor, right next to the elevator. I went over and rapped gently on the door. "Summer?" I called. "Are you in there? It's Shell McMillan. I need to speak with you."

Silence. I tried again. "Summer? Are you in there? I really need to talk to you."

No response. Maybe she was sleeping off a headache after all. I hesitated, then reached out and turned the knob. The door swung inward on creaky hinges. The room was in total darkness. I reached out, felt along the wall, found the light switch. I turned on the light, then blinked and froze in my tracks.

Andrea Palmer lay across the bed. Her left arm was thrown out, and her head lolled to one side. A thin line of drool escaped one corner of her lips. Her wide eyes were staring right at me, but I knew she didn't see me.

She was dead.

Chapter Twenty-two

For a moment all I could do was stare at the grisly tableau before me. Who would have wanted to kill Andrea Palmer? And why?

I started to reach into my pocket for my cell phone to call Josh, then paused. I gave a quick look around. No one else was in the room. I steeled myself and walked over to the bed. A wool scarf was around her neck, wound so tightly that I imagined that was what had killed her. Her sightless eyes bulged, her tongue protruded over her lips, and the fingers of her right hand were dug into the scarf as if she were trying to free herself. I pulled out my phone and snapped a few quick pictures of the body, being careful not to touch anything. Then I turned to survey the rest of the room.

A black backpack lay on its side in front of the dresser. I pulled my scarf off my neck and wrapped it around the fingers of my right hand, then lifted the backpack up. I shook it, then felt inside. Empty. No clues there.

I started opening the dresser drawers. They were all empty until I came to the last one. Inside that was a small white box. Inside the box was a heart-shaped gold locket on a thin gold chain. I opened the locket. Inside was a small black-and-white photograph of a curly haired girl in a pinafore dress. I took a photo of the locket and the photo with my phone's camera, then replaced the box in the drawer. As I turned I noticed something sticking out from underneath the far corner of the bed. I went over and pulled it out. It was a canvas cloth tote bag. I crossed over to the high-backed chair in front of the desk and sat down, then turned the tote bag over on the desktop. A plain white letter-sized envelope was at the bottom of the bag. The envelope was unsealed, so I opened it and let the contents spill out onto the desk. I gasped when I saw what they were. Old newspaper clippings about Lina Lawley! One of them was the one I'd seen on the Internet about the broken engagement, and I noticed that Venery's name was circled in bright red ink.

Significant? Possibly.

I spread all of them out and quickly snapped photos. I'd go over them later. I swept the clippings back into the envelope and put the envelope back in the tote bag, which I returned to its place underneath the bed. I was just about to check out the closet when I heard voices in the hallway. I hesitated, unsure of just what to do, when I heard a familiar voice call out, "Shell, are you here?"

I popped my head outside the door. "Gary! What-what are you doing here?"

"Doug and I split up looking for his camera. He went up to the second floor. I was going to take the third floor, but when I went past the reception desk the girl there recognized me."

"Simone. She mentioned she'd seen the show. So she's another of your adoring fans?"

"A helpful one, at any rate. She told me you were probably here looking for Summer, so I figured I'd check in, see if you needed any help." He paused and gave me a searching look, then pointed to the scarf that was still wound around my hand. "Something's wrong."

"Very wrong," I said. I swung the door wide and pointed to the bed. "Summer's not here, but I found Andrea like this."

Gary stared at the body then started to move closer. I put out my hand to stop him. "Don't touch anything," I cautioned.

He shot me a look. "Like it's my first time at this rodeo," he said. He walked over, stared at Andrea for a few moments, then came back to stand beside me. "Well." He scrubbed at his chin with his hand. "That's certainly an odd turn of events. Who on earth would have wanted her dead? Unless . . ." He raised his gaze to mine. "Do you think that girl Summer had something to do with this?"

"I have no idea. I don't even know if Summer was even in this room. But . . . I did find these."

I turned my phone to camera mode and called up the photos I'd taken of the locket and the clippings. Gary looked at them, scratching behind his ear all the while, a gesture he usually made when he was deep in thought. Finally he said, "Those articles about Lina Lawley are an interesting find. Any idea who the little girl is?"

"None. But all this makes me think that someone who had something to do with Venery's murder was in this room, and not too long ago."

"The killer?"

"Possibly."

"Lina Lawley?"

"Her, or maybe someone close to her."

"Hm." He was silent for a long moment and then he said, "We'd better call Josh. This could throw a whole new light on things. If Andrea's murder isn't related to Venery's, then we might have a psychopath on our hands."

"It could be a case of wrong place, wrong time," I said. "Maybe

Andrea was looking for Summer and came in here and surprised the killer."

"That, or . . ." Gary ran his fingers through his hair, mussing up the sides. "Do you think Andrea was involved with Venery's death?"

"I had that thought too," I admitted, "but I really don't know how she'd fit in. Then again, this case seems to have a lot of screwy angles."

Gary pulled his own phone out of his pocket. "I guess we should notify Josh there's been another casualty."

I thrust out my hand. "Wait," I said.

He stared at me. "What do you mean? We have to tell him."

"I know, but . . ." I gestured with my scarf-covered hand at the closet. "I didn't finish going through everything. Maybe there's something here that will give us some sort of clue to the killer's identity."

"Okay then." Gary pulled a handkerchief out of his jacket pocket and wrapped it around his hand. "Which do you want, closet or bathroom?"

"I'll take the closet."

Gary moved gingerly toward the bathroom and I opened the closet door. I saw a row of empty hangers and a garment bag. The bag appeared to be bulging at the bottom. I zipped it down and let out a little cry.

Nestled there was a Nikon camera with a red and black strap. A camera that looked suspiciously like Doug's.

"Gary," I called out. "Come here."

He was at my side almost immediately. "Doesn't seem to be anything in the bathroom other than mouthwash and some bottles of aspirin. Did you have more luck?"

"It would appear so." I pointed to the garment bag. "Take a look inside and tell me what you see, but don't touch anything."

Gary gave me another dirty look then peered inside the bag, let out a sharp breath. "That—that looks like Doug's camera!"

"That's what I thought. And if it is Doug's, how did it get here? Did Summer take the camera, or Andrea? Or someone else?"

Gary pulled out his phone. "Too many unanswerable questions for me. No more stalling. We've got to get Josh involved."

• • •

Needless to say, Josh was less than pleased when he arrived to find not only another dead body but Gary and me right in the thick of it. "This is turning into a regular thing for the two of you," he remarked in none too pleasant a tone. "Finding bodies, that is."

"It's not exactly a goal we aspire to," said Gary. "And for the record, Shell found this one."

I punched him lightly on the arm. "Thanks."

Josh had walked over to take a closer look at the body and now he straightened and whipped out his notebook. He pointed his pen at me. "Okay, Shell. Tell me just how you happened to find this one."

I explained about talking with Simone and the confusion over the free room. "I wanted to talk to Summer and get some clarification. If she was in this room and not one ten, then it is possible she was telling the truth about being asleep. She could have gotten the room numbers mixed up."

Josh's pen stilled over his notebook. "So Summer was supposed to be in this room recuperating from another headache? And instead of her, you found Andrea Palmer's body? Any idea what she might have been doing here?"

"Simone thought she was also looking for Summer. She might have come to this room and found someone else instead."

Josh frowned. "Or maybe Summer was in this room after all. She and Andrea didn't get along, right?"

Now it was my turn to frown. "Andrea was strangled. Summer is a very slight girl. I doubt she'd have had the strength to strangle Andrea. Besides, not getting along with your supervisor isn't a popular motive for murder."

"You'd be surprised," Josh muttered. He gave both of us a sharp look. "You didn't touch anything, correct?"

"Of course not," I said quickly. "We know better than that." I paused and gave Gary a nudge in the ribs. "There's something else you should know, though."

"Doug Harriman's camera is missing," Gary said. "He's been taking photos all night for the *Fox Hollow Gazette* and I wanted to look at some of them. When he went to get his camera out of the coatroom it was gone. He and I were looking all over for it, but so far . . . nothing."

"Let's see." Josh thumbed through his notebook. "So far I've got two murders that may or may not be related, a missing camera, and Louise Gates's jewels that she gave to Venery but somehow turned up in Patrick Hanratty's luggage."

"That's right," I said. "These events are all connected somehow, I just know it. We just have to figure out how."

"No, Amy and I have to figure out how," said Josh. "I think you and

Gary have done enough for one night." He whipped out his phone, punched in a number. "Amy? I need you here in room one ten pronto. Oh, and ask Al Linden to come along as well." A pause and then Josh let out a long sigh. "Yes, there's been another one."

He hung up and made a shooing motion with his hand. "Okay, get out of here, the two of you. Either I or Amy will take formal statements later. In the meantime . . ."

"We know." Gary made a motion of locking his lips and throwing away the key. "Mum's the word."

Gary and I stepped out into the hall and we walked halfway down, stopping in front of one of the supply closets. "What are the chances Doug will get his camera back tonight?" I asked.

"Not good," Gary replied. "It will be considered evidence now. Darn— maybe we should have looked at the photos that were on it when we had the chance."

"Probably," I said. "Although we've taken quite a few chances tonight. That said, what's our next move?"

"Maybe we should find a quiet place and look at the photos you took of those newspaper clippings. Try and figure out just how this Lina Lawley figures into all this, because I'm inclined to agree with you that she does."

"Thanks," I said. "But before we do that, I need to talk to Vi."

"Vi? What can she do?"

"Just a hunch I have," I said, tapping at my gut. "I think she might be very helpful, or at least, that's what I'm hoping."

"Well, I've learned to trust your hunches," remarked Gary. "So let's see if we can find her."

We made our way back into the main lobby, where even more people seemed to have congregated. Luck, for once, was on my side—the good kind. I saw Vi and John standing near a small alcove, drinks in hand. I pushed my way toward them, Gary right behind me. "There you are," I said as I approached. "I've been looking for you."

Vi twirled her wineglass in one hand, while John raised a glass with a pale amber liquid I assumed was Scotch. "Hello, Shell, Gary. We've been indulging at the bar," she said with a laugh.

"And then we took a walk around the inn," added John. "It's really a rather quaint place. If I'm not mistaken, this was once a private home. It still retains much of its charm. I like the fact that they have photos of the old owners on some of the stairwells, as well as beautiful watercolor paintings. And the desks on each landing with the Tiffany-style lamps are also a nice touch."

Gary chuckled. "I have to say you're the first accountant I've met that was into interior design."

Vi laid a hand on her husband's arm. "Believe it or not, one of John's hobbies is decorating. Every time we go to an antique mall or flea market he's always looking at furnishings."

"Hey, you love that vintage Weiman end table I found." He thrust out his chest and added, "Got it for a song, too. The guy thought it was a piece of junk."

"That's true. And that set of cast iron pots was a good find as well." Vi sighed. "I only wish he'd add cooking to his list of hobbies. It would give me a few nights off."

John grinned. "You can't have everything, dear," he said. "Then again, you never know. I could be tempted." Then he looked back at me. "Have they any idea when people will be able to leave yet? The storm sounds as if it's calmed down considerably. We haven't heard any loud gusts of wind or thunder in a while."

"Probably not yet," I said. "The roads are still too flooded. They'll want to be sure everyone will be able to get home safely. But in the meantime . . ." I looked earnestly at Vi. "I wanted to ask you something. Earlier tonight John said that it was always a dream of yours to be an actress?"

Vi's cheeks colored slightly. "It's true. There is a part of me that still wants to be onstage. I was always in the drama clubs in high school and college. I never had a leading role, but I thrived on it just the same."

"I was just wondering . . . would your idol happen to be Lina Lawley?"

Vi's mouth dropped open. "You've heard of her? I have to say I'm a bit surprised. She hasn't acted in twenty years. Most people go 'who?' when they hear her name."

"Of course it's logical that Shell knows who she is," John put in. He gave me a sideways glance. "After all, you're from Hollywood." He took another sip of his drink and added, "Vi really loved her. Like I said, every time she got that newsletter there was no talking to her until she finished the darn thing."

I looked at Vi. "So then you must have belonged to the Lina Lawley fan club?"

Vi raised her chin. "I most certainly did, up until a few months ago when it disbanded."

"It disbanded? Why?"

Vi was silent for a moment, and I thought I saw a tear form at the corner of her eye. Then she looked straight at me and said, "Because Lina Lawley is dead."

Chapter Twenty-three

You could have heard a pin drop in the alcove, the silence was so thick. I wasn't even certain I'd heard correctly. Finally I found my voice. "Dead? Are you sure?"

Vi looked slightly insulted. "Of course I'm sure. Her obituary was in the final newsletter. She died a few months ago. It was a sudden heart attack." A tear rolled down Vi's cheek. "It makes me sad to think of it."

I squeezed her hand. "I can see how devoted you were to her," I said. "If it bothers you to talk about her . . ."

Vi shook her hand free and waved it in the air. "No, no, it does me good to talk about her. She was such a free spirit—and had such a tragic life at the beginning. But like a true trooper, she rose above adversity. I saw every one of her movies. Every one!" She reached up to dab at the corner of her eye. "She was so talented. She could have gone so far in movies, maybe even won an Academy Award—if not for him!"

"By *him* I assume you mean Reynaldo Venery?"

"And the broken engagement? Of course," Vi sniffed. She looked over at her husband. "Venery being here tonight, in charge of the menu and really the main attraction, well, it was the reason I resisted coming, but John managed to talk me into it. I have to say, I'm glad he did. Not only did Venery keep a low profile, thankfully, but now we have a fifty-dollar gift certificate to spend at Sweet Perks."

I smiled at John, who gave me an enthusiastic thumbs-up. "That's great," I said. "But getting back to Lina Lawley and Venery, most of the articles I read were pretty sketchy. I was wondering if maybe you had more information."

"More information?" Vi's eyes narrowed. "What sort of information are you looking for, Shell?"

"I'm curious about her relationship with Venery. From what I could gather, it seemed as if it was . . . quite intense?"

Vi's lips twisted into a bitter smile. "Like Romeo and Juliet. She really loved him, you know. She had it all, and then, well, what happened was a travesty. I don't care what anyone says, that man destroyed her life. She was never the same after that, and she virtually vanished from making movies. She went away somewhere for a time, then ended up getting married and giving up a promising career."

John made a tsking sound. "You make it sound like Lawley's situation was unique. The affair ended badly, true, but she bounced back, met someone else, fell in love and left Hollywood. She's not the only actress to do that. Look at Grace Kelly, Kim Novak." He cast a pointed glance at me. "Even Shell. Her show was canceled, her fiancé cheated on her, but she came to Fox Hollow and started her life all over again." He chuckled. "You gave your life a reboot, isn't that the show business term for starting over?"

I gave him a thin smile. "Pretty much."

Vi's eyes slitted. "True, but Lina had *real* talent—no offense, Shell and Gary," she added quickly. "Who knows what heights she might have gotten to if Venery hadn't destroyed her confidence," Vi shot back.

"I did some research on Lina and Venery myself," I said, "and there are very few details on just what happened between them. I know Lina broke off the engagement, but all of the articles I've read are very vague. They don't give a reason."

"That's because she didn't want what happened to her publicized," said Vi. "Only the 'inner circle' members of her fan club were ever privy to the details."

"Inner circle? I've never heard that term applied to a fan club," I said.

"Me either," added Gary. He looked straight at Vi. "I'm betting you were in that inner circle, right, Vi?"

Vi nodded. "Oh, yes. It cost me two hundred dollars a quarter to be one, but I consider it money well spent. Inner circle members were responsible for spreading the word about Lina, her movies, what she was up to. We were always kept informed, but we were also sworn to secrecy on some matters, and I've never broken that vow. And I tell you, when I found out what happened, I was sick for days." She glanced around, and then added in a low tone, "I imagine it's all right to speak of it now. Lina broke off their engagement because she found out Venery'd been cheating on her."

Gary and I exchanged a glance and then I said, "That's not uncommon. It's why I broke off my engagement to Patrick."

Vi sniffed. "That wasn't the worst of it though." She leaned in closer to us and whispered, "Venery was also supposed to have fathered an illegitimate child! At least your ex didn't do that!"

"At least not that we know of," said Gary, which earned him a jab in the ribs from me. As he rubbed at his side I looked at Vi. "Are you absolutely certain of that?" I asked.

"Oh, yes." Vi's head bobbed up and down. "Gillian Carter, her fan club president, phoned each of the inner circle members individually to relay the news. We were all sworn to secrecy. Venery had a reputation as a ladies' man, but we'd all thought those days were behind him once he fell in love with Lina. Well, guess again! I guess that old saying is true, that a leopard can't change his spots, and neither can a cheating man!"

I was struggling to process this new information. "Just how did Gillian Carter find all this out?"

Vi looked at me and then at Gary and shook her head. "You don't know? Didn't you guys have fan clubs?"

"Sure we did," said Gary. "Mine was run by a woman in Minnesota. She used to text and email me several times a week for updates on different things."

"A woman in Tallahassee ran mine," I said. "Same thing. And I know for a fact mine didn't have an 'inner circle' of secret information."

"Mine either," said Gary.

"Hmpf," said Vi. "Maybe if you and Gary had, your show would still be on the air. Fan club presidents are closer to the stars they represent than their own mothers. It's all part of the job. A good fan club president can make or break a star, and Gillian was an excellent one. She was in constant contact with Lina. Sometimes I think she was even more devastated over what happened than Lina."

"So Lina herself told Gillian what happened?"

"She told her part of it. The rest Gillian hired a private detective to find out."

"The fan club president hired a detective?" Gary rubbed at his forehead. "That sounds a bit obsessive to me."

John shook his head. "Maybe, but it sounds very believable to me. Remember *Misery*? And *The Fan*? Some fans can border on the psychotic when they're obsessed with a celebrity."

"I guess that's true," Gary said slowly. "Sandy Bullock did go to court over a fan who was stalking her, right? And look at all the stars who died at the hands of a deranged fan—Selena, John Lennon . . ."

I shuddered. "Thank goodness our fans weren't that obsessed with us."

"Well!" Vi gave us all a withering look. "Don't put me, Gillian or any of the other girls in that deranged category. We may have gone a bit overboard at times, but none of us would ever have harmed her, or anyone else."

"Shell and Gary know that, sweetheart," John said smoothly. "We were all just trying to make a point."

"Right," I said quickly. "What we were trying to say was that maybe a fan club president using her own money to hire a private detective wasn't exactly beyond the realm of possibility."

"Okay, well . . . thanks, I think," Vi said grudgingly.

Gary rubbed his hands together. "So, what did Gillian's detective find out—if you feel like sharing that information with us, that is?"

"Well . . ." Vi hesitated, then moved in closer. In a low tone she said, "He told her that Venery had been carrying on an affair with a waitress in his restaurant while he was engaged to Lina! The girl had gone to Venery and told him she was pregnant. When Venery told her that it was her problem, she threatened to tell Lina unless he helped to support her and her baby. He told her that he wouldn't be blackmailed, and Lina would never believe that he'd cheated on her. Then he gave her a thousand dollars to either end the pregnancy or give the baby up for adoption, and said he never wanted to see her again."

Vi paused for a breath and I put in, "And then he confessed his indiscretion to Lina?"

"Oh, Lord no! He never said a word and never would have, but Lina got an anonymous letter telling her that her fiancé had been unfaithful. She confronted him. At first he tried to lie his way out of it, but finally he confessed. He said the woman meant nothing to him, but Lina was more upset over the fact he'd sent the woman away. That's when she ripped off his ring and told him she never wanted to see him again." Vi's eyes started to fill with tears. "Lina was such a caring person, she even tried to find that woman. She was so afraid for her and she thought she could even offer her financial assistance. But by then the girl had vanished."

"She knew the woman's name?"

"Well, it wasn't too hard to find out. After all, she'd worked at the restaurant with Venery. I remember the first name was Ariana, and her last name was something regal-sounding. Like King, or Lord, or something like that, except I'm pretty sure it wasn't either one of those." She paused, her finger tap-tapping against her chin. "I'd call Gillian to ask, but she's on a monthlong vacation in Italy and her husband made her leave her phone at home. The trip of a lifetime, she called it. And I'm afraid I never kept in touch with the other four girls who were in the circle."

John had been silent while Vi was telling her story. Now he looked at me. "There's a reason why you want to know all this, Shell, and I'm betting it's got something to do with Venery."

"It does," I said. "Unfortunately, I can't go into detail at this time."

John tapped his finger against his chin. "Funny. Venery takes a powder right after that little speech of his, and then the police show up. Josh, who's supposed to have the night off, suddenly goes into cop mode, and they want us to believe it's all because of the storm. Something just doesn't smell right."

Vi gave her husband a fond look. "Honestly, just because you won one of the prizes in that murder skit doesn't make you a full-fledged detective." She threw Gary and me an apologetic look. "He's always doing this. He's a frustrated Columbo. Does this every time we watch one of those old shows, or see a mystery movie. He always tries to guess the killer."

"Yeah? And how do you do?" Gary asked John.

John took another sip of his drink before he answered. "I'm usually right eight out of ten tries."

"Not bad odds," Gary said.

John tapped at his stomach, which protruded slightly over his belt. "If I were to take a guess, I'd say someone was murdered here tonight, and the police are keeping it quiet for now. Most likely because no one can leave because of the storm, and they don't want people to panic, thinking we're all trapped in here with a killer."

"Oh, John, for goodness sakes." Vi rolled her eyes. "See how he gets. You know, dear, I think maybe you should give up your CPA job and start writing murder mysteries." She turned to me and closed one eye in a wink. "You've certainly got the imagination for it."

• • •

Gary and I left Vi and John a few minutes later. Once we were back in the hallway Gary leaned in close to me. "I'm thinking what Vi told us wasn't what you expected to hear."

"It wasn't. I was hoping that she might have been able to give us a clue as to Lina Lawley's whereabouts. I wasn't expecting to hear it was the cemetery."

"Well, at least now we know Lina Lawley wasn't the one who killed Venery, and possibly Andrea Palmer," said Gary. "We've eliminated Louise and Tessa Taylor, so that leaves us with . . . who?"

"Patrick and Summer," I replied. "And if we eliminate Patrick . . ."

"We're left with Summer. She might have a motive, a flimsy one but a motive nonetheless to kill Andrea, but why would she kill Venery?"

"Maybe she wasn't telling the truth about how she felt toward Venery. Maybe they were . . . involved," I murmured.

"Well, she's hiding something. We need to figure out just what that is, and if it has any connection to Venery and/or Andrea."

I put a hand to my forehead and rubbed. "Talk about getting a migraine," I said. "We're almost at the cat room. Let's check in, see if Charisma has returned. Maybe she's come up with something."

Chapter Twenty-four

When we got to the cat room, Sissy and Roz were still focused on their game of Clue. Both looked up as we entered and I said, "Everything all right here? I didn't get any frantic texts, so I'm assuming all went well with Mrs. Dalton?"

Sissy wrinkled her nose. "As good as could be expected. She filled out the forms, complaining all the while, and then I took her over to Jerome's cage." The teen paused. "I've got to tell you I'm not sure she's serious about adopting any cat, let alone Jerome or Dahlia."

"What makes you say that?"

"Well, I took Jerome out of his cage and put him right in her arms. She held him like he was a bomb about to go off. Jerome could sense she was uneasy so he started squirming, and she dropped him." Sissy chuckled. "I never saw a cat run into their cage so fast. So then I brought her over to Dahlia. I didn't take her out, but Ms. Dalton put her fingers inside and petted her."

"So she seemed to really like Dahlia."

Sissy put her finger to her lips. "I'm not sure. She seemed to like her, but all the while she was billing and cooing she seemed . . . I don't know. Distracted, as if her mind was on something else entirely."

"I wouldn't make too much of it. From what I gather the woman lost her husband not long ago and she's lonely. I think Ms. Dalton is just confused about what she wants," I said.

"Maybe," Sissy said. "Anyway, she didn't stay too long after that. I put her forms in the pending file, even though I was tempted to rip 'em up."

"Relax." I put my hand on the teen's arm. "If she couldn't hold Jerome I doubt she'll want to adopt him. Dahlia might be another story though."

Sissy frowned. "Well, I for one hope that Taylor woman ends up with Dahlia. She seemed to really like her too, and vice versa." She paused and then added, "Your cats didn't seem to like that Mrs. Dalton much. Purrday and the princess seemed, I don't know, watchful? Wary? They just seemed to be keeping an eye on her."

"They're very intuitive cats. They probably sense the woman is a handful and they felt sorry for Dahlia."

"A handful, that's putting it mildly." The teen made a lemon face. "I've got to say, I feel sorry for whatever cat that woman ends up with, and I hope it isn't any of ours."

Sissy went back to her game and Gary and I continued to the back of the room. Charisma had indeed returned. She was hunched over the laptop I'd abandoned, a half-full glass of wine and a half-empty bottle of rosé beside her. The cats had awakened from their naps and were scattered about. Kahlua was on the floor, playing with the catnip mouse Serendipity had earlier. Serendipity was on the table, curled up in a ball beside Charisma. Purrday and the princess, though, were flanked on the opposite side of Charisma, their eyes fixed on the computer screen. Charisma glanced up as we approached. She picked up her wineglass, took a sip, and held it aloft. "The sleuths return," she said. "Any luck tracking down your friend, Shell? Did your hunch pay off?"

"You might say that," I said. "At the very least, I think we've homed in on that secret of Venery's the email you got hinted at."

"Really!" Charisma's face lit up. "Well, don't keep me in suspense. What is it?"

I looked at Gary, who nodded. "First I think there's something that we need to tell you, Charisma. We haven't been completely honest with you either."

Charisma's eyes narrowed. "No? Regarding what?"

I leaned forward. "What I'm about to tell you has to remain between the three of us," I said. "It can't go any further, not until Josh gives the okay. But I'm hopeful we can get this resolved tonight, and you'll have one heckuva story for your blog."

Charisma folded her arms over her chest. "Now you're scaring me."

"Sorry." I looked her straight in the eyes. "Venery's dead."

Charisma's facial expression didn't alter. She stared at me for a moment, then threw her head back and barked out a laugh. "Gosh, is that it? I wondered when you—or someone—would spill the proverbial beans."

"You knew?" I cried. "But how . . . who told you?"

"No one told me," she said. "It just seemed logical. I mean, all of a sudden the guy, who's as big a publicity hound as they come, suddenly disappears in the middle of a benefit where he's the star chef? I'm surprised more of those armchair Sherlock Holmeses out there haven't reached the same conclusion—or maybe they have." She turned to smile at Gary. "I have to admit, though, you and Doug Harriman cinched it for me when the two of you practically fell over yourselves trying to keep me out of the kitchen."

Gary shot her a sheepish grin. "Were we that obvious?"

"For me, yeah," she said with a laugh. She leaned back in her chair. "So tell me. How did it happen? Are there any suspects? Is that the real reason this place is in quarantine?"

"He was stabbed with his own knife, the suspect list is dwindling fast, and yes, it's the prime reason, although the storm is also a real concern," I replied. "And there's more. There's been another murder."

Now Charisma's eyes popped and her mouth fell open. "Another one! Who?"

"Andrea Palmer, the night manager."

"What?" Charisma's lower lip tugged downward. "Who would want to murder her? She has no connection to Venery—does she?"

"That's what we've been puzzling over," I said. "Right now it appears the suspect list is down to two. The receptionist, Summer . . . and Patrick. Of course, that's only for Venery's murder. We haven't started one for Andrea yet."

"Hm." Charisma leaned back and laced her hands behind her neck. "If your ex did kill Venery, which I greatly doubt, why would he kill the night manager? He'd have no motive, but maybe that Summer did. They didn't get along, right?"

"It didn't seem so," I replied. "We know that Venery made a pass at Summer, which she rejected."

"So maybe he tried again, and Summer killed him in self-defense," suggested Charisma.

"I might buy into that, except for the fact Patrick had the murder weapon in his possession until he was knocked out. The person who knocked him out clearly meant to use that knife to murder Venery."

"Which rules out self-defense." Charisma sighed. "Maybe the night manager figured out what happened and threatened to expose Summer, and she killed her too?"

"There's another possibility," said Gary. "Maybe Venery's and Palmer's murders aren't connected, which would mean there are two killers loose here."

I shook my head. "I don't think there are two killers," I said. "I think the same person murdered both Venery and Andrea. I'm not sure if it's Summer, but I think that she's involved in all this somehow."

Charisma splayed both hands on the table. "In that case, there has to be a common denominator among them, something that links the three of them together. But what could that be?"

"If we knew that, we'd have this thing solved," said Gary.

I looked at Charisma. "Remember I said I thought I'd discovered Venery's secret, the one that email hinted at? Apparently Venery fathered a child out of wedlock while he was planning his wedding to Lina Lawley."

"No," breathed Charisma. Her eyes had widened to gargantuan proportions. "Is that why she broke off the engagement?"

"It appears that way, yes."

"Considering the guy's reputation with the ladies, though, people might not have cared," said Gary. "Some people might actually have expected something like that of him."

"I'd agree with you, but I understand that the networks Patrick and Tessa were pitching their shows to are all family networks, the kind who promote squeaky clean, good wholesome entertainment. They wouldn't have been pleased with something like this in Venery's past at all."

"So something like this coming out would definitely have endangered Venery's being tagged for that show," mused Gary. He rubbed at his chin.

Charisma nodded. "Absolutely. Now, are you sure this info is on the up-and-up? That it's legit?"

I nodded. "The source is very reliable."

Charisma cocked her brow at me. "This source, it's your friend, this Vi?"

I nodded, then explained about the inner circle. When I finished, Charisma's nose wrinkled. "I've heard about fan clubs with those special circles. Nine times out of ten, it's true what they say is reliable, but . . . it wouldn't be the first time a reliable source got erroneous information. You understand, Shell, this is huge. I—we—have to be absolutely certain it's true."

Gary had been silent while Charisma and I were talking. Now he cleared his throat. "I think there's something we're overlooking."

I turned to look at him. "You've got an idea?"

"I have." He leaned back in his chair and crossed his arms over his chest. "What about the mysterious Renata? You looked it up and it's a feminine derivative of Ronald, right?" When I nodded he went on, "You originally thought that Lina Lawley might have come here to exact revenge on Venery, but she's dead, so that's out. But what about the child?"

"The one he fathered?" I frowned. "Why, I don't know. Vi said the mother went away and no one ever heard from her again. Venery gave her money to end the pregnancy."

Gary leaned forward and steepled his fingers beneath his chin. "What if the woman didn't? What if she went away and had the child—and maybe it was a girl. A girl she named after the father, a man she was still in love with in spite of everything. Renata." He leaned back, a self-satisfied smile on his face.

"That could work," I said. "And if she decided to keep the baby, she probably wouldn't have gone far. Vi said the woman Venery cheated on Lina with was a waitress, so she probably didn't have much money. She would most likely have had the baby in New Orleans, so maybe we should check birth records of girls born in New Orleans twenty years ago."

"Every birth record? That will take forever," cried Charisma.

"We don't have to check every record," I said. "Vi said the mother had a regal-sounding last name, so we check names like King, or Lord, or Duke . . . like that."

"It will still take forever," grumbled Charisma. "And just how do we go about doing that anyway?"

Gary had been fiddling with Roz's tablet while Charisma and I were talking, and now he looked up. "I've found a database for birth records in Louisiana," he announced. "But you have to be a member to get the info, so one of us will have to fill out a form. On the plus side, it's free."

"Yeah, free, but you probably go on a list and get a ton of spam emails," said Charisma.

I went over and looked at the tablet screen. "You only have to put first and last name and email," I said. "My old account at Hotmail is still active from when I was on the show. I was going to close it but never got around to it. We can use that one, and when we're done, I'll just close the account."

Charisma pushed the laptop over to me. "Fine. Be my guest."

I filled out the form, using my stage name of Shell Marlowe and my Hotmail address, Spygirl. Once I was in, I typed "Renata Duke" into the search engine along with the birth year, twenty years prior. I thought it was fortunate they didn't ask for an exact date. I hit enter and we all held our breath.

No hits.

"Darn," I said.

"Broaden the search," suggested Gary. "She might have gone to a neighboring town to have the baby. Just put in Louisiana and see what happens."

I complied. Still no hits.

"Give me another name. What else sounds regal?"

"How about King?" suggested Gary. "Can't get more regal than that."

I typed in "Renata King." That got a few hits, but none were the one we were looking for. I got the same result with Renata Lord, Knight, and Baron.

"We're running out of regal names," muttered Gary.

"Yeah, Duke, Baron, King—wait!" I held up a finger. "We forgot Prince. Second-most regal name, right, after King?"

I typed in "Renata Prince" and held my breath. This time I got six hits. I clicked on the first one. This Renata Prince was born in Westwego, parents names were John and Cecily Prince. I shook my head. "Not her," I said, and went on to the next record. The second Renata Prince was born in Baton Rouge, mother Viveca, father Herman Prince. Nope, no good either.

"Okay, you know what they say. Third time's the charm," I said, and clicked on the next record. When the information flashed on the screen I let out a breath. "Bingo," I said softly.

This Renata Prince was born in Gretna, Louisiana, on June twenty-first, twenty years ago this year. Gretna was only three miles away from New Orleans. The mother was Ariana Prince. On the line where the father's name should be was a large stamp that read "Unknown." I looked at the child's full name and my heart started to pound in my chest.

Renata Été Prince. I'd taken French in both high school and college, and I knew exactly what the English translation for Été was.

Summer.

Chapter Twenty-five

"Earth to Shell. Earth to Shell. Come in, please."

I looked up as Gary snapped his fingers in front of my face. "There you are," he said. "You looked as if you zoned out for a moment."

"I did," I admitted. I pointed to the screen. "Look at that."

Both Gary and Charisma peered over my shoulder. "Wow," Gary said. "That's quite a combo. Renata is Italian or Spanish, and Été is French, I believe."

"It is. And the French translation of *été* just happens to be . . ."

"Summer," cried Charisma. "So you think that's the connection? Summer is Venery's illegitimate child?"

"It makes sense," said Gary. "But we still don't know how Andrea Palmer fits into the equation, unless there is another killer, as Charisma suggested."

I snapped my fingers. "Remember that note I found?"

"The one that said admit the truth or suffer the consequences?"

"I'm more positive than ever it was meant for Venery," I said. "Andrea Palmer had access to everyone's personnel files. What if she discovered something in Summer's that led her to believe she might be related to Venery? Maybe Andrea decided to blackmail Venery."

"Of course!" Charisma jumped up and down in her chair in her excitement. "She met him and Venery was probably going to give her the jewels he got from Louise. They argued, things escalated and she killed him!" Charisma leaned back in her chair, smiling triumphantly.

"There's a big flaw with that." Gary shook his head. "If Andrea were blackmailing Venery, it would have made more sense for Venery to have killed her, which didn't happen. I agree, Shell, that note was most likely meant for Venery, but I don't know if Andrea was the one behind it. I'd say if Summer is really his daughter, it would make more sense for her to have written him the blackmail note. She might have been the person arguing with him, and when she left and saw Patrick and the knife in his pocket, everything came clear to her. She whacked him over the head, got the knife and killed Venery, then dragged Patrick to the basement, figuring he'd take the fall for her crime." Now Gary was the one to lean back and cross his arms over his chest, a self-satisfied smirk on his face.

I stood up and faced him. "Now let me point out the flaw in your

165

theory. As with Tessa Taylor, Summer is a very slight girl. She might have been able to knock Patrick out with the element of surprise, but no way could she have carried him down to that basement on her own."

"So she had help. Maybe she and Andrea were in on it together," Gary suggested.

I nibbled at my lower lip. "Andrea apparently disliked Summer. Why would she help her?"

Gary rubbed his fingers together. "For money, honey. Remember the jewels? Summer or Andrea could have hidden them in Patrick's luggage, figuring to get them later. Maybe she and Andrea were going to leave, but the storm put an end to that." He looked at Charisma. "What do you think, Charisma?"

Charisma frowned. "Both theories have good points. If Summer is indeed Venery's daughter, she had an excellent motive to want him dead. But I agree with Shell, the girl's a toothpick. She could never have gotten Patrick Hanratty down to the basement by herself." She tapped at her chin. "Maybe her feud with Andrea was an act, you know, to throw people off the scent."

"I'm wondering if Summer planned to kill Venery all along," said Gary. "When was she hired anyway?"

"I'm not sure, but I gathered she was fairly new," I responded. "If Andrea did write that note to Venery, then there must have been something in Summer's personnel file that tipped Andrea off as to Summer's true identity."

"Like what?" asked Charisma. "Andrea wouldn't have known about Venery's illicit affair, would she? And for that matter, we could be wrong about everything. Maybe Renata Été Prince isn't Summer at all." She rubbed her fingers lightly at her temples. "I don't know how professional detectives can do this for a living. This all is giving me a migraine."

"What we need is a good look through Summer's personnel file—and maybe Andrea Palmer's too," I said. I nibbled at my lower lip for a few moments before I continued. "The files are in Louise's office. She's supposed to be there resting with a migraine. I could go there and pretend I have a headache too. I'll ask her for some medicine and then Gary, maybe you could provide some sort of distraction to get her out of the office so I can go through those files."

"A distraction? What sort of distraction?"

I waved my hand impatiently. "Oh, I don't know. Use your imagination.

Just make sure it keeps her away long enough for me to get into that file cabinet."

"Which, no doubt, will be locked. What if the key isn't in the office, or Louise keeps it on her?"

I reached into my hair and pulled out a bobby pin. I held it up. "That's what these are for. I also have my debit card in my pocket. Either one should work."

Gary wagged a finger in front of my face. "Have you been taking courses in breaking and entering without me?"

I made a face at him and made a hurry-up gesture with my hand. "Let's get going," I said. "It sounds as if the storm is winding down, and people will be getting restless."

Charisma suddenly held up her hand. "Maybe there's something else we're overlooking," she said. "We don't know what happened to Ariana Prince, Summer's mother. What if she's the one who's here, the one who's behind Venery's murder?"

Gary and I looked at each other, then at Charisma. "Never thought of that, but it's a good point," I admitted. "Someone had to write that note Tessa Taylor found and sign it LL. Judging from the date Tessa told me, Lina Lawley was already dead."

"Maybe that could be the connection," said Gary thoughtfully. "What if Andrea Palmer isn't Andrea Palmer at all. What if that's an alias and her real name is . . ."

"Ariana Prince," Charisma cried. "Of course! Even the initials are the same! Maybe mother and daughter planned Venery's demise together."

"And afterward Summer killed her own mother?" I said with a frown. "That's a bit Machiavellian, don't you think?"

"You hear about things like that all the time," said Charisma. "It's not that unusual."

"We can discuss all this later," I said and looked at Gary. "We should get going."

"Wait," Charisma cried out as he headed for the door. "What should I do?"

"You can research Ariana Prince, see if you can get any sort of a lead on her, where she might be today, or even if she's still alive. Who knows, maybe your theory will turn out to be right and Ariana Prince is—was—Andrea Palmer."

"On it." Charisma settled herself in front of the laptop. "I have a few sources who owe me favors. I'm sure I can count on them to help." She whipped out her phone and hit a button. As Gary and I started for the door, I heard a soft meow behind me. I looked over my shoulder and saw Purrday and Princess Fuzzypants padding toward us.

"Uh-oh, no," I said. I bent down and gave each cat a pat on the head. "You guys stay here, okay. Gary and I have an important errand to run, but we'll be back very soon, I promise."

Purrday and the princess cocked their heads at me, then looked at each other. Purrday raised one paw. "Merow?" he said.

"Honest, we'll be fine," I said to the cat. I made a shooing motion with my hand. "Now go on, go back to Kahlua and Serendipity. Keep an eye on things here. Maybe Charisma can use your help."

Both cats looked at me, then they turned and walked back toward the table where Charisma was talking earnestly into her cell phone. They flopped down beside the table and glared at us. "Think they'll stay put?" asked Gary.

I sighed. "Probably not," I said. "But we can only hope."

We hurried toward the door. On the way I paused at the table where Sissy and Roz were deep in another game of Clue. "Keep a good eye on Purrday and the princess," I said. "They seem a bit restless and I don't want them wandering around."

"Sure thing," Sissy said. She reached for a card and groaned. "Lose a Turn! Swell."

Gary and I headed straight for the main lobby. We saw Josh talking to Doug Harriman, so we headed in that direction. Josh was standing with his back to us, but Doug saw us and waved us over. "Good news and bad," he said. "Josh found my camera, but it's evidence and I can't get it back yet."

Gary looked at Josh. "I know the camera is evidence, but I was wondering if maybe we might just look at the photos? Under police supervision, of course," he added.

"Why do you want to do that?" Josh's eyes narrowed as he looked from Gary to me then back to Gary. "This wouldn't have something to do with either murder, would it?" He jerked his thumb at Doug. "I had to tell him why I couldn't let him have his camera back yet."

"And I had to swear on a stack of Bibles not to say a word," said Doug. He made a crossing motion over his heart. "But boy, if I could get this story over to the *Gazette*, old Quentin might even give me a bonus." He chuckled. "And Leila Simmons would be green with envy."

Gary turned to Josh and said, "Clarissa wanted us to take another look at the photos. There were quite a few of her that she wants to use for publicity purposes. She'd like to get a jump on it because once Quentin gets his hands on the photos, he'd most likely give her a hard time."

"I can vouch for that," added Doug. "He'd say those photos are the paper's intellectual property or something like that."

Josh thought for a few moments, then finally nodded. "Okay. But the two of you wear gloves, and Amy is with you the entire time."

Gary cast an appealing glance my way, and I waved my hand. "It's okay, Gary. Go. Looking at those photos is important too." I swallowed. "I'll—I'll ask Olivia to come with me, or maybe my mother."

"Okay if you're sure." He looked at Josh. "Okay, Joshy. Lead the way."

Josh started off, Gary and Doug behind him. As they moved away from me I heard Doug whisper, "Are we really looking for photos of Clarissa?"

I proceeded to the Appalachian Room, where I spotted my mother seated alone at a corner table. I made my way over there and flopped down into the chair opposite hers. "Mother. Where is everyone?"

"They all went to the bar." She held up a half-full glass. "I didn't feel like imbibing." She leaned forward and said in a low tone, "People are getting very restless. If something doesn't give soon, your boyfriend isn't going to be able to keep Venery's death secret much longer. People are very suspicious."

"Hopefully it won't be too much longer, especially since the storm sounds like it's winding down," I said. "I need to ask a favor, Mother."

My mother's eyes narrowed. "What sort of favor?" She set her glass down, reached across the table and grabbed my hand. "Crishell, does this have to do with your boyfriend's investigation?"

"In a way," I said. "We need to find out something from the inn's personnel files, which I understand Louise keeps in her office. I heard she's holed up in there with a headache, so I—I need you to make up a ruse to get her out of there for a while."

"I see." My mother tapped one perfectly manicured nail against the lace tablecloth. "So you can what? Break in and go through those files?"

"It would really be a big help."

My mother let out a very slow, drawn-out breath before she answered. "Would it move things along? Help everything get settled so people can know the truth and maybe leave?"

Now it was my turn to draw a slow breath. "There's a very good chance it will."

My mother looked at me for a long moment, then shook her head. "No, Crishell. I will not go to Louise's office and make up some story to get her out of there so you can play Nancy Drew."

I let out a wail—a soft one to be sure, but a wail. "Oh, but Mother. You don't understand. This might be the only chance—"

My mother held up her hand. "I won't help you, because it isn't necessary."

"What do you mean, it isn't necessary?"

My mother's lips curved upward in a self-satisfied grin. "Louise isn't in her office, she's in an empty room across the hall, sleeping soundly. The poor thing is so frazzled by tonight's events that I gave her one of my sleeping pills. She'll be out for a few hours, so—"

I jumped up before my mother could finish her sentence and walked around the table. I bent over and gave her a resounding kiss on the cheek. "Thanks, Mom," I said. "I'll let you know how this all turns out."

"You'd better. And for goodness sakes, be careful," she called after me as I hurried out of the Appalachian Room and down the hall.

• • •

A few minutes later I was standing in front of Louise's office. I tried the door but it was locked. I pulled out the bobby pin and went to work. I stuck the flat end of the pin into the top of the lock and bent it, then I folded the rest of the pin until it was flush against the doorknob. I bent the wavy end of the pin to form a handle and then I took another bobby pin out of my hair and shaped it to form a tension lever. I inserted the tension lever into the lock and then felt for the pins, pressing down on the makeshift handle to push the pins up. Twenty minutes later I heard a click and I reached out to twist the knob. The door swung open, and I breathed a sigh of thanks to the YouTube gods for the handy how-to video I'd watched.

I stepped inside the office, shut the door, slid the bobby pins into my pocket and looked around. My gaze went immediately to the large file cabinet in the far corner of the room. I hurried over to it, checked the labels on the drawers. The third drawer was labeled *Files O–R*. I jerked that one open and started thumbing through the neat row of manila folders. I thumbed through them and let out a sharp breath when I found one labeled *Prince, S.* I whipped the folder out and took it over to Louise's desk. I eased myself into her chair before opening the folder. There were two sheets of paper inside. The top one was Summer's job application. I picked it up, then frowned when I saw the name written on the first line:

Summer Dalton.

"Dalton!" I flopped back in the chair as the paper fluttered from my hand onto the desk. "Then Summer isn't Venery's illegitimate child?" I remembered seeing Summer and Doris earlier in the cat room, talking. "Summer must be the relative Doris Dalton mentioned who works here. But if that's true, why is her application in a file marked Prince?"

I picked up the folder and looked at the second paper in the file. It was a copy of a petition for a name change. The petitioner was listed as Renata Été Prince. The form indicated that she wanted to change her name to Summer Dalton. According to the form, the petition had only been submitted recently and had not yet been approved by the court.

"So Summer has to be Venery's daughter," I murmured. "But how could Andrea have known that, unless . . ."

I went back to the cabinet and pulled out the file for Andrea Palmer. This one was a bit thicker. I sat back down at the desk and opened the folder. Andrea's job application was right on top and I gasped as I saw the name: Andrea Dalton Palmer.

"It's no coincidence Andrea and Summer both have the name Dalton," I cried. "They must be related somehow. Maybe Andrea knew the backstory about Summer's parentage, and when Venery showed up here, she saw an opportunity to blackmail him. Maybe during a confrontation she killed him. But then did Summer find out what happened and kill Andrea?"

"Wrong on both counts," said a voice behind me.

I spun the chair around and my heart started hammering in my chest. I'd been so engrossed that I hadn't heard the office door creak open, and now Doris Dalton stood framed in the doorway, a revolver clutched in her hand.

A revolver that was pointed directly at my heart.

Chapter Twenty-six

I struggled to remain outwardly calm, despite the butterflies that were rapidly churning my stomach. Everything suddenly clicked into place. "Mrs. Dalton," I managed to croak out. "Don't-don't do anything foolish."

"Good advice," the woman barked out. "You'd do well to follow it yourself, Ms. McMillan."

I tapped at the personnel folder. "Summer is related to you, isn't she? And so is Andrea Palmer?"

Doris's lips thinned. "Andrea was my sister-in-law. Summer is my granddaughter." She shook her head. "I knew you had a penchant for getting involved in investigations, and I had an idea you were getting close to figuring this out. I kind of liked you though. You were so nice to me at the shelter. I tried to keep you out of the way, but you're just like that bad penny. You keep coming back."

My gaze roved over her as if seeing her sturdy frame for the first time. "You're the one who knocked me out and dragged me down to the basement, aren't you?"

"Guilty as charged. Like I said, I tried to keep you out of the way."

I swallowed. Doris Dalton's eyes were alight with madness. The one bright spot was that Gary and my mother both knew exactly where I'd been headed. When I didn't return soon it should sound off an alarm. If I could manage to keep her talking until then . . .

Her skirt rustled, and I glanced down at her feet, at the scuffed black shoes. "You lied," I said. "You originally had on black heels. You switched your shoes."

Her head jerked up. "Pardon?"

"Your shoes. You said you wore those scuffed ones because of your bunions, but that was a lie. You had black heels on originally, but you had to ditch them after you got Venery's blood on them, didn't you?" When she remained silent, I decided to try a bluff. "There are photographs that were taken that will bear that out."

"You're lying. I got rid of all those photos," snapped Doris. "My late husband was a photographer, so I know how to work a camera. I lifted that photographer's camera from the coatroom and I erased the photos he took of me that showed my black heels." She reached up with her free hand and tapped at her temple. "I'm no dummy. I knew once I got Venery's blood on

my shoes I'd have to ditch them. I'd visited Summer here enough to know where all the help's lockers were. Fortunately most of them never lock them. I just kept going through them till I found a pair that would do."

"How clever," I said. I took a deep breath. "I'm guessing that when you heard Venery was going to be the chef at this benefit, you contacted him about Summer being his daughter?"

"Oh, I'd been in contact with him well before that," Doris growled. "I didn't think it was fair that my daughter should be dead, and he had a good life and a daughter who had virtually nothing. I wanted him to acknowledge Summer as his daughter, so she could claim her birthright. He got very nasty with me. Said that he didn't care one whit about Summer, that he'd made that clear to her and it wasn't his concern that she'd decided to have the child. He'd washed his hands of all parental responsibilities twenty years ago and he wasn't about to take them up now. I said I'd tell the press about his fathering Summer, and you know what he did? He laughed at me. He said that his name wasn't on the birth certificate, and besides, he wouldn't be the first celebrity to have a child out of wedlock, and most of those children were viewed as money-grubbing brats. He'd make sure Summer was painted as such, he said, and as for his money, well, she'd see as much of it as her mama had . . . nothing!"

"I see how that would make you upset," I said slowly.

"You don't know the half of it," Doris said. Her voice rose to a high-pitched wail. "Do you know what he had the nerve to say to me? That my Ari seduced him, that she came onto him. It was her own fault she got pregnant. He refused to take responsibility for his actions right up to the end."

"It's evident you loved your daughter very much," I said, trying to make my tone soothing.

"She was my only child, the apple of my eye," Doris said with a loud sniff. "Of course I loved her. I'd do anything for her." She paused. "I *did* do anything for her."

I decided to take a chance, even though I didn't have all the facts. "Your daughter died quite young, didn't she?"

"Too young," Doris sniffed. "She came home after that cad dumped her, with what was left of the measly thousand he'd given her. My Ariana had never been a well girl, and this put her over the edge. She was bedridden for most of her pregnancy, and we all held our breaths when little Summer came into the world. It's a miracle Ari didn't die in childbirth."

"She named her daughter after Venery, didn't she?" I said. "You didn't like that."

"No, I didn't." Doris waved the gun around for emphasis. "My daughter was a lovesick fool where that man was concerned. Renata was a popular name at that time, and since my husband and I drew the line at her naming the child Veronica, it was as close to Ronald as she could get." She made a small sound of disgust deep in her throat. "I wanted her to name the baby Summer, because she was born on the summer solstice. What does she do? Makes it her middle name, but in French! Another tribute to that man, who was always talking in French like he was some high-class chef. He was a nothing! A nobody! You know his real name? Ronald Payson! He thought changing his name made him a better person. Hah! As for being a great chef, well, he could brag all he wanted, but he was no Gordon Ramsey or Emeril, let me tell you. The only reason he got all those fancy positions was because he romanced the wives of the restaurant owners, and they persuaded their husbands to hire him."

"I didn't know that," I said in a soothing tone. At this point, agreeing with everything Doris said seemed the way to go.

She gave her head a brisk shake. "I never could understand that man's appeal, but apparently most women bought it. None of them could see through him, my own daughter included. He was a snake, a lousy excuse for a human being!"

"I agree," I said in a soothing tone. "From what I've heard he doesn't sound like a very nice man."

She let out a loud snort. "That's putting it mildly. He was the lowest form of animal life. Snakes in the grass have more class." She let out a loud sigh. "My first husband passed away. Dan Dalton was my second husband. He knew everything that had happened, and he always tried to get me to calm down about it. 'Let it go, Doris,' he always used to say to me. I pretended I did for his sake, but I didn't. How could I? Venery is the reason my baby girl is dead."

I glanced casually at my watch. It had been at least a half hour since I'd left my mother and Gary. With any luck, one of them should be starting to wonder where I was. I had to keep the woman talking. "How did your daughter die, Mrs. Dalton?" I asked softly.

"It was all *his* fault," she said stonily. "It was the week after Summer's sixteenth birthday. He'd just gotten that job on the cable show. Ariana hadn't been feeling well, but she insisted on driving over there. She was going to finally confront him, she said. She was going to make him come over and acknowledge Summer as his daughter. We tried to talk her out of it, we even hid the car keys, but she found them and took off. Like I said, she hadn't been feeling well, and she was on medication—" Doris Dalton paused as her voice caught, and tears started to flow out of her eyes. "My baby girl," she murmured. "She drove right through a red light. A truck hit her head-on. She died on impact."

I could visualize the accident, and I could feel Doris Dalton's pain. "How horrible," I murmured.

"Summer got a bit antsy after her mother died," Doris continued. "She'd always been an independent little thing, and now she was even more so. She went to college and graduated early. Then my husband got sick and died, and a few months later Summer came to me and said that it was time, she was going to move out. She was an adult now, and she wanted to be on her own." A strangled sob escaped her lips. "Something else I had to thank Venery for."

"Summer knows Venery is her father?"

She shook her head briskly. "No. I made certain of that. Ariana didn't want to tell her, either, not unless Venery owned up to the fact. That's why she rushed off that day. She'd still be alive if not for him!"

"So Summer was the reason he came to Fox Hollow, the secret he wanted to keep quiet?"

A crazed light had entered Mrs. Dalton's eyes, and she waved the gun around in the air. "Yes. Once I found out he was coming here, I pestered him for a face-to-face meeting. He kept saying he wasn't interested. I thought I could force his hand. I even sent an anonymous email to that Charisma Walters. I knew she was trying to up her game in the world of internet influencers, and I thought maybe that would stir something, that she might start an investigation, but . . . she didn't."

"And you wrote that note, 'Admit the truth or suffer the consequences,' and gave it to him hoping to force his hand?"

Her brows knit together. "No. That was my sister-in-law. Dan had told her the whole story about Venery, over my objections. Andrea wasn't the saint Dan always made her out to be. She was always criticizing Summer for one thing or another. Never mind the girl was putting herself through college. She thought Summer should be more of a go-getter. Anyway, when she found out Venery was coming here for that benefit, she decided she'd put the squeeze on him. She told Venery she knew all about what happened, and she had concrete proof. She told Venery if he didn't give her a hundred thousand dollars she was going to expose him."

"You'd already tried that tactic with Venery, though. And it didn't work."

"Yes, but Andrea was convinced she could get something out of him where I'd failed. The only reason it worked was because the contracts the network wanted him to sign had a morals clause. It wouldn't have mattered if the accusation were true or not, just the merest hint of scandal would be enough to blow his million-dollar deal. So he agreed to pay Andrea."

"And he went to Louise and threatened her with something he was holding over her head so she'd give him her jewels."

"Those diamonds belong to Ms. Gates? I didn't know that," said Doris. "I took them out of his pocket after I killed him and stashed them in some luggage for safekeeping. I planned to get them later when the storm died down and everything went back to normal."

"So you were the person Patrick heard arguing with Venery?"

She nodded. "Yes. It was another exercise in futility. He dismissed me, said he had another important meeting and I should know better by now. I left and saw Mr. Hanratty and the knife in his pocket, and I recognized that as Venery's knife. I grabbed a tray I saw lying around and whacked him over the head, then I took the knife, went back to the storage area and killed Venery. Then I dragged Hanratty down to the basement and left him there. I figured he'd be tagged as the prime suspect, because I knew he and Venery had been at odds."

"Why did you kill Andrea?"

"Because she'd gone to keep her appointment with Venery and saw me dragging Hanratty to the basement. She found Venery's body and confronted me. She wanted me to give her the money Venery had promised her, or else she was going to the police. I had to shut her up. I told her I'd meet her in the free room and give her the jewels, but I never took them out of the luggage. I went to the cloak room, grabbed a scarf out of someone's pocket and got there ahead of her. When she walked in, I got her around the neck and choked her."

I swallowed. "Does Summer know any of this?"

Doris's mouth thinned to a straight line. "No, and she's not going to." She waved the gun in the air. "Well, it's been nice chatting with you, Ms. McMillan, but unfortunately, you now know way too much for me to let you live. Just come with me now, please."

She took a step toward me and my eyes scanned the desk frantically, looking for something, anything, that I might be able to use to defend myself. My eye fell upon a silver letter opener on the edge of the desk. Honed from silver, the instrument looked to be exceedingly sharp and capable of inflicting a serious wound.

Unfortunately, Doris Dalton spied the letter opener at the same moment. Keeping the gun trained on me, she reached out and knocked the opener to the floor with her free hand. Then she kicked it into a corner, where it skidded to a stop half under the file cabinet. "Nice try, Ms. McMillan," she said. "Unfortunately, I doubt that would have been a match for this gun."

Keep her talking, my brain cried out. "Mrs. Dalton, it seems to me Summer is the real victim here. Don't you think that your granddaughter will be more than a little distressed to learn what you've done? Murdered two people."

"I did what I had to do. And it's three murders," she added, giving me a hard stare. "The only one I'm sorry about is yours." Keeping the gun trained on me, she reached out and grabbed my arm. I winced as her fingers dug into my flesh. Mrs. Dalton was indeed strong! She jerked me to my feet and I let out a sharp cry as she twisted my arm cruelly behind my back. "There's a lovely pagoda out in back. You're going to have a little accident there. It will be a tragedy that will never be solved."

I twisted my neck so that I could look into her glittering eyes. *Keep her talking*, the voice inside my brain repeated. "Haven't you forgotten something? The storm. They have guards stationed at the exits to prevent people from leaving, remember?"

"Correction. It *was* raging. In the last half hour it's calmed down considerably. The winds have died down, and it's not raining quite so hard now. I'm sure the guards will be called off shortly, if they haven't been already." Her lips quirked slightly. "What, are you afraid of getting wet? Cheer up, soon that won't matter."

I swallowed. Unless something happened quickly, this woman would indeed follow through on her plan and I'd be a dead woman!

"Grandmother!"

We'd both failed to hear the office door open and now Summer stood in the doorway, her face ashen, her eyes wide. "Grandmother, what are you doing?" she demanded.

"Get away, child," Doris Dalton cried. "This doesn't concern you."

"I think it does." Summer stood her ground, hands on her hips. "What are you doing with Ms. McMillan? And what's that in your hand? Is that—good Lord, is that a gun?"

"You never listen, do you?" Doris growled. "I told you to get out of here."

Summer, however, had other ideas. She moved a bit farther into the room, her gaze never leaving her grandmother's face. "I was outside the door, listening. You killed that Chef Venery and Aunt Andrea and you knocked out that other man and put him in the basement, and now you want to kill Ms. McMillan? For heaven's sakes, have you lost your mind?"

"I'm doing this for you, Summer," she cried. "I'm doing it to get justice for your mama. That man I killed, Venery. He was your father, but he'd never admit it. He refused to acknowledge you. He told me that he'd see you were painted as a money-grubbing little brat."

Summer's face screwed up into a puzzled expression and she gave her head a vigorous shake. "You're wrong about that," she said. "Venery wasn't my father. Mama told me that my father was in the Army, and he died overseas."

"That was just a story we made up. Reynaldo Venery was your father, and he would never acknowledge you. As a matter of fact, he never even wanted you born. And now he's dead. I killed him to avenge your mama."

Summer's gaze flicked to me, then back to her grandmother. "Even if that's true, my mother certainly wouldn't want you to kill anyone, Grandma. And certainly not Ms. McMillan."

Doris paused. A myriad of emotions flicked across her face, uncertainty one of them. Summer took a decisive step forward and held out her hand. "Now give me that gun," she said.

The uncertainty vanished from Doris's face, replaced by an ugly sneer. "Oh, no. I see what you're doing. I almost forgot your major in college was psychology. Well, that won't work on me."

Summer faced her. "What are you going to do?" she asked softly. "Kill me too?"

"No. But I am going to tie you up until I can figure out what to do with you."

Summer turned and started to run toward the door. Mrs. Dalton released me and then reached out with her free hand and grabbed the girl by the hair and jerked her backward. I considered making a run for it, but they were grappling right in front of the door and there was no other exit out of the room. It appeared that Summer was losing the battle, when suddenly there came another loud yowl and a white streak shot through the door and through the room.

"What the heck is that?" cried Doris.

That was followed by another loud yowl, and then a red streak followed the white one. Both leapt on top of the desk. Purrday and the princess sat calmly, heads cocked, their eyes fastened on Doris. "Merow," they chorused.

"What the heck?" growled Doris. "How did these cats get in here?" She looked at her granddaughter. "You mustn't have closed the door all the way. Too bad now."

She raised her gun and leveled it at Purrday. Summer let out a scream and I sprang forward and grabbed Doris's arm. "You're not going to hurt my cats," I growled.

Doris gave me a push that sent me reeling to the other side of the room. Purrday and the princess both let out another loud wail and then they were off like twin rockets, dashing madly around the room.

"Stand still," Doris growled. She waved the gun around madly as the cats dashed back and forth. "Stay still, for pity's sakes. I can't get off a good shot when you're running around like that."

"You are not going to shoot two defenseless cats," cried Summer. She lunged for her grandmother. Doris whipped around and smacked Summer full on the face with the back of her hand. Stunned, the girl went down. Mrs. Dalton stared at Summer for a moment, almost as if she couldn't believe what she'd just done, then turned her attention back to the cats, who had abandoned their mad dash. Purrday was nowhere to be seen, but the princess was now perched on top of the high bookcase at the far end of the room.

"You mangy thing," Doris cried out. She held the gun straight out and pointed it right at the princess. Her fingers slid down the revolver's handle, and that's when I noticed that it was encrusted with pearls. Could it be?

"Nooooo," I screamed. "You're not killing anyone, cat or human, with that gun." I made a dive for Mrs. Dalton. I grabbed her arm and brought it down hard. She clung to the gun like it was a lifeline, and gave me a shove that sent me reeling back against the desk and down on the floor. Then she whirled and pointed the gun right at me.

"Never mind the cat," she growled. "I was going to try and make your death as painless as possible, but under the circumstances . . ."

"Hey!"

We both looked toward the doorway. Purrday crouched there, and right behind him was Gary. He rushed forward to charge Mrs. Dalton and they struggled with the gun. The next second the gun went off, and Doris staggered backward, grabbing at her shoulder. "I'm shot," she shrieked. "Help me."

Summer, who had been staring wide-eyed the whole time, suddenly cried out, "Grandmother, are you sure you were shot? I don't see any blood."

I went over and picked up the gun from where it had fallen on the floor during the struggle. I held it up. "Mrs. Dalton, where did you get this gun?"

The woman appeared dazed and didn't answer for a moment. Then she said, "I found it hidden underneath a cushion on one of the chairs that had been set up on the murder mystery set," she said. "I took it and snuck it under my blouse. I figured it might come in handy."

"It's a prop gun," I said. "The bullets aren't real."

Mrs. Dalton let out a moan and started toward me, but just then the door was flung back and Josh and Amy burst in, guns drawn. I stepped back, twirling the gun, and cocked my head.

"It's about time. What took you so long?" I demanded.

Chapter Twenty-seven

"As the Bard would say, all's well that ends well."

Charisma raised her glass of sweet tea and grinned at me. It was late Sunday afternoon. The storm had ended right around the time I was having my confrontation with Doris Dalton in Louise's office, and now there was no evidence that a nor'easter had ever hit Fox Hollow. The sky was a radiant blue, there was a gentle breeze, and the sun was shining brilliantly. Charisma, Gary, Olivia, Doug, Patrick, me and the four cats were all gathered in my backyard for a barbecue and a rehash of the previous evening's events.

I leaned back in my swing chair, my glass of sweet tea cupped in my hands. "Well, I aged about twenty years before I realized Mrs. Dalton had the prop gun," I said. "I swear, that woman was nuts. She definitely would have killed me."

"Yes, poor Mrs. Dalton. Her elevator definitely didn't go all the way to the top," said Charisma. "I have to confess, in a way I do feel a bit sorry for her. Not that I condone what she did," she added quickly.

"I know," I said. "Her daughter's death really made her come unhinged." I looked over at Purrday and the princess. "Thank goodness they snuck out and found me. Their wild antics kept Doris Dalton from shooting me—not that she would have killed me with that gun." I looked at Gary. "I thought the cavalry would never arrive."

"Sorry. We got a bit sidetracked looking at Doug's photos."

"It was Mrs. Dalton who stole his camera," I said. "She said she erased photos that showed her wearing black heels instead of those scuffed loafers."

"She did, but she forgot entirely about erasing table photographs. When we got to the one of table thirteen, there sat Doris Dalton, right in the center, and right in Venery's line of vision. We figured that it had to have been seeing her that upset him, and we showed the photo to Josh. Then your mother came hurrying over and said that you'd gone to Louise's office quite a while ago, and she was a bit concerned. And when Purrday appeared, meowing up a storm, well . . . that was all I needed," said Gary. "Josh went to get Amy and they followed. He told me to wait but . . ." He shrugged.

Olivia leaned over and put her arm around Gary. "Well, I think you were very brave," she said. She leaned over and gave him a peck on the cheek.

He looked at her playfully. "That's all the hero of the piece gets? A peck on the cheek?"

"Now, now." Olivia patted his hand. "We'll wait till we're alone."

I cleared my throat. "No offense, Gary, but I think we know who the real heroes are."

Both Purrday and the princess sat up straight and meowed loudly.

Charisma grinned at me and stroked Serendipity, who was napping on her lap. "A feline hero and heroine," she said.

"That's absolutely right," I said fondly. "Purrday for going for help, and the princess for distracting Doris Dalton. If Doris hadn't tried to shoot her, I might not have noticed that she had the prop gun and not a real one. I was never in any real danger after all."

"Don't bank on that," piped up Patrick. "That woman would have found a way to do you in." He touched the back of his head and added, "I can speak from experience, she can pack quite a punch."

"Merow!"

Gary looked around. "Speaking of our erstwhile detectives, where are they? Or didn't you invite them?"

"I invited Josh," I said. "He said that he had a lot of paperwork to process, but he'd try and get here later." I sighed. "So much for his having the whole weekend off."

Patrick rolled his eyes. "Such is the life of a law enforcement official," he remarked.

"I'm surprised Leila isn't here," said Doug.

"She's busy basking in the glory of scooping every newspaper and TV station with the story about Venery's murder," I said with a chuckle. "After she got done chastising me for not taking her into my confidence."

Olivia took a sip of her sweet tea and then set the glass down. "So Mrs. Dalton's original plan wasn't to kill Venery then? She just wanted him to acknowledge Summer as his child?"

"Yes. Her unstable state of mind was triggered by her daughter's untimely death. Both her first and second husband tried to talk sense into her, but she wasn't listening to either one. She brooded over it constantly, and convincing Venery to do right by his daughter, Summer, was all she cared about. She left messages that he never returned, and then she started sending him letters, telling him there was a girl who could use his help. She signed some of them LL hoping to rattle him. Tessa Taylor even saw one of them on Venery's desk, pushed under a pile of papers."

"That showed just how much he thought of them," put in Gary.

"When that didn't seem to faze him, she threatened to expose Summer as his daughter unless he acknowledged her as his heir. It annoyed him more than anything, and that's why he agreed to cater our benefit. He was determined to see Doris face-to-face and get her to back off once and for all, and the benefit was the perfect cover."

Patrick took a sip of his tea. "But she didn't back off. If anything, she became more determined."

"No. If anything, his indifference incensed her more. But she didn't get the idea to kill him until she saw Patrick with Venery's knife. She realized she could kill him and set Patrick up as the perfect patsy."

"What she didn't count on was Shell and Gary believing in my innocence," said Patrick.

"Venery was also getting flack from Andrea, Doris's sister-in-law. Andrea was the one who sent Venery the note that said 'Admit the truth or suffer the consequences.' Venery'd discovered there was a morals clause in that deal for the network, so he determined to take Louise's jewels to shut Andrea up. But he met with Doris first, and they argued. He sent her off so he could meet with Tessa, but in the interim Doris saw Patrick with Venery's knife and figured that was her golden opportunity. She knocked Patrick out, grabbed the knife and went back to confront Venery. They struggled, and the lights went out. When they came on again, the knife was in Venery's chest. She shoved him against the rack and the boxes came down on top of him. She knew Tessa was due to meet Venery soon, so she left his body for her to find, went out and dragged Patrick down the hall and threw him into the basement. She figured that would keep him away for several hours and make him look suspicious."

"It's startling that seeing the knife gave her the idea to kill Venery."

"I figured she reasoned it would be poetic justice for him to be killed with his prized knife."

"She used pretty sound reasoning, if you ask me," observed Patrick. "It will be hard to get her off on temporary insanity."

"Oh, I'm not so sure," I said. "A good lawyer these days can argue just about anything. Personally, I think being in an institution where she can get good psychiatric help would be the best choice. After all, it's not like Venery was a saint."

"People would say he got what he deserved, although does anyone really deserve to be murdered?" asked Patrick. He slid me a glance. "Even you don't hate me that much." He lifted his head and added, "I think more guests are arriving."

The gate creaked open and we all looked over to see Vi and John Kizis arrive, each carrying a large tray. "All hail our resident Nancy Drew," said Vi. "Another close call, huh?"

"Not as close as it could have been," I responded with a chuckle. "All I can say is thank God that gun looked so realistic, otherwise Mrs. Dalton might have been carrying another sort of weapon around with her, one that might have been effective."

Gary, Olivia and Patrick all sniffed at the air as Vi and John set down their trays. "Is that apple turnovers I smell?" Patrick asked.

"The best Sweet Perks had to offer," said Vi. "We splurged that fifty-dollar gift card on these goodies for your celebratory barbecue."

"Oh, you shouldn't have done that," I said. "After all, John earned that gift certificate."

"It's fine." John patted his bulging stomach. "As my wife pointed out, I don't need an abundance of sweets or caffeine. Best to share my bounty with friends."

"So tell me," Vi asked with a twinkle in her eyes, "are we too late to hear the recap of last night's events?"

"I think we can give you the CliffsNotes version," I said. "But let's wait until after lunch. We've got hamburgers and hot dogs, and we've got chicken wings and thighs, too."

The gate creaked again and this time Marianne strolled in. She held a covered plate, which she also set on the table. "Brownies," she said. "Home-baked." She looked at me and added, "I've got good news to report. Dahlia has been adopted. Tessa Taylor came by the shelter this morning with a five-hundred-dollar check and took her."

"That's great," I said. "For both Dahlia and the shelter."

"Well, according to Tessa Taylor, her dream of a cooking reality show isn't dead in the water. Apparently two other chefs who previously reneged have now changed their minds, so she's hoping to sign a big fat contract later this week."

I shot Patrick a side glance, saw his lips droop. I reached out and patted his hand. "Cheer up, Patrick," I said. "Your day will come."

He stretched his long legs out in front of him. "Oh, I totally agree. As a matter of fact, I've decided to abandon my idea of a cooking reality show in favor of something else entirely."

Gary and I both said at the same time, "Not another spy show!" which caused everyone to chuckle.

Patrick shook his head. "No, not another spy show. At least, not one without the two stars who made the first one such a hit."

"So," Gary demanded as Patrick fell silent, "don't keep us in suspense. Tell us what your new project is."

Patrick fixed his gaze on Charisma. "Actually, it was Charisma's idea."

Charisma looked startled. "My idea? Really?"

"I read your blog today," he said. "You did a great job of reporting on not only the event but on the wonderful job that the police did in solving the two murders—with a little assistance, of course."

Charisma colored. "I was hoping everyone would like it." She looked at me. "Detective Bloodgood did ask me to downplay your and Gary's participation but . . . I couldn't help but give you a little kudos. I did keep your confrontation with Doris Dalton entirely out of it, though." She turned to Patrick. "How did my blog give you an idea for a new project?"

"You mentioned in it how much people enjoy playing armchair detective, particularly when there are prizes at stake, so . . . that got me thinking. A reality show where a murder—or another sort of crime—is committed, and participants play detective to win big prizes." He scratched at his head. "There are a few out there, mostly in Europe, so I have to come up with a new slant on the topic." He looked hopefully at me. "I thought maybe you or Gary might have some ideas along those lines."

Gary gave Patrick a look of mock horror. "What do you think we are, murder experts?"

Patrick grinned. "If the shoe fits . . ."

"Gee, thanks," I said. "But you're on your own with this one, Patrick. Short of having the participants solve an actual murder, I've got nothing."

"Maybe they could try and solve a cold case," suggested Charisma. "There are plenty of those. Or maybe murders or crimes inspired by works of fiction."

"Both sound like good possibilities," said Patrick. He tossed Charisma an engaging smile. "I don't suppose you'd be willing to have a sit-down with me sometime, maybe hash out a few ideas?"

Charisma's cheeks colored prettily. "I'd love to," she cooed. "I can ask my blog followers for some ideas as well. You'd be surprised with what they can come up with."

The gate creaked again and this time Josh stepped inside. He held up his hand. "I'm sorry, but I can't stay," he said. "I just wanted to let you all know that Mrs. Dalton has lawyered up."

"We kind of expected that," said Gary. "Who'd she get? Someone local?"

"He's from Hartford. Fred McIntosh," replied Josh.

Gary let out a low whistle. "That's a surprise. He's one of the best criminal lawyers around—and he doesn't come cheap."

"I think he might be doing it pro bono," said Josh. "More for the publicity than anything else. He'll probably try for a reduced sentence on grounds of temporary insanity. He knows she's not going to get off scot-free."

"People could be sympathetic to her story though," said Charisma. "Daughter knocked up by future famous chef, has daughter out of wedlock, killed tragically while on way to tell chef about daughter. Her mother's struggle to get chef to acknowledge the daughter—it is drama-filled, like a soap opera."

"Well, Summer did tell us that it was her grandfather—Dan Dalton—who kept Doris on track. Once he passed, she started to slip slowly back into her obsession. I've no doubt that McIntosh will try his best to get Mrs. Dalton a reduced sentence, or possibly to serve time in a mental institution where she can get the help she needs."

"That would be a good thing," said Charisma. "And what will become of Summer now that her grandmother is going away and her aunt is dead? Did she go to the jail to see her grandmother?"

Josh shook his head. "No, and I don't expect she will. She made it clear in her statement how she feels about her grandmother. She went away to college because she felt the woman was too controlling. As for her aunt, Andrea did pick on the girl, but deep down they cared about each other, at least according to Summer. I think she feels worse about the grandmother killing her aunt than anything."

I sighed. "It is a shame, though, that Summer can't get any of Venery's money. The guy was filthy rich, and he has no other heirs—as least, not as far as anyone knows."

"From what I understand, Venery didn't have a will, either. I guess he thought he'd live forever. Or else he just didn't get around to it." Josh looked down at the ground for a few minutes, then looked back at me. "I gave Summer the name of a good lawyer who specializes in these types of cases. Maybe he can get something for her, I don't know. She didn't say yes, but she didn't say no either."

"Well, I hope she looks into it. Something good should come out of all this. I bet she could use a little extra cash, although Mother mentioned that Louise was going to keep Summer on at the inn for as long as she wanted."

Gary stood up and clapped his hands. "Okay, now that we've rehashed everything to death, it's time to eat!" He walked over to the grill and lit it, then picked up a pair of tongs. A white chef's cap lay on a nearby chair. He put the cap atop his head, then got some hot dogs and burgers out of the cooler and put them on the grill. He brandished the tongs and said, "Come on, now, who wants what?"

"I'll take a hamburger to go," offered Josh. He leaned over and squeezed my hand. "I'll call you later, okay? If I can get this darn paperwork done, maybe we can go to dinner one night this week."

I leaned over and gave him a peck on the cheek. "I look forward to spending some quality time with you, Detective."

He grinned. "You and me both."

Josh moved off and Vi piped up, "I'll have a burger too, but I'll eat mine here."

Charisma rose, Serendipity in her arms. "I'll take a hamburger, and maybe just a tiny piece of meat for my precious baby?"

John chuckled. "I'll have two burgers and a hot dog. Gary, do you need any help?"

"Oh, no, John," I said with a grin. "Cooking is Gary's forte. Give him some time and I think he might even be as good as Venery was."

As everyone clustered around the grill with their plates, Patrick looked at me. "Gary might be as good as Venery, eh? Then maybe I should do a cooking show after all."

"If I were you I'd wait a few years," I advised. I hesitated, then held out my hand. "I think it's time I put the past behind me too. I don't want to brood over things like poor Doris Dalton. I guess what I'm trying to say is, Patrick . . . I think we might be able to salvage that friendship."

Patrick took my hand, held it for a moment before releasing it. "That means more to me than you know, Shell," he said softly. "Thank you."

We were both silent for a few moments, then Patrick rose from his chair and stretched. He cleared his throat and said, "I'd best get going. I've got an early flight tomorrow, and I promised your mother I'd stop by her house later to say goodbye." He shifted his weight from one foot to the other. "Truthfully, I thought she'd be here."

"I invited her but she declined. I think she's still a bit miffed at me for getting involved in a murder case . . . again. Plus, hot dogs and hamburgers really aren't her thing."

Patrick laughed. "She should know by now she can't change you," he said. "I think I'll tell her that she might want to plan something a bit less . . . exciting for her next benefit? Something where there are no dead bodies."

"She'd probably tell you that wherever Gary and I are, the bodies naturally follow." I wrinkled my nose. "As for her next project, I think she's already got something in mind. Believe it or not, I think it has something to do with a cat show."

"A cat show? Well, well, that would certainly be a change of pace," said Patrick. He looked over at the cats. "I'm sure the cats might enjoy something like that. Maybe you could enter one or two of them."

At that, both Kahlua and the princess sat up straight. Purrday flopped over on his side and yawned.

I chuckled. "Well, we have two interested parties, anyway. I think we can count Purrday out. He'd only be interested if there was a mystery attached to the cat show."

Patrick waggled his finger. "Be careful what you wish for, Shell," he said. "Sometimes those things have an uncanny way of coming true."

Purrday looked up, let out a soft meow, then blinked his good eye in agreement.

About the Author

While Toni LoTempio does not commit—or solve—murders in real life, she has no trouble doing it on paper. Her lifelong love of mysteries began early on when she was introduced to her first Nancy Drew mystery at age ten— *The Secret in the Old Attic*. She and her cat pen the Urban Tails Pet Shop Mysteries, the Nick and Nora mystery series, and the Cat Rescue series. Catch up with them at Rocco's blog, catsbooksmorecats.blogspot.com, or her website, tclotempio.net.